D1035078

J M C P L
DISCARDED

A TOWN NAMED PARADISE

Recent Titles by Julie Ellis from Severn House

THE HAMPTON SAGA

THE HAMPTON HERITAGE
THE HAMPTON WOMEN
THE HAMPTON PASSION

BEST FRIENDS
THE GENEVA RENDEZVOUS
THE HOUSE ON THE LAKE
SECOND TIME AROUND
SINGLE MOTHER
VILLA FONTAINE
WHEN THE SUMMER PEOPLE HAVE GONE

Wapiti regional library

A TOWN NAMED PARADISE

Julie Ellis

This first world edition published in Great Britain 2001 by
SEVERN HOUSE PUBLISHERS LTD of
9–15 High Street, Sutton, Surrey SM1 1DF.
This first world edition published in the USA 2001 by
SEVERN HOUSE PUBLISHERS INC of
595 Madison Avenue, New York, N.Y. 10022.

Copyright © 2001 by Julie Ellis.

All rights reserved.
The moral right of the author has been asserted.

British Library Cataloguing in Publication Data

Ellis, Julie, 1933–
   A town named paradise
   1. Detective and mystery stories
   I. Title
   813.5'4 [F]

ISBN 0-7278-5737-1

Except where actual historical events and characters are being
described for the storyline of this novel, all situations in this
publication are fictitious and any resemblance to living persons
is purely coincidental.

Typeset by Palimpsest Book Production Ltd.,
Polmont, Stirlingshire, Scotland.
Printed and bound in Great Britain by
MPG Books Ltd., Bodmin, Cornwall.

One

New York City
2 a.m., Wednesday, August 27, 1997

A record-breaking heatwave – sultry and humid – hung over mid-Manhattan, lent the city an aura of defeat. But behind exterior walls air-conditioners provided relief for those who could afford such amenities. The muted symphony of these purveyors of comfort in high-rise apartments and rows of townhouses and brownstones were the only sounds that broke the 2 a.m. quiet. Most office buildings were night-lighted but silent.

On Madison Avenue in the high-forties the elegant law offices of Clifton, Ambrose, Taylor & McNeil – which occupied four floors – provided twenty-four-hour air-conditioning service since, inevitably, some staff members labored far past the conventional hours on any given summer night. In one of the rows of tiny spartan offices situated beyond the ostentatiously expensive reception room and the ornate offices of the partners, Karen Mitchell – for the past fifteen months a lowly member of the firm – slid papers into folders, switched off her desk lamp, and sighed with relief. She reached for the phone to call the company car service. Another seventeen-hour day was behind her.

She pulled on the pale yellow linen jacket of her suit – a 'must' at Clifton, Ambrose, Taylor & McNeil, though women lawyers in other equally prestigious groups had abandoned such garb, ran one hand through the mass of near-black hair that framed delicate features. Blue eyes reflected her distaste for the lifestyle that had seemed so desirable during her years in law school.

1

Walking down the cold, spare hall she heard the whispery sounds of computer keys. Why must the bottom tier of lawyers in the firm work these insane hours? Bob, too, was still here. Perhaps he was finished for the night, she thought hopefully. They could go home together.

'Hi—' He glanced up from a brief on his desk with a smile. The charismatic smile that had lured her into moving in with him their final year of law school. It was Bob who had convinced her that corporate law was the way to go: '*Don't be a dork. Go where the big money is.*' 'I'll be stuck here another hour at least.' But he didn't seem unhappy. 'You go on home.'

'You look smug.' Probably because this was Tuesday of the week before the Labor Day weekend, and by Friday noon they'd be headed for the Hamptons. They hadn't had a real day off in a dozen weeks.

'You got it.' He radiated triumph. 'Guess who's taking over the Compton account?'

She was startled. 'But that's Arnie's—'

'Not any more. I talked to the old man. I made him see that Arnie's too slow, too cautious. He—'

'This is a conservative firm.' She hadn't meant to sound so sharp.

'Not when it comes to bottom lines. If I handle this right, it'll be a long leap to the associates rank.' When they were both associates they'd be married: '*On our way to a great condo, a house in the Hamptons, a top-of-the-line Mercedes.*' 'You know me,' he drawled. 'I'm the impatient type.'

Karen was disturbed. Sometimes Bob's steamroller tactics were unnerving. 'I'd better go down and wait for the car service.'

'Oh, some change in plans just came up,' he said with an air that warned her this was not something that would please her. 'We have to cancel the weekend at Montauk.'

'We've been counting on that for weeks!' She stared at him in disappointment.

'I can't turn down an invitation from the old boy. Ambrose asked me out to Southampton for the weekend. To go over my plans for the Compton people.' He paused, his eyes wary. 'Hell, I couldn't turn him down.' Reproach laced his voice because Karen seemed unreceptive.

'No, of course not.' For weeks she'd been looking forward to this escape from the firm. She was so tired, so tense. But for Bob the career came before everything else. 'We'll talk later.'

She hurried to the bank of elevators – her mind in chaos. It didn't bother Bob that he was cutting Arnie's throat. It didn't bother him to abort their weekend at Montauk, which for her was a lifeline to sanity. Nothing mattered to Bob except climbing the ladder. *It would always be that way with Bob – no matter how successful he was.*

All the small pieces that troubled her about their relationship jogged into place now. They'd never have a real life together. There'd never be time for family. The view of their future was an ugly, empty blob.

In the lobby she remained inside – as the night watchman always advised – until the car pulled up at the curb.

'Night, Joe—' She waved to the watchman and hurried out to the car.

Leaning back in exhaustion she forced herself to face the rebellion that surged in her. Because of her mother – whom she and Paula had always called Eve, while Grandma was 'Mom' – she'd longed for material success. It had always been so important to impress Eve. To impress was to be loved.

Eve was in the South of France now with her fourth husband. Eve was forever searching for a rich husband, a luxurious lifestyle – but she had a talent for marrying losers. The first husband – her and Paula's father – walked out when Paula was three and she was thirteen months. The second was serving a prison term for stock fraud. The third went through a substantial inheritance and left Eve. The current husband had a trust fund that supported them comfortably in whatever European country the dollar was strong.

She and Paula had spent hardly a third of their lives with
Eve. Just those times when Eve was freshly remarried and
came to scoop them up from Mom. Each time for a little
while she and Paula had been entranced by their glamorous
mother – yet always relieved to be dumped again on Mom.
Mom was reality. Eve was a fairytale with a disappointing
ending.

Karen had done all the right things in college – earned
top grades, worked hard at being a campus leader, spent her
summers working in law offices. The summer after her first
year at law school she'd worked for a legal aid group, the
second summer she'd wangled a job in a prestigious law firm
because Bob had insisted that was important if they were to
move into an important law firm after school. She'd loved
the months she'd spent with the legal aid group, gritted her
teeth and worked hard at the important corporate law firm
that hired her that second summer.

In minutes the car service delivered her at the smart East
Side apartment – where the monthly rent she split with Bob
was a constant shocker. Their once-a-week cleaning woman
had been here today – everything was shipshape. The blinking
red light on the answering machine told her there was a call.
She touched the 'message' button.

*'Nothing important, Karen. No need to call back. I know
your crazy hours.'*

Even on an answering machine message Mom managed to
convey her love. It disturbed her sometimes that Mom had
never met Bob – though she'd urged him to go up with her
on the weekend visits she contrived at intervals. She knew,
too, that Mom was unhappy that she was living with Bob.
But Mom was too cool to let on about that.

She prepared for the night – knowing it'd be a while
before she would fall asleep. Mom was right about their
crazy hours. Bob was willing to keep on this wild track
for the next three or four years. He was ready for whatever was necessary to promote them into partnerships. *Was
she?* She was uncomfortable with Bob's taking over the

Compton account. Arnie was a decent guy – bright and knowledgeable.

An hour later – when she was at last drifting off to sleep – she heard Bob come into the apartment. She fought off wakefulness. She couldn't erase her discomfort over Bob's latest action. They'd talk tomorrow, she told herself – and feigned sleep.

7 a.m., Wednesday, August 27, 1997

The clock alarm went off. Karen rushed to turn it off. Bob lay sound asleep on his stomach in their king-sized bed – his head burrowed in the pillow. Smothering yawns Karen headed for the bathroom. Last night's brief encounter with Bob before she left the office replayed in her mind as she stood under the needle shower. A warning light had gone off in her head in those few moments. *This wasn't the life she wanted for herself. She couldn't stay with this rat race.*

She heard the phone ring in the bedroom, turned off the shower, stepped out and reached for one of the lush bath towels Bob favored.

'You've got the wrong number!' Bob shouted. She heard the phone slammed back into place. 'Rotten bastard.'

Bob wouldn't go back to sleep – not in that frame of mind. Go out and talk to him now. She'd give a month's notice, look for something with less pressure. She wouldn't be the first one.

She left the bathroom, dressed except for her jacket, slid a light robe about her shoulders while she focused on the morning make-up routine. Bob climbed aboard the stationary bike for his customary fifteen-minute race before going in to shower. Working what she called her magic with eyebrow pencil and mascara, she sought the words to convey her feelings to Bob. What had been simmering within her for months now strained to be voiced.

She swung around from her dressing table and slid her

feet into a pair of bone pumps. 'Bob, I have to tell you something—' She struggled for poise. 'I've had it with the firm. I can't take any more of this insane treadmill.' He continued to pedal, but his eyebrows were raised in reproach. She took a deep breath, continued. 'I'm giving a month's notice at the office. I'll—'

He stopped pedaling, hung in place in disbelief. 'Have you gone berserk?'

'This is no way to live. I'm burnt out. I want a chance to do something besides fight for a partnership. I—'

'What about our pact? You're letting me down! You're not holding up your end!' His face was flushed, his voice harsh.

What pact? 'I'm giving a month's notice. I'll look around for something else.' She saw the cold rage that glistened in Bob's eyes. Couldn't he understand what this job was doing to her? Didn't he care?

'You're walking out on our future!' he yelled. 'And everybody at the office knows there's something going between us. Damn it, it'll reflect badly on me! I won't let you do this!'

'Maybe there is no future for us—' She'd told herself she was in love with Bob. She was in love with his vision of a successful future. But that was fast turning sour. 'If that's the way you feel.'

'That's right. You're out of your mind. If you quit, we're through.' A stranger glared at her. They'd known each other for four years. They'd lived together for over two years. They were a team – that's what he always said.

They were going to spend their lives together. 'You're reneging on your responsibilities! You're not holding up your end. You walk out on the firm – it's over for us.'

Why couldn't she stop trembling this way? This was unreal. 'I'll move out as quickly as I can.'

'Do that!' He left the bike and stalked into the bathroom, slammed the door behind him.

Could a two-year relationship end in two minutes?

10 a.m., Wednesday, August 27, 1997

Karen gaped in shock as Carl Ambrose heaped obscene invectives on her.

'I don't want a month's notice!' he wound up. 'I want you out of these premises by 5 p.m. today. Turn over whatever you're working on to Tim Evans, fill him in on the details. I want you out of here by 5 p.m.,' he reiterated. 'You don't belong in this profession.'

Karen walked out of the offices of Clifton, Ambrose, Taylor & McNeil a few minutes before 4 p.m. Tim Evans had trouble concealing his triumph at moving into her slot. She struggled to deal with her new situation. She mustn't allow herself to fall apart. She could handle this. She'd drive up and spend a couple of weeks with Mom while she reassessed her future. Mom had always been there for her in every crisis. She'd pack up at the apartment, load everything into the Dodge. In a corner of her mind she remembered that Bob had reserved a rental car for the weekend.

'The Hamptons are awash with Mercedes and Jags. It would be gauche to arrive in your beat-up seven-year-old Dodge.'

Mom had given her the Dodge her sophomore year at college – so she'd be able to drive home at intervals. *'And bring your laundry with you.'* Mom had re-mortgaged the house to help her through law school. Bob thought it was absurd that she'd fought to be able to pay Mom back out of her fancy salary, diminished by their exorbitant rent and the expensive garaging in the building. It had been Bob, too, who ordered her to stop bargain-hunting for clothes – *'Buy designer stuff – the job demands it.'*

It was close to midnight by the time she'd loaded the car. Bob hadn't come home. She suspected he was avoiding an encounter. A desire she shared.

Drive out of the city, spend the night in a nearby motel, she plotted. Drive up to Paradise in the morning. It would be traumatic for Mom if she pulled up in the driveway at three in the morning. She felt a rush of love as she visualized Mom's pleasure at her arrival. Mom was such a fine person, so involved in local groups out to do good for her town.

Oh, it would be great to spend a couple of weeks back home! She clutched at this prospect. Paradise was a different world. A quiet, serene place where nothing bad ever happened.

Two

Paradise, New York
12.10 a.m., Thursday, August 28, 1997

Not a leaf moved on the towering old trees in the two-acre swathe of woods that separated the half-dozen houses that were Paradise, New York's closest claim to mansion status from the modest development of three-bedroom, two-bath ranches and small Cape Cods. Dark clouds hung overhead, warning of an imminent summer storm. A faint hum of air-conditioners intruded on the night silence. No such disturbance from the weather-shingled ranch closest to the dividing woods.

He stood at the edge of the woods, his eyes fastened to the open window of the bedroom where he knew six-year-old Debbie Norris had long been asleep. His heart pounding. His muscles cramped from the long, covert wait. Earlier – concealed behind a clump of trees, with the additional protection of the night – he'd overheard the conversation between Debbie's parents, Doug and Jeannie Norris. They'd been so proud of their central air-conditioning – until it broke down in this latest August heatwave. Tonight bedroom windows must be open to bring in what meager relief was available. Tomorrow – hopefully – the repairman would show.

Perspiring in the khaki trench coat he wore in anticipation of a downpour, he reached into a pocket to assure himself the sedative-drenched washcloth lay there in readiness. The roll of duct tape available to silence any outcry. In another pocket the knife to slash the screen. No dog to yap and alert the others. He churned with anticipation, his breathing

9

rapid. No problem about getting into the bedroom where the little princess lay sound asleep for sure. Cut the screen and climb inside.

His throat tight with excitement, he'd waited almost an hour after the lights went out in the other bedroom. Everybody asleep in the house at close to midnight. He knew the little boy – maybe three years old – was sleeping tonight in the parents' bedroom after an earlier nightmare. He'd planned this with the care of a major military operation – or a well-plotted mystery novel. And he was within minutes of his reward.

OK, make his move. Every ounce of blood in his body was pounding! No more waiting around. In and out of that bedroom – the open window a blatant invitation – in three minutes. That sweet, beautiful little body in his arms – to do with as he wished.

All right, go.

Three

Paradise, New York
6.55 a.m., Thursday, August 28, 1997

Without opening her eyes Jeannie Norris reached out to the night table to shut off the raucous intrusion of the alarm clock. In a corner of her mind she was aware of heavy rainfall sometime during the night. Maybe the heatwave would let up now, she thought hopefully, pulling herself up into wakefulness. Doug would cling to sleep until she jogged him back into the real world in another ten minutes. Tommy sprawled on his stomach in the crib they'd moved into their bedroom last night. Not even a bomb would awaken those two, she always declared.

She left the master bedroom and crossed the narrow hall to Debbie's small, daintily wallpapered room. Debbie was such a dawdler in the morning. She stopped dead at the sight of the empty bed. The flowered top sheet thrown to the foot, the pillow crumpled. Had Debbie awakened earlier and gone out to watch television – the way she did on rare occasions? But no sounds emerged from the living room. Her eyes darted about the room in soaring alarm, then fastened on the cut-out section of window screen.

'Doug!' she screamed, and then again. 'Doug! Oh, my God!'

She darted to the window, stared out into the morning sunlight. Debbie's teddy bear lay on the sun-parched grass. She always slept with it clutched in her arms.

Doug charged into the room. 'Honey, what's the matter?'

11

'Debbie's gone! Somebody took her.' She pointed to the open screen-shorn window.

He gaped at the tell-tale sign. His face drained of color. 'I'll call the cops! They'll find her!'

Four

K aren turned off the highway on to the road that led into Paradise, New York. She'd slept little last night in her motel room about forty miles out of Manhattan. Life had suddenly become a surreal nightmare. For over two years her life had revolved around Bob and their work. Where did she go from here? She was a lawyer, she reminded herself with shaky defiance. She'd find a less pressured job. She wasn't the first to walk out on the rat race.

She'd stopped for a quick, light breakfast at a roadside diner – ate without tasting. She didn't need Bob to survive. She didn't need a man in her life.

She felt like a walking wounded, she derided herself. Yet in a corner of her mind she'd known for months that something was awry in their relationship. She'd fought against admitting it. She wasn't in love with Bob. He'd been her security blanket through the last year of law school and the past fifteen months. She'd needed someone to cling to – and Bob was there.

It was time to stand on her own two feet, make decisions that she could accept – intellectually and emotionally. She'd hurt for a while – but she'd be her own woman now. *It was time.*

Mom would be at the shop by now. She was always there at least half an hour before opening time. Folks in town teased Mom about her devotion to the shop. That was her lifeline to security. Widowed at thirty-six – with a daughter to raise

13

– she'd managed to open the shop with insurance money. People teased her about retiring – but she just said, '*Maybe when I'm ninety-two.*' The shop had made it possible for Mom to take in her and Paula in those long, lean periods when Eve declared she 'couldn't cope'. Mom had always been there for Paula and her.

She'd seen so little of Paradise since high school graduation, she thought guiltily. By taking summer classes she'd managed to graduate from college in three years – ever determined to have a successful career. To be able to say to Eve, '*Look, I'm making it.*' The little time she'd been here since college she'd wanted to spend with Mom. There'd been no socializing.

It was amazing how Main Street had changed so little through the years. Because people here wanted to retain the small-town aura. A huge public parking area had been provided years ago. The one mall had not become the focal point of shopping. Local stores didn't rush out to open branches there. National chains were slow in coming in. Paradise was considered backward by neighboring towns – but it was a good place in which to live.

Karen derived a sense of comfort in viewing the familiar stores as she drove along Main Street – en route to Mom's fashionable women's specialty shop. Yet she quickly became aware of a strange undercurrent. Clusters of people gathered at intervals – their voices inaudible to her in the window-tight car but their gestures, their expressions telegraphing an ominous situation. *What was happening here?*

Ah, there was a parking spot just two doors from the shop. Relieved, she slid into the space – reminding herself that here was none of the insanity that was part of driving in Manhattan. She left the car and hurried to the shop. Should she have called along the road to alert Mom that she was arriving? Would Mom be upset that she'd walked out on a high-paying, prestigious job? Everything she'd worked for most her life – thrown out the window. Doubts invaded her now.

She pushed the door open and walked inside. Mom was

in deep conversation with Della Andrews – who'd been with the shop almost since its inception. Again, she felt a sense of some horrible happening.

'Karen!' Her somber expression giving way to delight, Helen Lawson – still a lovely woman at sixty-four and appearing a dozen years younger – darted forward with outstretched arms. Slim, elegant, short hairstyle tinted a delicate blonde. 'Oh, honey, how wonderful to see you!'

'I needed to come home,' Karen said softly. Later they would talk.

'Karen, you look marvelous.' Della glowed with affection. 'It's been ages since you were home!'

'Too long.' Karen waved to the thirtyish woman hurrying into the shop. Frances had been with Mom almost eleven years now – ever since high school graduation.

'Has something just happened in town?' Karen asked. 'I mean, I saw people gathered together on the street and—'

'It's awful!' Della broke in. 'Nothing like this has ever happened in Paradise!'

'Little Debbie Norris was kidnapped sometime early this morning,' Helen explained. 'That poor little darling – she's only six years old. Everybody's so upset.'

'It's all we can talk about—' Frances joined in. 'Every parent in town – every grandparent – is terrified. If it happened to Debbie, it could happen to anybody.'

'I have an eight-year-old grandniece.' Della shivered. 'I talked to her mother a little while ago. Andrea isn't to stir outside the house until the kidnapper's caught.'

'Debbie's father is Doug Norris,' Helen picked up. 'He—'

'I remember Doug!' All at once the kidnapping was intensely personal to Karen. 'He was captain of the high-school basketball team—'

'Her mother is Jeannie Gilbert,' Helen continued. 'You two were friends your last year in high school. Both of you so involved in the drama club.' In truth, she'd known Jeannie since kindergarten.

'I'd forgotten she'd married Doug—' She recalled Jeannie

as a pretty, sometimes petulant girl whose father was the widowed mayor. It seemed another lifetime ago – yet suddenly
right at hand. Jeannie had been frank about not wanting to
go to college – '*I just want to get married, have a couple
of kids and a pretty little house.*' Karen felt cold with shock.
'Have they received a ransom note? Any word from the
kidnappers?'

'We don't know much of anything.' Helen's eyes – the
same incredible blue as Karen's – mirrored her pain. 'There
was just this announcement on the morning news program
– and of course, everybody's talking. Why would anybody
kidnap Debbie?'

'Isn't Jeannie's father the mayor?' Karen sought for a
handle. Was this some revenge deal to get back at him?
Any public official was sure to create enemies.

'Oh, Clay Gilbert's been mayor for the past eighteen years,'
Della said. 'You know the police are going to do everything
they can to find Debbie.' Della turned to Frances. 'We ought
to open up that shipment that came in yesterday afternoon.'

'Yeah, let's get cracking. We won't solve any problems
just standing here and yakking.'

Karen turned to her grandmother. Conscious of the questions in her eyes.

'I came to stay for a couple of weeks, Mom. If that's all
right with you?'

'Karen—' Helen clucked in reproach. 'This is your home
– you know that. You stay as long as you like.'

'I was getting burnt out – I need some time away from the
office.' She couldn't bring herself to say she'd walked out on
the job that had seemed so wonderful fifteen months ago.

'That's not surprising, considering the wild hours you were
putting in.' Helen exuded love and sympathy. 'You have your
house keys?'

Karen nodded. 'I'll drive to the house and unload the car.
See you later.' The serene little town she remembered had
erupted into ugliness.

Approaching the weather-shingled Cape Cod at 1402

Maple Drive – that had been home for much of her life – Karen felt a rush of warmth. Here she'd always felt secure, loved. Here existed a comforting stability. She smiled at the sight of Cindy Simmons – Mom's neighbor on the right – who'd moved here five years ago with her husband Todd and baby Laurie. Now Laurie had a three-year-old brother, Zachary. Both Cindy and Todd taught at the one private school in Paradise. They'd become almost like family, Mom said.

Karen pulled into the driveway. Cindy – small, slender, honey-colored hair cut short – looked up with a start. She'd been focused on weeding a flower bed on the small front lawn – Laurie and Zachary her absorbed helpers. Harry, their golden retriever/Collie mix, snoozed on the tiny double-columned porch. A transistor radio sat on the top step of the miniature white colonial – sound muted.

'Hi!' Karen thrust open the car door, emerged. 'How's the gardening?'

'Last night's rain helped a bit. It's been dry all month.' Cindy rose to her feet. Laurie and Zachie smiled shyly. 'Good to see you. It's been ages.'

'Too long.' Cindy seemed tense, she thought, and understood. 'I just stopped by the shop to see Mom. She told me about little Debbie Norris—'

Cindy flinched. 'I can't believe that something like that could happen here. Poor Jeannie and Doug – they must be out of their minds—' Subconsciously she dropped a hand to draw each of the children closer. 'Laurie was playing over at Debbie's house yesterday afternoon.'

'There's been no word yet?' Karen's gaze strayed to the transistor radio.

Cindy shook her head. 'I keep the radio out here just in case. Todd says there should be a ransom phone call soon—' Cindy hesitated. 'It's unreal – something you read about in the supermarket tabloids. You never expect it to happen in your town, to somebody you know. I called Jeannie as soon as I heard and offered to take Tommy, but she's afraid to let him out of her sight. Doug's home from the factory – he's

superintendent there now. Everything seemed to be going so
well for them – then this.'

Cindy's phone rang. She excused herself, hurried inside –
both Laurie and Zachary in tow. Karen began to unload the
car. Mom would know – when she saw how much stuff she'd
brought with her – that this wasn't a casual visit. But she had
no apartment in Manhattan. No job. Mom would realize she'd
broken off with Bob and would be relieved.

Five

N eil Bradford sat at his desk at the headquarters of the local TV station – phone at his ear. A long way, he thought subconsciously, from his role of roving foreign correspondent. He'd come home to recuperate from a bullet he'd caught in the leg in Bosnia, expecting to be here four or five weeks. Now he'd been here five months – because he knew Mom and Dad needed him until the station was on an even keel.

'Look, Chuck, any little news item you can give us will be helpful. People are distraught about this.' He listened to a repetition of what he'd been hearing all morning. No ransom note, no ransom call – all they could do at this point was to stand by and wait for word from the kidnapper. 'Yeah, I understand. You're doing everything you can—'

His father walked into Neil's tiny office – his face somber. 'Nothing yet?'

'Nothing,' Neil confirmed. 'They're doing the usual – checking for fingerprints. Last night's downpour washed away any footprints.' He ran a hand through unruly dark hair. His movie-star handsome face was grim. 'Not what you thought you'd find when you moved here three years ago.'

He was proud of the way Mom and Dad had handled themselves after Dad was 'excessed' from the middle management job he'd held at a Manhattan television station for twenty-two years. Mom had taken retirement from teaching. They'd sold their house in Westchester, scouted for a new way of life. It

19

took nerve for them to throw all their assets into buying this station, gambling on fulfilling a dream Dad had nurtured for years. His own TV station – tiny but his. What he called 'my voice in the wilderness'.

'Neil, what about taking a run over to the police station?' Frank Bradford suggested, and grinned. 'Yeah, I know it's not what you're used to – but maybe you can shake some news out of them.'

Dad and Mom were clutching at some weird idea that he'd be content to stay here after almost seven years of roaming around the world. He'd taken off right after journalism school – grabbing in brief reunions with them in London and Paris and Rome. '*Come home and write a book,*' Mom constantly encouraged, '*about all your experiences.*' He'd put that prospect on a back burner. He needed to distance himself first before re-living those years.

'I don't like this delay in their having some word. It could be the kid was snatched by some sick woman who wants a child. Do you know how many kids are missing each year, Dad? The figures are staggering.' He paused. 'Or she could have been taken by some sick pervert. Let's pray this *is* a "for ransom" deal.'

'How long is it now?' Frank glanced at the wall clock.

'The police figure she was kidnapped somewhere between midnight and 1 a.m. That's ten or eleven hours. Doug Norris remembers it was around eleven thirty or so before he fell asleep – his wife was asleep well before then. Then there's the lack of footsteps outside the window,' Neil pointed out. 'The rain hit shortly after 1 a.m.' He squinted into space. 'Maybe you're right. I should camp out at the police station for a while.'

Neil headed on foot for the station, only three blocks distant. Approaching the modest quarters – a red-brick two-story structure – he saw a familiar figure emerging from a well-maintained but far from recent-vintaged car. Clay Gilbert, his mind registered with triggered interest. Had the police alerted Debbie Norris's grandfather to some new development? He accelerated his pace. This could be a news break.

Inside the reception area he was conscious of an aura of excitement among the newspaper reporters waiting there along with several photographers. Not just locals, Neil pinpointed. The kidnapping of a young child always created strong public interest.

'The mayor's inside with the chief,' a reporter from the *Morning Enquirer* told him, one impressed by his newspaper background. 'We should be hearing something any minute.'

'This wasn't some guy floating through town,' a young reporter from the *Evening News* speculated. 'It was planned. And why hasn't there been a demand for ransom?'

'It could have been a woman wanting a child of her own—' Neil voiced an earlier thought.

'Maybe there was no kidnapping.' A tough-voiced, middle-aged stranger shrugged cynically. 'Don't the cops suspect the parents in most of these cases?'

'Not when the parents are Jeannie and Doug Norris,' the young reporter shot back. 'They—' He stopped short as a door opened and the police chief and Mayor Gilbert emerged.

'I have an announcement to make—' Pale, his eyes revealing his anguish, Gilbert surveyed the cluster of reporters and photographers. The atmosphere was suddenly electric. 'I'm offering a twenty-thousand-dollar reward for the return of my granddaughter. No questions asked. Just bring her back—' His voice cracked. 'Poor baby – she must be terrified. Debbie's never been away from her parents for one night. Even when Jeannie gave birth to Tommy and she was too young to be allowed in the hospital, Doug and I took her to the sidewalk beneath Jeannie's window, so she could see and wave to her mother. This is a terrible, terrible thing. I want to tell the – the person who took Debbie that we'll pay a reward of twenty thousand dollars for her return. No questions asked,' he reiterated with a defiant glance at the police chief. 'We just want her back.'

'Mayor Gilbert—' Neil moved forward. His expressive

21

brown eyes compassionate. 'I'd like to offer you the opportunity to make this plea in person on live television. At any time you prefer.'

Clay Gilbert hesitated. 'At 7 p.m. tonight?' He was striving for composure. 'When most folks in town are home for the evening?'

'At 7 p.m.,' Neil confirmed, while several reporters made a dash for the door. Intent, Neil pinpointed, on headlining the mayor's offer on the front page of the evening editions.

Twenty-four hours ago this was a quiet little town of ordinary people with ordinary problems. After what happened last night between midnight and 1 a.m., it would never be the same again.

7 p.m., Thursday, August 28, 1997

Karen and Helen ate dinner without tasting – their eyes fastened on the TV screen, repositioned to be visible from the dining area. Throughout the town, Karen thought, people in Paradise were listening to Mayor Gilbert's emotional plea for the return of his granddaughter. How awful for Jeannie and Doug! How awful for little Debbie!

'Please, whoever you are – bring back my granddaughter. Her mother and father will give you in exchange a package containing twenty thousand dollars in twenty-dollar bills – no questions asked. I swear this before God.'

'Clay Gilbert must have worked a fast deal with the bank to raise that much cash in so little time. But everybody wants to see that darling little girl returned safely.' Helen winced. 'I know how I'd feel if something like that happened to Jill.' Her own two-year-old great-granddaughter.

'Oh, Mom, don't even talk about it!' She wished that Paula and Ron and Jill didn't live so far away – but Ron was happy in his research job at Berkeley. Paula was proud of having made a good marriage. *'It's for always, Karen. Not like with Eve.'*

'Remind me to turn off the eye-round roast in the oven

in another forty minutes. You take it over to Jeannie in the morning. Whether Debbie's been brought home or not, Jeannie's not going to feel like cooking meals.'

'I don't dare call and tie up the phone in a situation like this.' Yet Karen felt guilty that she had made no personal contact with Jeannie. Cindy said she'd gone over to the house to offer again to take Tommy for a 'sleep-over'. *'Jeannie and Doug are too distraught to let him out of their sight.'*

'You read about things like this happening, but you never expect it to happen in your own home town – to people you know.' The thought reiterated endlessly tonight.

The tragedy that descended on the town thrust Karen's personal crisis into the background. She was relieved that Mom made no effort to probe into her reason for this unannounced arrival. It seemed crass to consider watching TV tonight – though Mom called it her habit-forming sedative. Mom talked about mundane happenings in town, expressed her usual gratitude to the inventors of air-conditioning because last night's rain had done little to alleviate the heatwave.

'Let's listen to the news, then call it a night,' Karen urged as 10 p.m. approached. 'It's been such a draining day.'

They watched the local newscast for a few minutes – with no new word on the kidnapping, then switched to CNN for national news.

'Let's call it a night, Mom.' Karen rose to her feet, crossed to flip off the TV.

'Last night Jeannie and Doug went to bed never guessing what they'd find in the morning. Let God give them the strength to see this through. I know how they're hurting.'

Sleep was slow in coming to Karen. Of course, Mayor Gilbert had made his plea just four hours ago, she told herself with an effort at optimism. Maybe the kidnapper was working out in his – or her – mind just how to collect the reward without being ambushed by the police. Maybe the town would wake up in the morning and discover Debbie had been returned to her parents.

7.45 a.m., Friday, August 29, 1997

After a night of fretful sleep Karen awoke to morning sounds in the house. Mom was in the kitchen putting up coffee. Straining to hear, she was aware that the kitchen radio was relaying the morning news in muted tones. Despite the horror that rocked this town, life must go on its usual path. Mom would go to the shop, open up – as businesses through Paradise would do.

Karen lay in bed and contemplated her own situation. She was *glad* she'd pulled the plug on that insane existence with Bob and the firm. She didn't have to redesign her life overnight. Just relax, try to unwind for the next week or two.

She smiled affectionately as Mom arrived at her bedroom door with a mug of coffee.

'I didn't grind beans this morning,' Helen apologized. 'I didn't want to wake you with that infernal noise.'

'Oh, Mom, you always spoil me—' Karen pulled herself into a sitting position, reached for the coffee mug.

'There's been no word yet from the kidnapper.' Helen's eyes were somber. 'Cindy popped over before she and Todd left for school. They're getting ready for Wednesday's opening. She baked chocolate chip cookies last night. I told her you'd take them over to Jeannie along with the roast.'

'Sure.' What a weak, palliative offering when Jeannie and Doug were in such pain.

By a few minutes past 9 a.m. Karen was in the kitchen and preparing to take over the roast and cookies to Jeannie. Probably they'd been swamped with such offerings, but what else could people do to show their support and compassion?

'I'm taking the kitchen radio in to the shop,' Helen reported, preparing to leave the house. 'In case some word comes through.'

'I'll drop by later,' Karen told her. 'Maybe I can drag you out for lunch.'

She debated about driving or walking to the Norris house.

This early in the morning the heat was already oppressive. Drive, she decided. Behind the wheel of the car she tried to gear herself for this first meeting with Jeannie in more than seven years. They'd both been totally immersed in the high-school drama club, though neither harbored any professional ambitions in that area. For Jeannie it had been a game. For her a kind of escape from reality. She'd been so serious about a career in those days. She was serious now, she told herself defensively – but not in the way Bob had been serious. *Where did she go from here?*

This was Jeannie's block, she pinpointed, and began to watch for numbers. There, the grey, yellow-trimmed ranch on the corner. Nothing to identify it as a house of pain, she thought. Yet the stillness of the neighborhood hinted of unusual circumstances. Though school had not yet opened for the year, no children played in the yards nor rode bikes along the neat sidewalks. Backyard gyms were deserted.

She parked at the curb – consciously avoiding the space before the house, reached for the parcel of roast and cookies. Her throat tightened as she left the car, walked the thirty feet to the flower-bordered fieldstone path to the house. Would Jeannie and Doug consider her an intruder? She'd stay just a few minutes – just long enough to express her sympathy. In truth, what else could she do?

She hesitated a moment, then touched the bell. Would they be upset that this was not some caller with news about Debbie? Perhaps she shouldn't have come. She heard the chimes inside, then the sound of approaching footsteps. The door opened. Jeannie stood there – her eyes reflecting both hope and fear.

'I didn't dare call,' Karen said shakily. 'I know you want the phone line open—'

'Oh, Karen—' The intervening years evaporated. For a moment they were back in happier days. But only for a moment.

'I wish I could be helpful.' Karen juggled the parcel in one arm to embrace Jeannie with the other. 'I just arrived in town yesterday. When I heard about Debbie, I had to come—'

'It's been so awful,' Jeannie whispered. 'Nobody's called. Nobody's left any message. Dad insisted the police stay away from the house – lest whoever took Debbie be frightened away. Karen, who would do such a horrible thing?'

'Let me take that.' Doug appeared, reached for the parcel. 'Everybody's been so kind. You two go into the living room. I'll bring us coffee.'

'We sat up all night – Dad was here till past three – thinking maybe somebody would show up—' Jeannie gestured futility. 'Not a word from anywhere—'

'Go inside and sit down,' Doug ordered with synthetic calm.

Karen and Jeannie went into the small, pleasant living room. They heard the voices of Tommy and his sitter in the rear of the house. Jeannie brought out a scrapbook laden with photographs of Debbie and Tommy from infancy to the present. Jeannie was trying so hard not to fall apart, Karen felt with anguish. What could you say to make things easier at a time like this?

Over coffee and Cindy's chocolate chip cookies the three pored over the scrapbook, the other two filling Karen in on special moments in the past. But the phone didn't ring. Nobody arrived at the front door.

'Daddy! Daddy!' Tommy summoned from the rear, over-riding a feminine voice.

'I have to referee.' Doug rose to his feet and headed for Tommy's room.

Moments later the two women heard a car pull up in front of the house. Jeannie stumbled to her feet. Her face incandescent.

'Debbie?' She darted from the living room to the tiny foyer. Without waiting for a ring she pulled the door wide, Karen a few paces behind. 'Yes?' Her voice was harsh with excitement as she stared at the handsome thirtyish man in khaki chinos and sports shirt who stood before her. He belonged, Karen calculated, to the truck at the curb – the property of the local TV station.

'I'm Neil Bradford,' he told Jeannie. 'From the local TV station. I just spoke with your father – he said there'd been no word yet.'

'I thought you were—' Jeannie gestured in despair.

'I'm sorry.' He was contrite. 'I talked to your father – he's raising the reward to fifty thousand dollars, and—'

'Where can Dad get that kind of money quickly?' Jeannie stared in disbelief.

'A man in town will put it up,' Neil explained. 'Jake Rhodes. It just might help if you make a personal plea on television. We can arrange for it to be carried nation-wide and—'

'No way!' Karen moved forward in anger. 'Get out of here! If you ever set foot here again, we'll ask the police for a restraining order! Jeannie will not make a personal plea! You can't do that to her!' She pulled Jeannie back into the foyer, slammed the door shut. 'How dare he pull something so low!'

'Karen, maybe he's right—' Jeannie was bewildered. 'I'll talk to Dad—'

'Your father wouldn't want you to do that.' Karen strived for calm. 'Not once he's thinking clearly. Don't you realize how that'll look to the public? They'll remember Susan Smith. They'll remember her emotional plea for the return of her two boys. Half of America cried while she lied. She knew her two little boys lay dead in the water!'

'Debbie's alive!' Jeannie's voice soared hysterically. 'Why doesn't he bring her back to us? Whoever came in through that window. She's alive! I know she is!'

Six

K aren sat across from her grandmother in a rear booth of the comfortable restaurant favored by business people in the area for lunch. They'd given their orders, talked briefly with the longtime waitress about the atmosphere of shock and pain that engulfed the town. Now – alone with her grandmother – Karen reported on the encounter at Jeannie and Doug's house with the man from the TV station.

'How awful of him to try to put Jeannie in a position like that!' Karen said. 'And he wasn't an out-of-town reporter. He's from the TV station here in town. I think his name is Bradford—' She searched her mind. 'Neil Bradford.'

'Oh, my God—' Helen flinched.

'What, Mom?' Karen was bewildered. 'He knew everybody who saw Jeannie on TV would remember Susan Smith going on TV to plead for the return of her little boys – and how everybody reacted with such sympathy.'

'Neil didn't know about the Susan Smith horror. He's been out of the country almost since he got out of journalism school – until about five months ago. He's been involved in all the ugliness in Bosnia. He was shot in the leg there. His parents persuaded him to come here to recuperate.'

He hadn't known. He'd meant to be helpful. 'Are his parents friends of yours, Mom?'

'We've become close in the three years Arline and Frank have been in town. We have dinner together once or twice a month. They're two of the finest people I've ever met.'

28

A *Town Named Paradise*

Mom was trying hard not to show how upset she was, Karen interpreted.

'I'll call him and apologize,' Karen said. 'He'll understand my reaction when I explain the situation.'

'I don't want to put you through that—' But Helen was upset.

'I'll call him.' Karen felt suffused with guilt.

'It's not good, is it, that nobody's contacted Jeannie and Doug?'

'It's not good.' Karen sighed. 'Everybody feels so helpless. And I suspect the local police haven't called in the FBI because they hope the reward offer will create some action.'

'Cindy says Laurie's hanging on to her every minute she's in the house. She didn't want Laurie to know – but how could Laurie not know? It's all everybody's talking about. And the police have come up with nothing.'

'They weren't happy about Mayor Gilbert's offering a reward for Debbie's return – with no questions asked,' Karen surmised. 'He's demanded they abort any thoughts about a surveillance of the house or a phone tap. He doesn't want the FBI brought in. But it's over twenty-four hours since Jeannie discovered Debbie missing. If they have no response to the reward offer by tonight, the police will want to push ahead.'

'Nobody in this town will sleep well until Debbie's found.' Her eyes were troubled. Karen knew her fears. *Was Debbie still alive?* 'They're holding a prayer service tonight at the Baptist church.' Helen hesitated. 'You meant it about calling Neil?'

'I'll call him,' Karen promised.

Unexpectedly Helen smiled. 'He's caused a lot of excitement among the young women in town. Several are out to snare him.'

Back at the house Karen stalled on making the call to Neil Bradford. She frolicked with Harry while Cindy and the two children concentrated on the tiny rock garden that was their current project.

29

'Thank goodness, the heat spell's letting up.' Cindy turned to Karen while Laurie and Zachary abandoned the rock garden to cavort with Harry, whose energy was boundless. She frowned, as though dealing with some disturbing thought. 'Do you believe in fate? If the air-conditioning at Jeannie's house hadn't been down, the bedroom windows would have been closed. Debbie might not have been kidnapped.'

'We never know what lies just around the corner.' Karen leaned forward to scratch Harry behind the ears. If Bob hadn't taken away Arnie's client – if he hadn't casually broken their weekend date at the Hamptons – she might still be on that crazy treadmill. 'I'd better get moving. I have a phone call to make.'

She sat before the phone and tried to frame a polite apology. For Mom she must do this. All right, do it.

She dialed, expecting a receptionist to pick up. She recognized Neil's voice immediately.

'Hi, this is Karen Mitchell—' She strived for casualness. 'I'm calling to apologize. I was the one who yelled at you at the Norris house this morning. I didn't know then that you'd been out of the country for years – that you didn't know about the Susan Smith murders and her pathetic appeals to "the kidnappers who took my little boys." And then she was revealed as the killer.'

'My parents clued me in.' His voice was deep and warm. 'I understand why you were so upset. At a time like this Jeannie and Doug Norris need a friend like you.'

'I wish there was something I could do to help.' She felt a fresh surge of frustration. 'I've known Jeannie since we were in kindergarten. I haven't seen her since our last year at high school. I was away at college, then law school, and working in New York for over a year.'

'My old hunting grounds.' For a moment he sounded nostalgic. 'I grew up in Manhattan's West Eighties.'

'I just came in town yesterday morning. It – it's been a traumatic homecoming.'

'We want to run a human interest segment about Jeannie

and Doug on the station.' He was serious now. 'To counteract those sly remarks that are coming through from the out-of-town media. You know, the insinuations that the mother or father is hiding some ugly secret.'

'I hate that!' Karen said passionately. 'Much of the media is so cynical – ready to jump at any sensational possibility. Anything that'll make a great headline or shock radio or TV audiences.'

'You go way back with Jeannie and Doug – you could be a big help pulling together a human interest story. They're an average couple thrust into a terrible situation that could happen to any couple anywhere in America.' He hesitated a moment. 'Could we get together and talk about them?'

'Yes—' She was startled by this invitation, but she understood where he was heading. Thank God some media people felt protective towards Jeannie and Doug. The local newspapers, at least – and now the TV station.

'What about dinner tonight? I don't know Jeannie and Doug. Instinct – and others in town – tell me they're good people. I don't want to see the media give them a rough time. Shall I pick you up around seven thirty?'

'That'll be fine. Let me give you my address—'

She sat by the phone for a few moments and pondered Neil Bradford's request. He shared with her a fear that speculation – never mind facts – was becoming acceptable to the media these days. They were driven to increase print circulation, raise TV or radio ratings. Neil worried about how this would affect Jeannie and Doug. He was what Arnie called a *mensch*.

Later Karen reported her conversation with Neil to Helen.

'If Neil Bradford can make the situation easier for Jeannie and Doug, I'm all for it.' Mom sounds almost defensive, Karen reproached herself. Because of what she had said about his being pursued by local women. There was nothing personal here – just a shared wish to do the right thing.

'I'll finish off last night's chicken and salad, then go over

Julie Ellis

to the church for the prayer service,' Helen decided. 'But let me turn on the TV. I hear Clay Gilbert's going on at seven to announce the reward is being raised to fifty thousand dollars. No questions asked,' she emphasized.

At exactly seven thirty Karen saw a white station wagon draw up before the house. Neil Bradford emerged and strode up the path to the house. Never once in their relationship had Bob arrived anywhere on time, she thought involuntarily.

'We saw Mayor Gilbert's appeal on the 7 p.m. news,' Karen said. 'He came across very determined about no police intervention.'

'It's thirty-six hours since Jeannie discovered Debbie was missing.' His face was somber as they walked together towards the station wagon. 'If there's no word by morning, the police figure there'll be no response. It's time to bring in the FBI.'

'Have they come up with anything concrete?'

'If they have, they're keeping it quiet. I'm sure they've done the usual stuff.'

En route to the restaurant – The Colonial, a new and popular spot, Neil confided – he questioned her about the family's history in the town. He knew the mayor was a fourth-generation resident. Fighting self-consciousness, Karen explained about her on-and-off residence in Paradise.

'This was home for most of my growing-up years. From nursery school I knew the same people – you know how it is in a small town. Jeannie was popular in high school – a cheerleader, member of the drama club. A fair student. Doug was the big basketball star of Paradise High. He went to a community college for a year, then right to work at the shirt factory. I understand Jeannie works at the local bookstore.' She was sure Neil knew that Rhodes Shirt Factory was the major employer in this town – had been for the past twenty years. 'They were married when Jeannie was nineteen and Doug twenty.'

The restaurant was a restored 1798 white colonial residence, with the lower floor rooms converted to three charming dining rooms – tables well spaced to ensure diners' privacy – and the kitchen at the rear. Pricey for a town like this, Karen thought as she inspected the menu.

'After four years of eating garbage in the Balkans, I revel in a place like this.' Neil chuckled. 'I revel in a decent bed and a place to shower every morning.'

He talked about growing up on the West Side of Manhattan, going first to private school, then to Stuyvesant High and on to Columbia and Columbia School of Journalism.

'My parents went through the whole sixties scene together – and some of it never rubbed off. They've got this thing about being involved with their community, giving back to it. It rubbed off on me,' he conceded. 'I still balk at the way "liberal" has become a dirty word.'

Karen confessed that she had walked out on a prestigious law firm and a shockingly high salary. Astonishing herself at her candor with someone she'd just met. But Neil *understood*.

'Tell me about this guy Jake Rhodes – the one who's helping Mayor Gilbert with the reward money.'

'He's respected in town but not especially liked.' She searched for words to give Neil a concise profile. 'He comes from a working-class family, married the only child of the man who owned what was then a small shirt factory in town. He took over when his father-in-law suffered a bad stroke and built it into a major industry. Changed the name from Mellon to Rhodes Shirt Factory. His workers consider him a fair man but super-demanding – and he keeps a distance from most people. The only person in town that he's close to is Mayor Gilbert.'

'You scratch my back and I'll scratch yours? As mayor, Gilbert's probably useful to him in zoning deals and stuff like that.'

'That's the general opinion. He's always there for the mayor at election time – and the mayor fights for his causes. The way I heard, Rhodes' first wife died when his daughters were twelve and nine. He married again two years later. A twenty-year-old receptionist at the mill. He built that big house on Kenilworth Road when she became pregnant. The first one beyond that small stretch of woods. By the time Adam was two, Rhodes knew the marriage was over. He caught his new wife sleeping around, divorced her and drove her out of town. I guess that kind of soured him. Adam's about seventeen now, I think. He's been off at boarding school and summer camps since he was twelve. He has severe allergy problems that make it necessary for him to live above the timber line. At least, that's what Rhodes claims. People say he can't bear to have Adam around because he's the image of his mother. The older daughter – Olivia – lives about forty miles from here, the other out west. Why all the interest in Jake Rhodes?'

'I'm trying to get a handle on people in this town.' He grinned. 'Starting at the top.'

By the time they arrived at dessert Karen had diverted conversation to his hectic years in Bosnia and the surrounding areas. He talked with pain about the death and destruction he'd seen, glossing over his own injuries.

'Maybe what I saw over there made me want to help the Norrises. The worst thing over there was seeing children – babies – dying. Innocent little kids. Why the hell did they have to die? When will the world learn to live in peace? Not until you see war face to face do you realize its horror.'

When they at last prepared to leave, Karen was startled to realize they'd been at the restaurant over two hours. She sensed Neil's reluctance to end the evening, realized with self-conscious surprise that she shared this feeling. They walked out into the night where the temperature had dropped a dozen degrees. The sky was star-splashed. The moon lent a soft golden patina to the landscape.

Neil drove her home, parked in front of the house. They saw Harry tied to the Japanese maple on the Simmons's small front lawn – barking in reproach.

'Hey, fella, cool it,' Neil called out good-humoredly.

Cindy charged through the front door. 'Harry, be quiet!' She saw Karen and Neil sitting in the car and waved. 'He's indignant because Todd's at a meeting with some parents and not taking him for his usual late walk.'

'We can do that—' Neil turned to Karen. 'We can use a walk after that dinner, can't we?'

'Sure.' She thrust open the car door on her side and walked to join Cindy and Harry, rapturous at fresh attention.

Neil and Cindy knew each other from local affairs. 'Todd won the station's award for the town's favorite schoolteacher two years in a row,' Neil told Karen.

'Mom mentioned that,' Karen recalled.

'We'll give Harry a long walk,' Neil promised Cindy. 'He doesn't have to stay on the leash, does he?'

'No, he's a good boy. If he gets rambunctious, just order him to sit – and he'll obey.' She dropped a loving hand on Harry for a moment. 'Now don't make me a liar.'

Seven

K aren and Neil headed down the road with Harry off the leash and rapturous at this freedom. They walked without any real destination, their conversation darting from one subject to another. Harry seemed to be leading the way. Probably the route he took each night with Todd, Karen surmised. The soft night air was such a relief, she thought with pleasure, after the heatwave that had engulfed much of the Northeast. The night stillness a soothing balm.

They strolled from the older part of town into the new development of modest houses. The development where Jeannie and Doug lived, Karen realized.

'Isn't that the mayor's car in front of the Norris house?' Neil asked.

'Yes—' Every room in the house was alight. 'Neil, do you think there's been some response to his appearance?' Hope spiraled in her.

'I doubt it – I told Mom and Dad where we were having dinner. One of them would have called me.' His eyes spanned the area. 'The cops are keeping to their word. Nobody in sight.'

'Harry!' Karen scolded because he had taken off and was headed into the woods. 'Harry, sit!'

But Harry was in pursuit of a cottontail and too intrigued to respond.

'He won't catch it,' Neil soothed. 'But he's having fun.'

They followed Harry along a path beaten into the woods

36

by neighborhood children. The moon casting incredible light. Harry had stopped chasing the cottontail. He was digging with great insistence.

'Harry, are you trying to dig to China?' Neil joshed and then stopped dead. 'Oh, my God! Harry, sit! Sit!' Responding to the forcefulness of Neil's command, Harry sat.

'What is it?' Karen followed his galvanized gaze. A tiny white hand appeared from a mound of dug-up earth. 'Oh, Neil!' Her eyes sought his. He nodded in silence.

'I'll stay here,' Neil said. 'Phone for the police—'

Karen hurried from the woods, paused at the clearing – her eyes drawn to the Norris house. She shivered. No, they didn't have to know just yet. No doubt in her mind that the tiny hand protruding from the dirt was Debbie's. The house next to the Norrises' was dark. The family already in bed for the night. The house across the road was lighted. She hurried up the path to the door, rang the bell.

'I'm sorry,' she apologized when a middle-aged man in an undershirt opened the door. A stranger to her. 'There's an emergency – I need to call the police.'

'Sure.' He gestured her inside. 'The phone's on the end table by the sofa.' He pointed to the living room.

'Fred, who is it?' A rotund, fortyish woman in a robe came into the living room while Karen spoke with someone at the police station. He put up a hand for silence.

'Is this something to do with Debbie Norris?' he asked anxiously.

'We think so,' Karen said. 'But please, don't leave the house. The police are on the way.' She paused a moment, her heart pounding, her throat tightened. 'There's a body in a shallow grave. We saw one tiny hand—' Her voice broke. How were they to tell Jeannie and Doug?

'Oh, how awful—' The woman began to cry.

'Put up some coffee,' he told his wife. 'There won't be much sleep tonight.'

'Do they know?' the woman asked Karen.

'Not yet. We're not sure, of course, that it *is* Debbie.'

'Such a sweet young couple. Their lives will never be the same again.'

Karen left the house, hesitated at the curb. The lighted Norris house the focus of her attention. The police would want a family member to identify the body, she recognized with anguish. Not Jeannie or Doug. Mayor Gilbert, she pinpointed. Bring him to the woods with her.

She hurried across the road and up to the door, rang the bell. There *was* a chance that the small body in the shallow grave was not Debbie's – but her mind ridiculed such a supposition. She heard the chimes. The door opened. Mayor Gilbert stood there, his face tense, eyes questioning.

'I'm sorry,' she whispered. 'I think you should come with me into the woods. I've called the police—'

His face was drained of color. 'Sure—'

'Karen?' Jeannie rushed to the foyer. 'There's word?' Her eyes searched Karen's, saw only compassion. 'What's happened to my baby?' Her voice was shrill with terror.

'Doug, you and Jeannie stay here,' her father commanded.

'They've found my baby!' Jeannie struggled to free herself from Doug's restraining arms. 'Let me go to her! Let me go to her!'

'We're not sure yet,' Karen soothed, feeling sick. She was sure. 'Wait here—'

They heard police cars – their sirens silenced out of respect for the neighbors – but a quick glance told her that, yes, the two vehicles coming to a stop at the edge of the woods were police cars. In painful silence Karen and Clay Gilbert left the house and hurried to the wooded area. They heard a faint whimper from Harry, who sensed something awful had happened.

One of the police officers had brought a shovel from his car. Cold and fearful, Karen stood between Neil and Clay Gilbert while the officer swept the dirt away to reveal a towel-wrapped tiny body. Karen was conscious of an odd, heavy perfume that saturated the towel. The officer – his face revealing his pain – gently peeled the towel from the small face. A length of thin household rope about the slender throat. She had been strangled.

'It's Debbie—' Gilbert's voice was a shaken whisper. 'That's our baby! Oh God, how do I tell Jeannie her baby's dead?'

Eight

It seemed so natural, Karen thought, to be sitting here in Mom's large country kitchen with Mom and Neil. She was still cold and trembling from those harrowing minutes in the woods. She clutched her coffee mug and listened while Neil rehashed what they knew thus far.

'We have to wait for the forensic reports, of course – but I suspect she was killed between midnight and 1 a.m. yesterday morning. The police have little to go on at this point,' he conceded in frustration. 'The white bath towel had no identifying features – it could have been any towel from any place. The length of rope about her throat could have come from anywhere. I can't identify that heavy cologne, either on the towel or her body. Nor can you, Karen—'

'I heard one of the detectives say that the – the body had been washed clean,' Karen recalled. 'Could it be some ritual murder?'

'No. It was washed to rid it of semen.' Neil was blunt. 'To eliminate a DNA test that might identify the perpetrator.'

The other two gaped in shock.

'You think she was raped?' Karen felt sick.

'I'd take any bet.' He grimaced. 'That poor little kid. What kind of monster is hiding in this town? Of course, I could be wrong,' he conceded after a moment. 'I pray I'm wrong.' But he didn't believe that, Karen thought.

'This town will be crawling with reporters and TV people in the morning,' Helen predicted and shuddered.

'You've got a shop to open in the morning,' Neil reminded Helen gently. 'And I have a 7 a.m. newscast to do. Let me get out of here so we can all get some sleep.'

In her bedroom Karen slid beneath the sheet. No need tonight to flip on the air-conditioner. She knew sleep would elude her – aborted by the image of the tiny hand that emerged from the shallow grave. One moment life had seemed so beautiful for Jeannie and Doug – whose wants were modest. Then this nightmare. Perhaps life was meant to be good only in brief spurts.

At last – from exhaustion – she succumbed to troubled slumber.

6.42 a.m., Saturday, August 30, 1997

Karen came awake with a sense of plummeting through space. Immediately aware of last night's happening. Her eyes sought out the clock. 6.42 a.m. She frowned, reluctant to face the day ahead. Faint sounds from the kitchen told her Mom was already up.

She'd get up in ten minutes, she compromised. Catch Neil's 7 a.m. newscast. She mustn't allow herself to become emotionally embroiled with him – no matter how she was drawn to him. And she sensed he felt something special for her. But this was ridiculous! She was rebounding from Bob. *I can't afford another mistake.*

All at once restless, she tossed aside the sheet, reached for slippers at the side of the bed. The sensuous aroma of fresh coffee drifted down the hall from the kitchen. She'd splash water on her face, shower later. In ballerina-length printed nightie she left her room and headed for the kitchen. Now she heard the muted sound of the kitchen radio.

'Coffee's ready,' Mom said, kneading a mound of dough. In times of stress Mom baked. 'You feel like breakfast yet? I'll put biscuits in the oven in a couple of minutes.'

Karen managed a faint smile. 'Just coffee for now.'

Mom seemed to be fighting for composure. 'I heard the 6 a.m. news on the radio. Neil was right. The police said Debbie was raped before she was strangled.'

Karen closed her eyes in anguish. 'That poor baby—'

'I'll pour coffee for us, and let's go catch the 7 a.m. TV news.'

With coffee in tow the two women went into the living room. Karen flipped on the TV. The station wasn't waiting for the 7 a.m. report. Its woman newscaster – visibly shaken – was relating last night's discovery.

'Dr Evans, the head of the forensic department, reports that Debbie Norris was raped before she was strangled. The district attorney vows that all efforts will be concentrated on finding and convicting the perpetrator . . .'

The sound of the doorbell was a harsh intrusion.

'I'll get it—' Karen hurried to respond.

'Karen, did you hear?' Cindy was ashen. She knew that Debbie's body had been found. Returning Harry to the house, Neil had told her this. Now she knew about the rape. 'It's shattering!'

'We heard—' Karen and Cindy walked into the living room – both anxious to follow the newscast.

'No child in this town is safe until that monster's found!' Cindy's eyes clung to the television set. 'I told Todd – Laurie's not to go out of the house unless both of us are with her.'

The camera switched to Neil. 'Sssh!' Helen ordered.

'We have with us this morning well-known businessman Jake Rhodes and his son Adam. Mr Rhodes has a statement to make.' Neil turned with a deferential smile and the camera segued to the other two.

Jake Rhodes stood at the microphone – tall, somber, slightly forbidding. His son seemed uncomfortable at being dragged into the limelight. Poor kid, Karen sympathized – it couldn't be easy living the nomadic life demanded by his severe allergies. Why did Rhodes drag Adam into this situation? No teenager appreciated this kind of exposure.

Probably Rhodes was already planting seeds that would lead one day to a political role for Adam in this town.

'I grieve deeply for Jeannie and Doug Norris. As a family man – with two daughters and a son—' He dropped an arm protectively about Adam. 'I know the anguish they feel. And I feel rage that something so despicable could happen here in our town. The reward that I offered for Debbie's return will now go to the person providing information that will lead to the arrest and conviction of the perpetrator.'

Now Neil added the meager fresh information available. The Norris family was pleading for an early release of the body so that they could arrange for the burial.

'Why are they holding up releasing the body?' Cindy was indignant.

'The police are searching for whatever evidence may be available,' Karen explained. 'They have to be sure they're overlooking nothing.' She frowned, her mind replaying last night's discovery. 'Neil and I both noticed a strange cologne that seemed to be on the towel wrapped about the body.'

'Is that a lead?' Cindy asked.

'It could be.' Karen was puzzled. Why wasn't it mentioned on the news? Because it was bizarre? Or out of respect for the family?

They watched absorbedly until the morning news moved on to matters outside the town. Now Helen switched off the TV.

'I just hope this town doesn't become a circus.'

'Todd says out-of-town reporters are already coming in,' Cindy told them. 'Now we'll be flooded. Every supermarket tabloid will send in crews. The television networks. But if it'll help ferret out that monster, then so be it.'

Labor Day Weekend, 1997

All Labor Day weekend festivities were cancelled. This weekend the town was in mourning – its grief spiced with rage. As feared, hordes of reporters, photographers, and TV crews invaded the town, camped before the Norris house. The police department set up barricades to protect the family from intrusion at this critical time. Only friends were allowed to approach the house.

On Monday the police released the body. Debbie Norris was to be buried on Wednesday. The day she was to have entered first grade. School would open a day late this year. Elementary students were to receive counseling before classes began. Businesses and local government offices would close for the afternoon of the funeral.

The citizenry was frustrated by the lack of bulletins from the police department. Most were indignant when word seeped through that Doug Norris was undergoing intensive questioning. A supermarket tabloid headline read: 'FATHER EXPECTED TO PLEAD INSANITY'. How dare they, Karen railed.

'It's routine to suspect the father,' Neil reminded Karen and Helen when he dropped by the house on Tuesday – the night before the funeral. Their discovering the body was a special bond between them, Karen told herself defensively. It was natural that he should be underfoot this way.

Was Bob reading about the case? The New York tabloids would headline the story. Did he wonder if she was here?

'Local people know Doug couldn't have anything to do with this.' Neil brought her back to the moment. 'But the father is always questioned.'

'Can't they do something more constructive?' Helen was acerbic.

'The pickings are slim.'

'What about fingerprints?' Karen probed.

'Not much available. They've been sent to the lab in Albany for identification. But these things take time.' Karen was conscious of the way his eyes sought hers. With questions. He was wondering how long she'd be in Paradise, she interpreted. She couldn't answer that. 'Every florist in town is sold out,' he said. Then frowned. 'You know, I'm still puzzled about that cologne. It reminded me of something – but I can't pinpoint it.'

'It was a man's cologne.' Karen was grim. 'Why was it there?'

Neil hesitated. 'To conceal the aroma for a time when the body began to decompose,' he surmised. 'The murderer wanted to delay discovery as long as possible. He didn't anticipate Harry's digging.'

'Have the police checked on enemies the family might have? Was there somebody with a grudge against the mayor – or Doug or Jeannie?' Helen echoed Karen's suspicions. 'Or was it a rape case that turned to murder?'

'I suspect that's the assumption,' Neil said after a moment.

10.20 p.m. Tuesday, September 2, 1997

On the way home Neil decided to stop off at Wheat's Drugstore – the largest and most popular in Paradise – to buy razor blades. It was weird how Wheat's – which normally closed at 7 p.m. – was staying open till 11 p.m. because of the influx of out-of-towners. The three hotels in town were close to being booked to capacity – which never happened. The restaurants had waiting lines at meal times.

Neil parked before the drugstore, hurried inside. He headed for the area where he'd find the needed razor blades. He was reaching for his quarry when he felt a heavy hand on his shoulder.

'Hey, Neil! Neil Bradford! What the hell are you doing in this one-horse town?'

He swung about to face a fiftyish man with sagging jawline and bags under cynical eyes. For a moment Neil couldn't identify him.

'The last time I saw you was in Herzegovina! It must have been four years ago. What are you doing on this beat?'

'I caught a bullet in my leg.' Hank Graham, Neil pinpointed. He'd been a roving reporter for some shaky magazine that went under while Graham was on his beat. 'My parents run the local television station. I'm here for rest and rehabilitation.'

45

'This rag I'm working for out of New York shipped me over to cover the rape/murder deal. You know, when a little kid is involved, everybody gets excited. The story doesn't seem to be going anywhere that I can see.' He shrugged. 'But they tell me to hang around – and they're paying the bills.'

'Hi, Neil—' Todd waved from a few feet away. 'Tell your father my kids love the new puppet show.'

'I'll tell him—'

Hank Graham stared curiously at Todd. 'Who's that guy?'

'Todd Simmons. He teaches at a private school here in town. Why?'

'He looks damn familiar.' Hank shook his head in dismissal. 'I can't place him.'

'Everybody has a double. Even you,' Neil joshed. 'I'll see you—'

Neil hurried to the line of customers at the one cash register. He had no desire to join Hank Graham at some gin mill for reminiscences. As he recalled, Hank loved to get tanked up and talk about old foreign correspondents he'd known in earlier years.

At home he found his mother settled on the sofa before the TV set – feet resting on the oversized coffee table. A cup of coffee in hand. In another twenty minutes the station signed off for the night. A ritual Dad enjoyed.

'Nothing new on the case,' she reported. 'And this is decaf,' she said with a glint of humor – forestalling reproach. 'I just made a pot if you'd like some.'

'I've had my quota for the day.' His eyes were somber. 'I hope the cops keep the media away from the funeral tomorrow.'

The sharp ring of the phone was a jarring intrusion.

'I'll get it, Mom—' Neil reached for the cordless phone atop the fireplace mantel. 'Hello—'

'Hey, it wasn't hard to find you. Just one other Bradford family in town.' Hank Graham's voice exuded excitement.

'What's up, Hank?'

'You know that guy we saw in the drugstore – and I said he looked familiar?'

'Yeah—'

'Something just clicked in my head! I know who he is. I covered his trial for rape – it must have been sixteen or seventeen years ago! He—'

'You're way off the mark,' Neil interrupted. 'Todd Simmons has been teaching school in this town for several years. He won an award for being the town's finest teacher. You're—'

'This is the guy! Same first name – Todd. Only then it was Todd Anderson. I remember the case because it had such a melodramatic climax. The jury announced their findings – "guilty as charged". His father leapt to his feet, yelled out something and collapsed. He died of a massive heart attack right there. Hey, you were a little kid – you never knew about it.'

'I can't believe this is the same guy.'

'It's the same.' Hank's voice was edged with triumph. 'And some character in town is offering a fifty-thousand-dollar reward for information leading to a conviction! Wow, could I use that loot!'

'Even if you're right,' Neil said uncomfortably, 'that doesn't mean he's guilty of this crime.' But he couldn't accept that Todd Simmons was Todd Anderson, who'd served time for rape. 'That's pure speculation.'

'But don't you think the cops will want to question him?'

'If he is Todd Anderson – and I don't swallow that – then the media will convict him,' Neil warned. 'All it takes these days is a rumor, and they're off to the races.'

'If he has an alibi, he'll be off the hook before anything can happen.'

'Hank, it turns me off—'

'Fifty thousand dollars doesn't turn me off. If he's innocent, then he'll clear himself.'

'But if he is Todd Anderson – even if he's innocent in this case – his life will never be the same in this town. *He teaches seventh graders*. He'll be driven out of the school—'

'He was seventeen when he raped a twelve-year-old girl. He was tried and convicted as an adult. Do you think he should be teaching twelve-year-olds? First thing tomorrow morning I'll be at the district attorney's office. I'm inviting you to be there with me – to get the scoop for your station. You'll be on nationwide TV. And when the district attorney interviews me on your station, I want you to tape it so I can FedEx it to my tabloid.' His eyes were brilliant with anticipation. 'I can see the headline: REPORTER NAILS RAPIST/MURDERER. Pick me up at my hotel tomorrow morning at 8 a.m. sharp.'

Neil put down the phone, stared into space.

'What was that all about?' His mother was anxious.

As succinctly as possible, Neil filled her in.

'That's absurd! How dare he even suggest such a thing!'

'I'll be there with Hank to see what comes up. I'm sure if the police go to the extent of questioning Todd, he'll clear up the matter fast.' But his mother grimaced in distaste.

Hank had over thirty years of reporting behind him. He had a keen memory for cases he had covered through those years. But no, Neil shot down doubts – Todd Simmons was a totally decent man. Hank was all wrong.

Nine

7.10 a.m., Wednesday, September 3, 1997

K aren awoke with an instant realization that this was the day the town would turn out en masse for Debbie Norris's funeral. Six days ago at just about this hour Jeannie had walked into Debbie's bedroom and found her missing. People were upset that the police had no lead. Neil said the district attorney was being bombarded by questions from the media and providing no acceptable answers.

She heard sounds in the kitchen. Mom was already up and about. Neither of them was getting decent sleep these nights. Both woke up exhausted from stress. Jeannie was under heavy sedation, they heard. Doug barely holding on. Mayor Gilbert moved about in a daze, to erupt at intervals into rage that no suspect had been seized.

The telephone rang. A raucous intrusion in the early morning silence. Karen glanced at her bedside clock. Who was calling this early? She hurried out to the kitchen. Mom was on the phone.

'Come right over, Neil,' Helen urged. 'It's not too early. You'll have breakfast with us.'

'What's up?' Was Mom developing romantic ideas about Neil and her? The possibility was unnerving. She wasn't ready for this.

'Neil is upset about something to do with the case. I don't know why he wants to talk with us about it. Anyhow, he'll have breakfast with us.' She reached into a cabinet for pancake mix. 'You think he'll like strawberry pancakes?'

49

'Mom, everybody likes your strawberry pancakes. Oh, I'd better get dressed—'

Karen was furious with herself for changing outfits three times this morning. Settling on a turquoise shift, she heard Neil pull up into the driveway. What had brought him over this early in the morning? Mom said he'd sounded very cryptic.

She headed for the kitchen. Mom was at the griddle making pancakes. Neil sat at the breakfast table with coffee mug in hand. She was too impatient to play games.

'The police have come up with a suspect?'

'Not exactly.' Neil seemed unhappy.

'What does that mean?' Karen poured herself a mug of coffee, joined him at the table.

Neil briefed Karen and Helen on his encounter with Hank Graham.

'I kept telling him he must be wrong about Todd, but he's going to the DA. I guess I need to hear you say you don't believe it, either.' His eyes searched Helen's.

'I don't believe it.' She was firm.

After Neil left, Helen settled herself at the table with another cup of coffee. Mom enjoyed these little interludes each morning when they could dawdle in conversation before she took off for the shop, Karen thought tenderly.

'Neil's very special. I was indulgent with his mother when she talked about all his fine traits – thinking, you know, she's another mother who adores her son. But he stands out from the crowd.'

'He thinks a lot like us—' Karen was evasive. She suspected where Helen was heading.

'He looks at you as though he thinks you're very special—' A hopeful glint in her eyes.

'Mom, stop building up romantic thoughts about us.' Karen managed to appear amused. 'I helped him on that story about Jeannie and Doug. And then, of course, we were both involved in—' She paused in pain. 'In finding Debbie that way. I'm no competition for those local women who're out to entrap him.'

'That's what you think,' Helen said airily. 'I see the way he looks at you—'

'I'm just out of a long-term relationship that turned sour,' she admitted. *That* pleased Mom. It annoyed her that Bob always managed an excuse not to come here. Not once in over two years. 'I'm in no mood to start up another so soon.'

8 a.m., Wednesday, September 3, 1997

As arranged, Neil went to Hank's hotel to pick him up. Hank was waiting in the lobby.

'I called the district attorney at his house,' he told Neil. 'He's expecting us at the office.'

'If you're wrong about this, he'll be teed off,' Neil warned.

'I'm not wrong.' Hank's eyes glistened with anticipation. He was mentally spending that $50,000 already, Neil interpreted. 'This will be a great story for both of us.' He was in high spirits. 'It could put your old man's station on the map.'

'Hank, there's got to be a mistake. My parents both know this guy – he's a sterling citizen. Two years in a row he was voted the town's best teacher.'

'But fifteen or sixteen years ago he raped a twelve-year-old. He served time in prison. And you think he has nothing to do with what happened here?'

'We'll find out soon enough.' He wasn't going with Hank for a great story. He wanted to clear up this nasty accusation.

At the courthouse they were immediately ushered into George Morrison's small, cluttered office. Neil introduced the two men.

'You said you have a lead on the perpetrator in the Debbie Norris case.' With a hint of skepticism, Morrison focused on Hank.

'I covered his earlier trial – over in East Sedgewick.'

'What earlier trial?' Morrison was suddenly alert.

'When he was convicted on rape charges.' A triumphant glint in Hank's eyes now. 'Only then his name was Todd Anderson. Not Todd Simmons. It's the same guy – even all these years later I recognized him.'

Morrison leaned forward, pushed a button on his intercom. 'Doris, tell Jim to get in here. Pronto.'

Neil listened with growing unease to the rapid-fire exchange between Morrison and Hank. Then they were joined by the assistant prosecuting attorney. Neil began to feel uneasy. *Was there a chance that Hank was right?*

'All right,' Morrison concluded at last. 'We'll pick him up for questioning. Meanwhile, you get on the computer, Jim. See what comes up.'

'You're making reports on the local TV station, then on radio,' Hank said to Morrison. 'As your source I'd like to appear with you on your next report. I rate that.'

'Hold it, Hank.' This was moving too fast. Neil turned to Morrison. 'There's no proof yet that Todd Simmons and Todd Anderson are the same.'

'We'll get the proof.' Morrison was brusque. 'And if it's true, the public has a right to know.'

'That's guilt by association!' A pulse pounded at Neil's temple. The kind of crap he loathed! 'It can't be introduced at the trial.'

'No.' Morrison smiled faintly. 'But it's a basis for bringing him in for questioning.' He paused in thought for a moment. 'We'll just say that he's being brought in for questioning. We'll hold him pending an investigation of his whereabouts between midnight and 1 a.m. on the night of the murder.'

While Helen talked on the phone with a neighbor about the memorial service at the school later in the day, Karen scanned the morning newspaper. She felt disconcertingly at a loose end. She was beginning to unwind after the trauma of those last two days in New York. To switch from seventeen-hour workdays to idleness was a culture shock.

Bob had made no effort to call her. He must realize she

was here. Not that it would matter, she thought defiantly. Bob was history. She'd known for months that it was a bad scene – she'd just been afraid to admit it, to look ahead at a life on her own. Her eyes swung to the wall clock. It was past nine thirty. Normally Mom would have left the house for the shop by now – but these weren't ordinary days.

She wished there was some way she could be helpful to Jeannie. For a few minutes time had seemed to hurtle backwards – and they were close. But there were too many years between those days and now. Jeannie made it clear she didn't want to see anybody except immediate family – and that was understandable. Her life would never be the same again. Or was it true that time heals all wounds?

Helen hung up the phone, reached for her purse. 'I'd better get moving – we'll be closing up at one o'clock.'

'Neil and that reporter must be with George Morrison by now—' Karen frowned. 'I can't believe the man could make such a ghastly mistake.'

'He'll be straightened out fast enough.' Helen grunted in distaste. Her eyes swung to a window that faced the Simmons house. All at once she stiffened. 'What the hell?'

'What is it, Mom?' Karen was startled by the alarm in her grandmother's voice. 'Mom?'

'Two police cars are pulling up into Cindy's driveway!' Helen's eyes clung to the view.

'They want to question Todd – it doesn't mean anything. That reporter made an accusation. They have to follow it up. It's just routine.'

'But how rotten to put Todd in that position!'

They watched while two detectives went into the Simmons house. The atmosphere tense. Moments later the two detectives emerged with Todd.

'Let's go over there.' Helen was brusque. 'Cindy must be distraught.'

Moments later – seeing Karen and Helen approach – Cindy opened the kitchen door before Karen's finger touched the bell.

'The detectives are taking Todd in for questioning,' she said, her face drained of color.

'It's just a formality,' Helen soothed. 'Some reporter made a mistaken identification.'

'You don't understand – it's going to start all over again. All the old insanity, the lies! They'll dig up the old case.'

'What case, Cindy?' Karen kept her voice even, but her mind was on full alert.

'Sixteen years ago – when Todd was seventeen – some little girl in town accused him of raping her. He was convicted.' Cindy struggled to continue. 'I've always felt responsible for what happened. Back then we were living in East Sedgewick. We were going steady in our senior year. We had a stupid fight, and I refused to go with him to our senior prom. This girl – Tiffany – gatecrashed. She was twelve but she looked seventeen. You know – she was wearing a lot of make-up and a sexy dress. She came on strong, coaxed him away from the prom. They had sex. It was Todd's first time – but not *hers*!' Cindy remembered with fresh rage. 'I never had a doubt. I knew Todd was innocent, but—'

'She got scared and told her mother she'd been raped,' Karen finished for her.

'She appeared at the trial. No make-up, demure hairdo, dressed like a twelve-year-old. Everybody believed her—' Cindy closed her eyes for a moment in remembered anguish. 'Even my parents at first. Todd had graduated at the top of our class – he'd been voted "Brightest" and "Most Likely to Succeed". My parents came to realize he was being railroaded. My mother sat with his parents every day at the trial—'

'But he was convicted,' Helen finished for her.

'He served three and a half years, then was released for good behavior. He earned college credit while he was in prison, got his degree and his masters in education when he got out.'

'You waited for him,' Karen said gently.

'My parents were upset, but then they realized how much

we loved each other. They knew nothing could keep Todd and me apart. I don't think I could have survived those three and a half years without their support. I chose a college close enough to Todd's prison so I could see him on visiting days. I was all he had that last year and a half. His father had died the day he was convicted, his mother two years later.'

'But the name change?' Karen was uneasy. As a convicted felon Todd had to register with the state. *Under his legal name.* 'How can he call himself Todd Simmons?'

Cindy sighed. 'I know it was wrong, but we managed to get around that. My parents legally adopted Todd when he was released. They did this down in Florida. By that time they'd retired and moved down there. I married him as Todd Simmons.' Her face reflected her fears. 'Now the case will be dragged out again. The newspapers will have a field day. They—'

'Todd must have a lawyer present when they question him,' Karen broke in. His previous conviction would be confirmed. He'd be a prime suspect – even though the earlier conviction couldn't be introduced into a trial.

'Karen, go down there!' Helen ordered.

'Would you?' Cindy's eyes pleaded with her. 'Todd was convicted of something he didn't do! And now they'll try to do that again!'

Karen wavered. 'I have so little criminal law experience—'

'You can bet no local attorney will take him on,' Helen said bluntly. 'Call downtown and tell them you're Todd's attorney. He's not to be questioned until you're present!'

'No! I won't!' Zachary's voice – raspy, hoarse – filtered from the bedroom where he played with Laurie. 'Mommie, Mommie!'

Cindy was immobilized, her eyes fastened to Karen.

'Mommie! Zachary's so bad!' Laurie complained. 'Tell him he's supposed to stay in bed!'

'I'll call downtown.' Karen strode to the phone. 'Let them know I'm Todd's attorney. They don't question him except in my presence.'

Off the phone with the district attorney's office, she sat frozen in place for a moment.

I've made a commitment to stay here in Paradise probably for months. Is this what I want to do with my life? Bob would say, 'Oh, what a sucker you are!' But Bob is out of my life. I know he was wrong for me. Why do I feel this little insidious doubt? Bob was a habit. I've kicked the habit.

But still – in the depths of the night – she reached over half-asleep, and was startled not to find him there. Deep in the recesses of her mind she had allowed a truant thought that he would call her here. He must have known she'd come home. Bad habits, she reproached herself, die slowly.

Ten

S unlight lent a specious air of well-being to the breakfast area of the Norris kitchen. Jeannie toyed with the scrambled eggs Doug had made for her. He worried that she was making no effort to take over the reins of the household, she realized. How could she think about such things?

Each morning at 9 a.m. Marie showed up to take care of Tommy – just as though she would be leaving to go to the bookstore. Doug made breakfast, brought take-out food home for dinner. Mr Rhodes insisted Doug didn't have to come in to work just yet, but Doug went in anyway. How could he do that, when their precious baby wasn't buried yet?

'Jeannie, eat,' Doug urged anxiously. 'We can't afford to fall apart. We have to think about Tommy.'

'If we'd taken care of the air-conditioning, the window in Debbie's room would have been closed. Locked.' She brushed aside the knowledge that windows in Paradise were rarely locked. 'Debbie would be here with us.' Her eyes were accusing. It was a husband's job to take care of such things.

Doug flinched. 'We can't go back and change things. We have to learn to cope. Honey, I'm eaten up inside, too – but we have to learn to live with it.'

Jeannie started at the jarring intrusion of the front door bell. Every unexpected sound alarmed her. 'It's too early for Marie—'

'I'll get it.'

Doug went to the door, admitted his father-in-law.

'Where's Jeannie?'

'In the kitchen—'

'Daddy?' Jeannie was accustomed to her father's appearance at the house at odd moments these past days, but the tone of his voice told her this was not another of his efforts to bring her comfort.

'They've caught the bastard!' Clay Gilbert charged into the kitchen. His face was florid, his breathing heavy. 'George just called to tell me.'

'Who?' The fork fell from her hands. Her voice was an agonized whisper. 'Who murdered my baby?'

'Todd Simmons! All the time pretending to be such an asset to this town. He—'

'Whoa, Dad,' Doug interrupted. 'Have they got any proof?' He turned to Jeannie. 'I can't believe it was Todd!'

'Oh, it was him, all right. George gave me the facts. He was seen speeding through town right after midnight that night. George says they have witnesses. And he was living here under an assumed name. We never knew the real man.' He paused, his face contorted with rage. 'He was convicted of raping a little girl over in East Sedgewick. He spent time in prison. He—'

'Why did they let him out?' Jeannie hovered at hysteria. 'Why didn't they keep him in jail? Monsters like that shouldn't be allowed out on the street. Daddy, you tell George we want him to die for what he did to my baby!' She closed her eyes in anguish. 'I don't want to think about what he did to Debbie. She must have been so frightened, so hurting.' She took a deep breath. 'I don't want to think about it. How do I live with that in the years ahead?'

'Jeannie, take one of your pills,' Doug ordered. 'I'll get it for you—'

'What good do pills do? I can't sleep for remembering what he did to Debbie. She was only six years old—' Her voice broke.

'I'll get your pill—' Doug crossed to the kitchen counter.

Jeannie turned to her father. 'Daddy, you tell George to go for the death penalty! His daughter is walking around live and well – and mine is gone forever.'

* * *

At long last Todd sat alone with Karen in a small room at the police station. He was exhausted, she thought compassionately – and haunted by memories of earlier such questioning. Her head reeled as she considered the incredibly swift escalation of Todd's situation. Yesterday he'd been the town's most beloved teacher. Now he was a prime suspect in a rape/murder case. A known felon.

'I saw no way to deny I was Todd Anderson.' He was almost apologetic.

'You did right. The police would have confirmed it through the computer system in a matter of hours. Even less.'

'That couple from the tavern who said they saw "a grey Dodge speeding through town not long past midnight". I wasn't speeding—' Todd frowned. That heretofore unrevealed evidence had unnerved her, Karen admitted to herself.

'Maybe I was doing forty in a thirty-mile stretch. I was anxious to get to that drugstore over in Thomasville, where the pharmacist is supposed to be available twenty-four hours a day. There's a phone number listed on the door—'

'Why the race to the pharmacist?' The former conviction wasn't supposed to enter into this case, but the word would spread fast. She'd fight for a change in venue – but could she swing it? No doubt in her mind that Todd would be arraigned tonight or tomorrow, go before a grand jury in a matter of days and ordered held for trial. 'Who was sick, Todd?'

'Zachie developed a wracking cough. Cindy gave him the regular cough medicine we keep for emergencies – and it seemed to work a bit. Then he had a bad bout about midnight. Cindy was uptight – she went to pour another dose of the medication and dropped the bottle, spilled what was left. I went to get a refill.'

'What happened at the pharmacist? I know,' she soothed, 'you told the detectives. But let's go over it again. I'm looking for something to help us.'

'I got the phone number, looked for a public phone. There

was one just a block away. I tried to call. There was no answer. I kept trying until I realized it was useless. I went back home. Cindy was giving Zachie hot milk and honey. It seemed to be helping. Early this morning I picked up the medication – it was the over-the-counter kind. Then – an hour later – all hell broke loose.'

Karen went home – her mind racing, in turmoil. This was going to be a rough case. Was she sharp enough – experienced enough – to clear Todd? He was innocent – she'd take any bets on that. No doubt in her mind, though, that the arraignment would lead to a grand jury appearance. First step – prove that the pharmacist Todd talked about was *not* available when Todd tried to reach him. That would lend a certain credibility to his being seen driving through town at that crucial time. Thomasville was about eighteen miles west. Drive over there now. Talk to the pharmacist. But first run over to try to comfort Cindy.

She found Cindy coaxing Zachary to open his mouth and take a dosage of his cough medicine. Cindy was struggling to mask her terror for the children's sake. Laurie was unfamiliarly solemn. She was old enough to understand her father was in trouble, that he'd been taken away by the police.

'If you don't get rid of your cough, you won't go to nursery school,' Cindy warned Zachary. 'You want to go, don't you?'

'Yeah—' He sighed philosophically and opened his mouth.

'Laurie, you and Zachie do puzzles now. Let's see which of you finishes first.'

The two women left the children in puzzle activity, walked down the hall to the living room.

'School's opening tomorrow. Todd won't be released by then?' Cindy's eyes said she expected a negative reply.

'It's going to be a rough haul.' No point lying to Cindy. 'I expect he'll be arraigned by tomorrow night. I've asked for that. Then he'll be held for a grand jury hearing.'

'I'll have to call the school and tell them—' A harrowing duty, her eyes proclaimed.

'I'll talk with you later,' Karen promised. 'I need to drive over to Thomasville and question the pharmacist.'

Cindy hesitated. 'I won't be going to the funeral. I won't be welcome. Karen, it's going to be so awful for Laurie and Zachie—'

Karen was sliding behind the wheel of her car when she saw Neil's station wagon approaching the house. He parked at the curb, strode to her car.

'Word gets around this town fast,' he said lightly, but his eyes were serious. 'You're Todd's attorney.'

'For now,' she hedged. 'He may need somebody with stronger background.' She shook her head in exasperation. 'Todd has friends among the local police – but already they're turning against him. They *know* him, Neil. How can they believe he's guilty?' But a jury convicted him in that earlier case.

'If I can help in any way, I'm available.' Neil cleared his throat in a gesture of unease. 'Morrison wants to go on TV with what they've learned.'

'You mean, about Todd's previous conviction?'

'No. He knows he can't do that.' Anger welled in her. But the media would spread the word. 'This business of Todd's being held – that he was seen allegedly speeding through town at the time the crime was committed.' Karen grunted impatiently.

'People have been on Morrison's back for not coming up with anything yet – he feels he has to make a statement. Dad stipulated he wait until after the funeral this afternoon.' He paused – his eyes dark with questions. 'How does the case look?'

'Not good. I'm driving over to Thomasville to talk to the pharmacist now. A man named Somers.'

'You realize that no local attorney – other than you – would touch the case?'

'I figured that. And I doubt that Todd and Cindy can afford a big city criminal attorney on teachers' salaries. I'll fight for him, Neil. I just pray that'll be enough.'

'Would you like company to Thomasville?' He contrived a shaky grin. 'I can write it off as a professional assignment.'

'I'd like that.' She was grateful for Neil's presence.

They located the pharmacist in Thomasville. Karen sensed he'd heard about Todd's being held for questioning. His eyes were wary when she asked about his unavailability when Todd tried to reach him.

'He never called,' the pharmacist blustered. 'I always hear the phone when it rings. He's lying.'

'But if you were sleeping heavily,' Karen tried again, 'perhaps you—'

'No! He's lying!'

Frustrated, Karen and Neil returned to the car.

'He's not telling the truth.' Karen churned with rage. 'He doesn't want it getting around that he wasn't available when he's supposed to be. He doesn't give a damn about Todd.'

'Let's make a note to do some checking on him. I'll do legwork for you on that.' Neil reached to pat Karen's hand in encouragement.

They drove back to Paradise – rehashing all they knew thus far about the case. On Main Street they noticed that some shops were already closing in preparation for the funeral.

'Come to the house with me, and let's scavenge for lunch,' Karen invited. 'Unless you have to be back at the station?'

He grinned. 'I'm allowed lunch.'

He knew how serious this situation was for Todd. He wanted to be helpful. She brushed aside a truant suspicion that he was pursuing a news story for his station – a story that might provide national prominence.

They were debating about sandwich makings when the phone rang.

'Answer it – I'll play chef,' Neil told her. 'After all those years in the Balkans, I have great affection for America's food supplies.'

Karen picked up the extension in the dining area. 'Hello—'

'Karen, I just heard about Todd! We were stunned—'

Jeannie was at the other end. 'All these years here he's been lying about his background. He—'

'Jeannie, he was railroaded in that other case,' Karen broke in. 'He—'

'Is it true that you're representing him?'

'Yes—'

'How can you?' Jeannie's voice spiraled into shrillness. 'He raped one little girl, and now—' Her voice cracked. 'How can you defend that monster?'

'Jeannie, he's not guilty – in either case!'

'He was here in this house that afternoon! Is that when he decided to take my baby?'

'Jeannie, he didn't do it! Todd's a fine person. He—' She paused as Neil walked into the dining room – eyebrows raised in question. 'Jeannie, don't hang up!'

'She knows you're acting as Todd's attorney,' Neil guessed.

'Laurie plays with – played with Debbie every day. Jeannie and Doug have known Cindy and Todd since they moved to town. They aren't personal friends,' she conceded, 'but they've always been so friendly. Yesterday everybody in town liked Todd, had great respect for him. Today he's a monster.'

'Not to everybody. There're people here who can't believe Todd could be guilty.'

'But I'm going to have to prove that to a jury.' Karen's throat tightened. 'That's going to be a tough deal – despite the lack of real evidence against him. The tabloids will label him guilty! He'll be convicted in the headlines!'

'Not just the tabloids.' Neil's face betrayed his own fears. 'The local papers will be out for blood. We're living in an era where the media convicts on speculation. To hell with proof. They'll run with any rumor that's melodramatic enough to seize attention.' He paused, took a deep breath. 'Karen, I want to be part of your team. I'll do whatever I can to help.'

Eleven

As though in tune with the mood of the throng gathered for Deborah Norris's funeral, the sun had given way to dark clouds that threatened to unleash a downpour at any moment. Townspeople simultaneously grieved and were outraged at what had happened. Nothing so monstrous had ever occurred in Paradise, New York. Its name a mockery today.

Hugging the conviction that no one – *no one* – knew that Debbie's killer stood among them as the minister read the service, he maintained the proper demeanor. He hadn't meant to kill her. But she woke up and was about to scream. *That wasn't supposed to happen.* The little bitch was supposed to stay out cold.

He'd put that length of thin rope in his pocket because his mind had subconsciously ordered him to be prepared for an emergency. He'd done everything right. The cops had picked up that teacher with a police record – he'd go to trial and be convicted.

Stop worrying – you're home free.

Twelve

W hile Debbie's tiny coffin was being lowered into the ground, Karen sat with Todd in the small, drab room provided for attorneys consulting with their clients.

'I can't believe this is happening again—' Todd shook his head in bewilderment. 'How will Cindy ever make Laurie and Zachie understand?'

'We've got to go back into that other case. I know – it shouldn't be even mentioned, but—'

'But the news media will have a field day,' he picked up grimly.

'Were you satisfied with your defense in that case?' Karen probed. It was urgent to disprove that jury's findings to turn around the unfavorable reporting Todd was receiving now. Otherwise, he'd never get a fair trial in this town – where every prospective juror knew about that earlier conviction. 'Did you feel he – or she – let you down?'

'My parents hired the best lawyer they could afford. He tried – but I was set up.' He gestured his frustration.

'Go back and tell me how it happened,' Karen pushed. 'I know it's difficult, but I need to know—' No doubt in her mind that Todd had been innocent.

'It was the night of our senior prom. A few weeks after my seventeenth birthday. Cindy and I got into some screwy argument – the way teenagers do. She refused to go to the senior prom with me. She didn't go at all.' He closed his eyes and forced himself to hurtle back through the years. 'It was sixteen years ago . . .'

9.20 p.m., June 22, 1981

The night was hot, humid. Todd was upset that Cindy refused to go with him to the prom. They'd been going steady for five months. They wanted to become formally engaged before they left for college in the fall. Both sets of parents insisted they wait. Hell, they knew they wanted to spend the rest of their lives together. Why had they battled that way over some stupid little thing?

When Eric Peters circulated among the senior class to invite a chosen few to a private party at his parents' fancy house, Todd had been surprised to be among those chosen. Eric's family was rich, did little socializing with local residents. His father was into politics – his father and mother were always running over to Albany for dinner parties and political gatherings. Eric was their only child – simultaneously spoiled and neglected.

Along with a cluster of other students, Todd left for further celebrating at the Peters house.

'Nobody's home,' Eric crowed in triumph. 'My parents are at some bash in Albany – they won't be back till 5 a.m. – and it's the help's night off. We'll have a ball!'

Eric promised they'd toast their graduation with champagne. Wow, he thought, Cindy would be disappointed to have missed this party! They gathered together in what Eric's mother liked to call the music room. Eric ordered somebody to put on his Bruce Springsteen album. In moments the air was filled with 'Born to Run'.

Eric produced a magnum of champagne. He shipped two girls – giggling in delight – to the kitchen to bring back champagne glasses. Most of them, Todd thought self-consciously, had never drunk anything stronger than beer. In moments Eric was struggling to uncork the champagne. The girls shrieked in approval when this was accomplished. They all pretended that the champagne was cool – but it tasted like sour ginger ale, Todd decided. Yuch!

He stared in surprise when he saw one of the French doors leading to the garden opened from the outside. A tall, bone-thin girl in a sexy dress walked inside, waved to Eric. Todd saw a smug, secretive, silent exchange between them. He was curious. Who was she? He didn't recognize her.

She wasn't wearing a bra, he noted. She had huge nipples that pushed through the soft material of her dress. She didn't seem comfortable in the high-heeled sandals she wore.

'Hey, Todd—' Eric crossed to where he stood alone and sipped his champagne with pretended enjoyment. 'Tiffany's giving you the eye—'

'Who is she?' Not from their class.

'Tiffany something or other,' Eric drawled. 'And she's available.' He winked. 'I had her twice already. Great.' He grunted expressively.

A lot of the guys pretended they were screwing all the time. He knew they were just bragging. But he believed Eric. He felt a sudden surge of heat. She was walking towards him. He took a deep gulp of the champagne – all at once feeling insecure, not sure how to respond.

'You're cute,' she whispered in a throaty voice that reminded him of some movie star he'd seen in a forties movie on TV. 'I'm Tiffany. Who're you?'

'Todd—' He cleared his throat. All at once self-conscious. Did she know what she was doing to him?

She giggled, leaned towards him till those unbelievable nipples were pushing against his chest. *She knew.*

'You want to do it with me?' She mouthed the words. 'I'm good. Ask Eric.'

'He told me—' He'd never been with a girl. He and Cindy wanted to wait until they got married. That's what they kept telling themselves.

He'd never felt this way before – like he'd go mad if they didn't. 'Where?' he asked after a moment. He didn't have a car – like Eric.

'My place—' Her smile was nonchalant. 'My mother's a cocktail waitress. She won't be home for hours.'

While the voice of Bruce Springsteen blared through the room, they walked together towards the French doors, strolled out into the humid night. He felt an odd, unfamiliar lightheadedness – from the champagne, the heat of the night, the closeness of Tiffany. This was unreal and exciting and – somehow – terrifying.

'She lived in this shabby little house about a dozen blocks away. It was a holdover from another era – a holdout from neighbors who probably were dying to see it demolished. I thought she was seventeen or eighteen. The way she looked – with all that make-up and the sexy dress and the way she wore her hair. It was over so fast – and she was telling me to beat it. All at once she seemed scared that her mother would show up. Her father died when she was little. She had no brothers or sisters. The next day my world exploded. Her mother went to the police and said I'd raped her twelve-year-old daughter.'

'What about Eric?' Karen was searching for an angle.

'He denied he ever knew her. He was scared to death Tiffany would drag him in, too.' Todd took a deep, painful breath. 'But she didn't. She nailed just me. I'll never know why she suddenly panicked. Why she lied like that—' He stared quizzically at Karen. 'But that's history. What are you looking for?'

'It would be good if we could prove that Tiffany deliberately presented herself as your own age. Not how she appeared at the trial—' He winced. She paused for an instant. 'But I would like to have the media understand that you were not guilty of that charge. That this case is not a follow-up to that. Todd—' She leaned forward urgently. 'If there's anything you think the police can dredge up about – about possible involvement in Debbie Norris's murder, tell me now.'

'Nothing—' He spread his hands eloquently. 'She was a darling little girl – she and Laurie had great times together. I was over at their house last Wednesday afternoon to pick up Laurie and bring her home. I told the police.' Would the police contrive to make something of that, Karen asked herself yet again.

She drove through the empty streets, conscious of the closed stores – knowing most of the town was attending Debbie's funeral. Mom was there, of course. But her own presence would not be welcome.

Arriving at her block she gaped at the line-up of cars parked there. A cluster of people – some with notebooks in hand, others equipped with cameras – roamed about before the Simmons house – trampling the lawn. Two TV trucks sat at the curb – neither from Neil's station. Inside the house – drapes drawn tight at every window – Harry alternated barking with ominous growls.

The media people were milling about here because they were barred from the funeral, her mind pinpointed as she drove slowly past the house. They hoped to interview Cindy or to nab photos of her and the children. Damn them! They were like vultures. She hated the way newspaper reporters – and television and radio reporters, clutching their microphones – buzzed around families dizzy with grief over some tragedy and plied them with questions.

She parked on the opposite side of the street. No way she could turn into her own driveway, dotted with restless groups. A man was swaggering up to Cindy's front door.

'Hey, Cindy!' he yelled. 'Did he ever abuse you? What about your little girl? How could you stay with him, knowing what he'd done?'

Swearing under her breath, Karen darted from the car, across the street and to her front door without any notice from the others. They weren't interested in her, she derided herself while she grappled with the key.

Inside the house she hurried to the phone, called Cindy. She heard the busy signal, waited a few moments and tried again. Still busy. Cindy had put the phone off the hook. She went out on the rear deck, peered towards the front. The news people were unaware of her presence. They were focused on the other house. Quick. Run across before they trailed her to an opened door.

'Cindy!' she called urgently. 'It's me!'

The door opened. Karen darted inside.

'Karen, it's been awful! They're hanging around like vultures. I had to take the phone off the hook – they kept calling on their cell-phones.'

'They'll leave soon,' Karen comforted. 'Once the funeral's over, they'll move back to the Norrises. What about food, milk? Do you need groceries?'

'We're out of some things.' Cindy was shaky.

'Make a list – I'll shop for you,' Karen told her. 'Then we'll talk about Todd.'

Karen drove through the closed-up town and out to the mall to shop groceries for Cindy – stocking up so that Cindy could avoid this chore for a few days. By the time she returned, most of the media people had decamped. Still, she knew Cindy was wary of emerging.

She went to the side door and knocked. Cindy opened it slowly, smiled in relief when she saw Karen.

'Let me take one—' She reached for a bag piled high with supermarket offerings.

Inside Laurie and Zachary rushed forward in welcome. Poor little kids – this was so rough on them, Karen thought in frustration. And there was a long road ahead. Now Harry charged towards her – eager for play.

'I'll take him for a walk,' Karen told Cindy. 'And I'll walk him again tonight.'

She battled with Harry to head in the opposite direction from his usual walks. *Not to the woods, please.*

'Harry, no!' she scolded while he strained in reproach. 'This way!' Poor baby. He couldn't understand what was happening.

Cindy said Laurie and Zachary were terrified. They clung to her, asked repeatedly about Todd. Tomorrow night he'd be arraigned. No point to pretend he might not be held for a grand jury. The best she could hope for was to postpone the trial until the end of the year. She needed time. She wasn't done with that lying pharmacist. There must be a way to pull the truth out of him.

Thirteen

N eil sat slouched over his desk. His eyes were fastened to the TV monitor on the opposite wall. Donna Jackson was just finishing up her heartrending report about the memorial service at the school and the funeral. He geared himself for George Morrison's nightly report. Probably every TV set within viewing range was tuned in to this channel.

He fumed, remembering the radio station's melodramatic report of Todd's earlier conviction. And now Morrison was about to make his own report. Why didn't Dad reject his bringing Hank on with him? But Dad couldn't do that, he admitted to himself. That was Morrison's five-minute spot to do as he wished. But how the hell would Todd ever get a fair trial in this town with that story circulating?

'Hey, Neil, did you arrange for the taping of Morrison's piece?' The daytime engineer – taking off for the day – hung in the doorway. 'One for the DA and one for his guest?'

'It's arranged.' Neil was terse. Hell, Dad didn't like this any more than he did. Still, he had to go along with it. But Dad and Mom were having trouble, he suspected, in dealing with two possible frame-ups.

Am I being incredibly naive? Am I allowing the way I feel about Karen to sway me? How could I have become so emotionally involved so fast? Even Mom and Dad suspect I've fallen off the deep end. Of course, they're all for it. I've got to cool this thing. I think Karen is responding. Maybe she's just

71

on the rebound. She told me she's just broken off a two-year relationship.

Then George Morrison began to speak – with Hank at his side, preening like a beauty contest winner. Scowling, Neil leaned back in his chair and watched the performance. Like Dad said, George was already running for the State Assembly – at least, in his mind.

Karen abandoned eating to gape at the TV screen. Damn George Morrison! He was prosecuting Todd even before he came to trial!

'Todd's in a bad spot, isn't he?' Helen was somber.

'He's cornered the "bad luck" market.' Karen was grim. 'Why do your friends, the Bradfords, let Morrison set Todd up this way?'

'I don't think there's much they can do about it. The district attorney is making a nightly report on a major murder case.' But Helen wasn't happy. 'He didn't bring up the other case,' she conceded grudgingly.

'But by bringing Hank Graham on the newscast with him, he allowed it to be introduced,' Karen said grimly. 'It can't be presented at the trial – but every possible juror will know about it.'

'Are you all set for the arraignment tomorrow night?'

'As set as I can ever be.' It was a farce, in truth. She'd insist that Todd be released, mention all his civic contributions – but they both knew Todd would be held for a grand jury hearing that was sure to order him to trial.

5.00 a.m., Thursday, September 4, 1997

Cindy was up at dawn, willing herself to go in to school as though this was the opening day of any other year. Thank God, Laurie would have the distraction of starting first grade. Zachie's nursery group wouldn't begin sessions until Monday. Until then Sara would be with him until she came home from school. Once he was in nursery school Sara would take him there in the morning, pick him up at noon. She'd do the house-cleaning while he was at his group. For the past two years Sara had been working for them in the course of the school year.

The hours dragged until it was time to leave. Sara was running late, she noted nervously. The first day of school was not the time for Sara to be late. She brightened at the sight of an ancient Chevie pulling up before the house.

'Hi.' She greeted Sara with an effort at casualness. Of course, Sara knew what was happening. That's why she looked so stern. 'Laurie and I will have to dash—' Why was she so self-conscious? Sara couldn't believe Todd was guilty.

'I'll stay today. But don't expect me back again,' Sara told her. 'I figured it was too late to quit last night – when I heard the district attorney on TV with that reporter. I'll do the right thing – I'll stay with Zachary today. But I don't work for no murderer.'

Cindy struggled to mask her shock. Pale and trembling, she managed a reply. 'I'll make other arrangements.' How dare Sara label Todd a murderer when he hadn't even been arraigned! She blotted out the realization that many others in this town harbored the same thought. But, thank God, Laurie and Zachie were back in their room. They hadn't heard Sara. 'Laurie, time to go to school!'

On the drive to school Laurie chattered effervescently. This new adventure had – for the moment – replaced her bewilderment and anxiety about her father's having 'gone to help the police find out about who had killed Debbie'. How long could she protect the kids from reality?

As planned, she and Laurie were among the first arrivals at the school. She remembered now that counselors would visit each class this morning to help them deal with the horror of Debbie's death. This time last year Laurie and Debbie had entered kindergarten here. Jeannie had been candid about Debbie's attendance. '*Doug and I couldn't afford it – Dad came through.*'

Beth and Fred Miller – owners and co-principals of the school – were supportive of Todd, she remembered with a surge of gratitude. It had been so painful to call and tell them that Todd was being questioned by the police and wouldn't be there for the first day of school. Not for months, her mind warned bleakly. They'd managed to round up a substitute on less than twenty-four hours' notice.

Cindy took Laurie to the first grade classroom. Two children were already there. Immediately Laurie joined them. The first grade teacher was busy at her desk.

'Hi,' Cindy called.

'Hi.' The other woman smiled briefly and focused on bringing materials out of her supply cabinet. Instantly Cindy felt an unfamiliar withdrawal. 'I'll see you at lunch, Laurie—' Fighting misgivings, she pulled Laurie to her for a quick kiss.

Now she went to the principal's office to check in. Beth was there alone. She seemed tense, Cindy thought – but that was normal on the opening day of school. And replacing Todd on such short notice must have been unnerving.

'Cindy, I – I tried to reach you at home – but you'd already left.' Beth was contriving not to meet her eyes.

'A problem?' All at once her throat was tightening.

'Fred and I talked about this far into last night,' she stammered. 'We could never believe Todd was guilty of such an awful act, but we've been bombarded by calls from parents. Cindy, I'm sorry. We have to replace you.'

'Why?' Her voice was strident. 'I've always had great rapport with the kids and the parents.'

'Parents are threatening to withdraw their children. They feel we let them down by hiring Todd without a real check on his background. Cindy, I know this is rotten – but what can we do? If parents withdraw their children, we'll have to close up. We've been here a dozen years. We can't afford to start all over again. I'm sorry, Cindy.'

'But I have a contract!' She gaped at Beth in disbelief.

'We spoke with our lawyer early this morning. There's a

morals clause in the contract. You brought Todd to us and failed to tell us he was a convicted felon. The contract is invalid.'

'I see.' But she didn't see at all.

'We must ask, also, that you take Laurie out of the school. Unless, of course, you're prepared to pay the usual tuition.'

'I'm not prepared for that.' Nor was she prepared for unemployment, she taunted herself. They had some small savings, but how long would that last? 'I'll take Laurie with me.' How did she explain this to Laurie? Would the nursery group ask her to withdraw Zachie? Her head reeled with these fresh hurdles. But for Todd's sake and the children's sake, she must keep her sanity.

8.40 a.m., Thursday, September 4, 1997

Karen ordered herself not to be nervous about the arraignment. She knew the outcome. Just put on the best show she could. Stress Todd's performance here in this town, all the good he'd accomplished. Mom would stay with Laurie and Zachie so Cindy could be there. Cindy was still shaken by her babysitter's reaction to Todd's being held by the police – she was fearful of trying to acquire another sitter. No need. Mom was happy to stay with Laurie and Zachie. Della and Frances could handle the shop for a while.

She was startled when she arrived at the courthouse for the arraignment to see the courtroom spilling over with people. A handful were to be arraigned on petty charges. The big attraction was Todd. Newspaper reporters lined the wall at the rear. She was instantly aware of the hostile mood. All right, get on with it. No doubt in anybody's mind that Todd would be held for a grand jury hearing – and that he would have to stand trial. But local people were here to see it happen. To be in on the kill.

Afterwards – leaving the courthouse – both Karen and Morrison were besieged by reporters. Cameras were in action. Karen knew that tomorrow morning's newspapers, tonight's late telecast, would shriek of the town's outrage. People who felt that Todd should not be pilloried before the trial were afraid to speak their minds. And they were few, Karen conceded privately.

10 a.m., Friday, September 5, 1997

Karen geared herself for a hostile encounter when George Morrison – whose youngest sister had graduated from high school with Jeannie and herself – summoned her to his office the morning after Todd's arraignment. By law the district attorney had to share with her whatever fresh evidence the prosecution had uncovered. *What had Morrison come up with now?* Todd had not lied to her, she told herself for the dozenth time as she walked into Morrison's spartan office. Every instinct insisted Todd had no part in Debbie Norris's rape and murder.

Now she sat in a chair across from George Morrison, who was leaning back with an unexpectedly conciliatory smile while he explained why he had called this meeting.

'Look, we can work out a plea bargain that will save this town a lot of anguish and the court a bundle of money. Karen, you know the guy is guilty—'

'I know no such thing!' She braced herself for trouble.

'The fax came through this morning.' His face exuded complacency. 'Your client's fingerprints were found in the Norris house. He—'

'Todd was in the house a few hours before the murder,' she interrupted. What was this craziness about a plea bargain? If he thought he had a strong case he wouldn't be pulling this. 'He made a statement to that effect. He went to the house to pick up his little girl, who'd spent the afternoon playing with Debbie. He—'

'His fingerprints were found in her bedroom. On the windowsill of the window with the ripped-out screen,' he emphasized. 'The family is screaming for the death penalty.

76

I'd prefer to avoid that. But remember – the victim was Mayor Gilbert's grandchild. Todd will serve time, of course – but I'll have an excuse not to ask for the death penalty if he cooperates. He'll serve time – but he won't die.'

Fourteen

K aren waited for Todd to be brought to the small conference room. She steeled herself to conceal her dismay
at this latest development. She was aware of the anxious
questioning in Todd's eyes as he sat at the small table across
from her.

'Todd, they've found your fingerprints on the windowsill
in Debbie's bedroom.' She took a deep breath. 'The window
with the cut-out screen—' Only now did a faintly accusing
note color her voice.

'I told you I'd been in the house. I went to pick up Laurie
– she'd had a play date with Debbie.'

'You didn't tell me you'd been in Debbie's bedroom.' Give
Todd a chance to explain. *Let him have an explanation.*

'When I arrived at the house, the sitter told me Laurie
was in Debbie's bedroom. They were sprawled on the floor
with Debbie's new Barbie doll and some doll clothes.' Karen
sensed he was fighting to recreate the scene for her. 'It was
hot in the house – the air-conditioning had broken down. I
went to the window and opened it wider, for whatever breeze
could come in. The sitter knows I went down the hall to the
bedroom to pick up Laurie—' A touch of anxiety in his voice
now. All at once he seemed to understand the implication of
his fingerprints on that windowsill. 'She was sitting on the
sofa and watching *Oprah*. Tommy was in the playpen. She
told me the two girls were in Debbie's room. I went there—'
His voice trailed off.

78

'I'll talk to the sitter.' Karen felt a trickle of relief. 'We'll get a statement from her.' She hesitated for a moment. 'The district attorney came up with a plea bargain. I told him you weren't interested.'

'A plea bargain is for the guilty,' he flared. 'I'm innocent.'

'I'll get a statement from the sitter,' Karen reiterated, trying to sound confident. She rose to her feet. 'That's important.'

She drove home, phoned Neil at the station.

'I'm sorry, he's out on an assignment,' the receptionist told her. 'May I take a message?'

'Thank you, no. I'll try him later.'

It was unsettling, the way she and Neil had become so close in a few days. But that happened in times of crisis, she thought defensively. Neil was as convinced as she that Todd was innocent – that justice had not been served in the earlier case. He shared her obsession to see justice win out. She heard Neil's voice tickertaping across her mind:

'You know, Karen, you and I are anachronisms – throwbacks to the sixties. Or maybe we're expressing the X-generation's new thinking. I'd like to believe that.'

Bob was X-generation – but his was a 'me-generation' approach, like in the eighties. How could she have closed her eyes so long?

Now she focused on the task at hand. She couldn't phone Jeannie and say, 'By the way, what's the name of your babysitter?' Ask Cindy. Cindy would know. Go over and talk to Cindy. And she couldn't dodge bringing Cindy up to date on the fingerprint problem. It was urgent to have the babysitter confirm that Todd was in Debbie's bedroom that afternoon.

She left the house and hurried next door, again utilizing the side entrance. Thank God, the media mob – except for a handful of discards – had given up on grabbing an interview with Cindy or photos of her and the kids.

'Hi.' She tried for a reassuring smile when Cindy opened the door.

'Hi.' Her eyes searched Karen's. 'Did you see Todd this morning?'

'We – we had a long talk.'

'Laurie, you and Zachie go into the living room with Harry. Play there, OK?'

'OK—' Laurie was so subdued, Karen thought unhappily. She couldn't understand what was happening, but she knew it wasn't good.

'We'll play school later,' Cindy called after her, then turned to Karen. 'Tell me about Todd. How's he holding up?'

The two women sat at the table at one side of the kitchen. No use stalling, Karen told herself. Cindy has to know about the fingerprints. She explained that the fingerprints placed Todd in Debbie's bedroom.

'I have to talk with the babysitter, have her give a statement to the police that Todd went to the bedroom to pick up Laurie. Do you know who she is?'

Cindy nodded. 'Marie Bingham. Her parents work at the shirt factory. She's about twenty, has been working as a sitter since she dropped out of high school at sixteen. She's been with Jeannie and Doug for about a year, I think.' She hesitated. 'I was never impressed with her qualifications.'

'I just need a statement from her that Todd was in the house on Wednesday a week ago and picked up Laurie in Debbie's bedroom,' Karen reiterated. 'That explains his fingerprints in the bedroom.' In truth – discarding Todd's earlier conviction – there was the flimsiest of evidence against him. Once she cleared up the fingerprint deal, Morrison had nothing to run with. So why was she so anxious? See Marie Bingham. Have her make a statement. She'd feel better once that was done.

'Have you come up with anything yet on the pharmacist?' A tic in her left eyelid betrayed Cindy's anxiety. 'Is he still claiming Todd couldn't have tried to call him?'

'Neil Bradford is working on that. We're trying to figure out why the man's lying that way.' It was *important* that they prove Todd did try to reach him. It explained his presence in town at that hour. 'Neil says he was probably some place he shouldn't have been.'

'Laurie can't understand why I'm home – why she can't go to school. She was so excited about going into first grade. I don't know what to tell her—' Cindy's voice broke. 'Zachie's too young to realize something dreadful is happening – but Laurie knows that her daddy isn't here and that it's somehow tied up with Debbie's death. I keep asking myself – who in this town raped and murdered Debbie?'

'Whoever he is, he's out there somewhere in this town. I can't believe it was somebody just passing through.'

'It's wonderful of your friend Neil to be helping us this way,' Cindy said softly. 'I hope he understands that Todd and I are so grateful.'

'Neil wants to see justice done.' Karen reached to squeeze Cindy's hand in encouragement.

Neil isn't just doing this to be with me, is he? I see the way he looks at me sometimes. The way a man does when he feels something special for a woman. I'm not ready for any kind of relationship. Or is he going after a story that could put his station in the national spotlight? No, don't be so cynical! He's not like that.

2.05 p.m., Friday, September 5, 1997

In his car, using his cell phone, Neil called Karen.

'I had to cover an assignment for the station this morning, but I squeezed in a side trip to Thomasville. I've just got back.'

'Any luck?'

'A very weak lead. But that's better than nothing. Shall I come over now?' Did he know how charming he was at times like this? Probably. Helen's voice tickertaped across her mind: *'He's caused a lot of excitement among the young women in town. Several are out to snare him.'*

'Come.' She was impatient to brief him on the fingerprint situation. She needed his reassurance that he would continue to work with her to clear Todd. He could be helpful. Cindy and Todd couldn't afford a team of expensive investigators. Damn, she wished she had more background in criminal law.

Ten minutes later Neil's car pull up at the curb. Karen rushed to the door to greet him.

'Did you have lunch?' she asked, conscious all at once that she was hungry. Her mind took rapid inventory of the refrigerator's contents.

'I stopped for coffee in Thomasville.' He grinned. 'You're in the mood to feed a hungry reporter?'

'I think I can handle that. I didn't get around to lunch, either.'

While she rummaged for sandwich makings and Neil put up coffee, she brought him up to date.

'I'll go over to talk with Marie Bingham this evening. She works for Jeannie until six thirty, when she normally gets home from the bookstore. I understand Jean's still under heavy sedation, so Marie comes in to take care of Tommy as usual.'

'Doug's back at the factory. I gather he felt he needed to be busy, though the word is that Jake Rhodes told him to take time off as long as he felt he needed.'

'What about Somers? The pharmacist?' Karen placed the two sandwiches on plates, carried them to the table. 'You said something about a "very weak lead".'

Neil chuckled. 'It seems Somers is something of a philanderer, judging from what the waitress at the coffee shop told me. I gather at one point she had something going with him – then she got dumped. Now gossip says he's hot for some married woman twenty years younger than he. His new love has a husband who travels a lot.' He lifted an eyebrow in silent comprehension.

'And he was in her bed instead of his own when Todd tried to call him that night?'

'And neither one wants to admit it.' Neil frowned. 'But we'll have one hell of a time proving that.'

They heard a faint shush from the coffeemaker.

'I'll get it.' Neil headed for the counter. 'Sit.' Bob had never made a move that was cooperative, Karen thought involuntarily.

Neil poured coffee into two mugs, returned to the table, his eyes quizzical.

'I surmise you plan on being around for a while – now that you're Todd's defense attorney.' It was obvious that he approved.

'The situation made that decision for me.' The way he looked at her was unnerving. She debated for a moment. 'I told you about walking out on the job – that insane rat race—'

'That was bright.'

'I walked out on a bad relationship, too,' she said after a moment. 'I knew for months it was wrong. But it was my security blanket.' She managed a wan smile.

'I never had time for any real relationship.' His eyes were tender as they met hers. 'In truth, I never met anyone that felt right. Until now—'

'Let's take this slowly, Neil. I can't afford a second mistake.'

'Sure. Slow and easy. I've been on a treadmill of my own. I needed this break. The job was exciting and fulfilling – and I could feel some great opportunities hovering overhead. But deep inside I had this weird feeling that I should slow down, get out of the fast lane. I promise you,' he said gently, 'we won't rush.'

Alone in the house, Karen focused on her next move. Call on Marie Bingham. Make her understand it was her duty to make a statement on Todd's behalf. She searched her mind for some impediment to this. No reason for Marie to balk.

She had one client with whom to deal – and she mustn't fail him. She settled herself at the desk in her bedroom – the same desk where she'd studied through the years of attending schools here in Paradise. Plot her approach. Break

83

down the problems to be solved. Damn that pharmacist! He was protecting his hide – and the young married woman with whom he was having an affair. How could she push him into making a statement that would be a plus for Todd? One small step – but it was important.

She'd wait until close to 8 p.m. to go over to the Bingham house, Karen plotted. She'd talk to Marie. Clear up this business of Todd's fingerprints at the crime scene. That was urgent.

The afternoon sped past. She left her improvised office, went out to the kitchen to prepare dinner. She was touched by Mom's obvious pleasure at having her here. Mom had always been the one constant in her life. Why had it always been such an obsession to please Eve?

There'd been no letter from Eve for weeks now – but that wasn't unusual. Her mother talked about going to Switzerland for some health treatment that was supposed to ward off aging. Already – still slim and beautiful via daily workouts at a gym and the magic of skillful make-up – Eve talked about a face-lift.

A car was pulling up in the driveway. That would be Mom. She hurried to the door.

'Something smells great.' Helen sniffed appreciatively. 'Garlic chicken,' she identified with approval.

'It's tasty, easy, and we'll have two dinners out of it.'

Helen's air of levity evaporated. 'I had lunch today at Claire's.' Claire's was her favorite lunchtime haunt. 'The talk there was disturbing.'

'About Todd?' The two women headed for the kitchen.

'Some people are screaming for the death penalty. They say, "It wasn't just rape or murder. It was rape *and* murder."' Helen grimaced in recall. 'Never mind he hasn't gone to trial yet.'

'The *Morning Enquirer* and the *Evening News* are sounding like tabloids.' The two local papers. 'The radio station is just as bad.' Neil's voice echoed in her mind. *'It's "what can we run to bring in a larger readership – or more listeners?"*

Rumors are pounced upon and accepted as facts. Dad and Mom insist on acting with responsibility. They refuse to cater to hysteria.'

Helen brought the salad from the refrigerator and carried it to the dining area table. Karen dealt with the chicken – all the while conscious of her grandmother's preoccupation.

'Mom?' Karen joined her at the table. 'Something's bugging you.'

'I suspect Neil didn't tell you—'

Karen stopped dead. 'Didn't tell me *what*?'

'The station's announced a nightly five-minute spot for George Morrison to present the latest developments on the case.'

'Why?' Karen stared in outrage. 'To stir up more hysteria?'

Helen's eyes were apologetic. 'They were probably pushed into it. You know they're on Todd's side.'

'The mayor's manipulations,' Karen pinpointed. 'And that newspaper reporter who's panting to collect Jake Rhodes's reward!' Again, she was assailed by doubts. Was she the right attorney to clear Todd? But she was what Todd had to defend him. Cindy and Todd couldn't afford 'dream-team' attorneys.

'I can't bear the way everybody's sure Todd's guilty because he was convicted in that earlier case. Damn it, Karen – he was just seventeen then – and it was sixteen years ago. He served his time.'

'He was framed for that. It *happens*.' It always unnerved her to pick up a newspaper and read that somebody in prison for years had suddenly been cleared. 'God knows why that girl lied the way she did.' In a corner of her mind she tried to deal with a taunting suspicion that Neil's TV station was not as truly concerned for justice as he professed.

His parents were allowing themselves to be used by local politicians.

7.50 p.m., Friday, September 5, 1997

Karen left the house to approach Marie Bingham. No intro-
ductory phone call, she'd cautioned herself. Just drive over
and ask to speak with Marie for a few moments. Perhaps once
Marie knew the object of the visit, she would be pleased to be
part of the investigation, to be in the spotlight briefly. Some
people ate that up. Cindy was blunt about Marie's level of
intelligence.

The Binghams lived in a part of Paradise that mocked its
name. Their white shingled cottage cried out for paint. The
steps that led to the porch were rotting. An ancient car sat in
the driveway. The Bingham parents both worked at the shirt
factory, Karen recalled – and while people conceded that Jake
Rhodes was a fair boss, he was known for keeping wages as
low as he could contrive. The cartons of empty beer bottles
on the porch indicated a major expense.

Karen discovered the doorbell was inoperative. She rapped
sharply on the screen door – hoping to be heard over the
too-loud television. A middle-aged man with a beer-belly –
in much-washed jeans and an undershirt that reeked of sweat
appeared at the door.

'Yeah?' He seemed mildly curious at her presence.

'Mr Bingham?' She was conscious of unpleasant vibes.

'Yeah—'

'May I speak with Marie for a few moments, please?'

'What's she done?' All at once he was pugnacious.

'Nothing wrong,' Karen rushed to reassure him. 'I'm Karen
Mitchell—' She saw recognition leap into his mind. 'Todd
Simmons' attorney.'

'What do you want with Marie?' he challenged. Karen saw
the young blonde in a too-tight T-shirt and shorts coming
towards them.

'I would just like her to confirm that Todd Simmons was
at the Norris house on the Wednesday before the Labor Day
weekend.'

'He was there.' Radiating hostility, Marie stood beside her father. 'I told the cops.'

'What we need to establish is that he went into Debbie's bedroom to pick up his daughter.' Karen strained for a cordial tone. 'He—'

'He didn't go to Debbie's bedroom,' Marie interrupted, shooting a nervous glance at her father.

'Try to remember, Marie. This is important.' Karen managed to combine politeness with firmness. 'It was a little past 4 p.m. You were watching *Oprah*, and—'

'I wasn't watchin' TV!' Marie's face was flushed. 'I was with the kids in the livin' room. I don't watch TV when I'm babysittin' durin' the day!' Her face exuded defiance. 'If he said I was, he was lyin'. He never set foot in Debbie's bedroom. Least ways, not when I was there.'

Fifteen

8.40 p.m., Friday, September 5, 1997

Fighting a headache – tense with frustration at the encounter with Marie – Karen debated about reporting to Cindy. She'd call later – Cindy would be getting the children to bed at this hour. She parked in the driveway, headed into the house. Helen was in the living room – engrossed in one of her stream of suspense novels. She glanced up with a hopeful smile.

'The little bitch lied through her teeth.' Karen collapsed into a chair. 'She didn't want her father to know the two little girls had been playing alone in Debbie's bedroom while she watched television. She doesn't give a damn about Todd's needing her confirmation.'

'The district attorney still has no real case.' But Helen's bravado was hollow. 'Oh, Neil called. You can reach him at home now.' She paused. 'Cindy's going to be upset.'

Karen's smile was wry. 'I'm upset. We need a statement from Marie Bingham that places Todd in Debbie's bedroom that Wednesday afternoon. Todd's fingerprints in the bedroom is the prosecution's major evidence.' She left her chair and crossed to the phone, punched in Neil's number.

'Hello—' Neil's voice was warm and anxious.

'I bombed,' Karen told him. 'Marie Bingham doesn't want it known that she left Debbie and Laurie alone while she watched television. Especially she doesn't want her father to know. I suspect he'd rough her up if he knew.'

'Shall I come over? Maybe together we can dig up an angle.'

'Come,' she said. 'We need some angles.' At the grand jury hearing on Thursday Todd would be indicted. *I mustn't let it appear that George Morrison has an airtight case.*

'I can't believe the way people have turned against Todd. After all he's done for this town.' Helen shook her head in bewilderment. 'Those few who doubt that he's guilty are afraid to open their mouths.'

'And meanwhile whoever murdered Debbie Norris is running around scot-free.'

'I'll put up coffee—' Helen laid aside her book, rose to her feet. 'Neil's a fine young man,' she said quietly.

'He's afraid Todd will be railroaded because of that earlier case. The press has made him appear a monster.' All at once she felt self-conscious. Mom was developing ideas about Neil and her. *I'm not ready for that.*

'I'll pull a coffee cake out of the freezer and pop it into the oven,' Helen decided. There was always a coffee cake in the freezer for such occasions. 'This could be a long evening.'

The phone rang. Karen picked it up.

'Hello—'

'Did you talk to Marie Bingham?' Cindy asked. 'I saw you drive up – I knew you were home—'

'I was waiting to call you later, once the kids were asleep,' Karen explained and hesitated. 'Marie lied. She wouldn't admit Todd had been in Karen's bedroom that Wednesday afternoon.'

'I was afraid of that. Mothers have complained that she's unreliable, that she lies. She didn't want it known she'd left Debbie and Laurie on their own that way.' Anger blended with alarm in her voice. 'I don't suppose Laurie's word would be accepted? *She* knows her father was there in the bedroom—'

'Don't let's worry about that just yet,' Karen hedged. 'I'm not finished with Marie Bingham. I'm just putting her on hold.'

'The grand jury won't release Todd?'

'No chance, Cindy,' she said gently. 'He'll be held for

trial. We'll ask that he be released on bail until the trial, but the judge will refuse.' She hesitated. 'I know it'll be hard on both Todd and you, but I hope to delay the trial as long as possible. To give me time to dig up evidence to clear him.'

'Delay as long as you can. All that matters is that you clear Todd. They *don't* have a strong case against him. Just flimsy, circumstantial evidence.' A defiance in her voice that was born of fear.

'Cindy, I'll talk to you later.' She heard a car pull up before the house. That would be Neil. She hurried to the front door.

Helen ordered Neil and Karen to the dining area.

'Coffee's coming right up, but you'll have to wait for the cake. It's still in the oven.' Delicious aromas – of coffee brewing and cake warming in the oven – infiltrated the dining area.

'I'm being so spoiled here at home.' Neil settled himself at the table with an air of pleasure. 'I may never leave.'

'That'll make your folks happy,' Helen told him.

Neil turned to Karen. 'Tell me about this Marie Bingham.'

She reported on the brief encounter at the Bingham house.

'We need to find some way to refresh her memory.' Now he provided the latest on Hank Graham's efforts.

'The creep's all upset that the reward isn't his on the basis of Todd's arrest. The exact wording was "on the arrest and conviction". So he's praying for an early trial.'

'I keep telling myself there's no real evidence against Todd. It's his word against Marie's about his being in the bedroom – and her reputation isn't impeccable. But Matt Somers is a problem. He's a responsible citizen.'

'We're not giving up on Somers yet. Though it won't be easy to turn him around.' Neil reached into a jacket pocket for a notebook and pen. 'Let me make a note to talk to that waitress in Thomasville again. Her name is Peggy Allen.'

'If we could unearth evidence that Todd was framed in that earlier case, we'd do him a lot of good with prospective

A Town Named Paradise

jurors.' Karen reached for hope in a dismal situation. 'Of course, none of this can be introduced at the trial.'

'What about digging into that?' Neil paused, frowned in thought. 'Maybe you ought to talk to Cindy, flesh out the picture.'

'Would you go over with me to talk to her? You might pick up on something I miss.'

'We'll have coffee, then go over.' He smiled as Helen approached the table with the coffee tray. 'God, that smells great! When I remember the bilge we were drinking in Bosnia, I wonder I stayed over there so long.'

Ten minutes later Karen phoned Cindy.

'Could I come over with Neil in a bit? We want to pick your brain. Or are the kids still awake?'

'They're in bed. Give me another ten or fifteen minutes to be sure they're asleep. OK?' Cindy seemed both eager and apprehensive.

Helen brought the cinnamon-laced coffee cake out of the oven, served generous wedges. Bob would never have fitted into this scene, Karen thought involuntarily as she lifted a forkful to her mouth. He'd always avoided coming home with her. Now she was glad that he had. He'd think she was crazy to have taken on Todd's case. But Neil was eager to help her. And it *wasn't* just to follow up an important story for the station.

While Neil swept up the last crumbs of the cake but rejected a second helping, Karen glanced at the clock. 'We can go over to Cindy's now.'

In Cindy's cozy living room – their voices low so as not to awaken Laurie and Zachary – Karen questioned Cindy about the earlier case. Painful but necessary, Karen told herself.

'Todd didn't have a chance,' Cindy reiterated. 'Tiffany set him up. The press had a ball.'

'Often when a girl that young is involved names are kept out of the press,' Neil said curiously. 'Why not this time?'

'Oh, Lottie – Tiffany's mother – wanted the whole world to know that a boy from a nice family on the right side of

91

the tracks had violated her daughter. She had a real chip on her shoulder. And Tiffany wallowed in all the publicity.'

'I know it's a long shot, but suppose – all these years later – Tiffany's suffered a change of heart? No,' she instantly discarded such a possibility. 'Not Tiffany nor her mother.'

'It's worth a try.' Cindy's smile was shaky. 'What have we got to lose?'

'I gather the town where you all lived is a couple hundred miles from here?' A long haul, but perhaps she ought to go there and explore the case.

'You're thinking of Sedgewick, New York. This is East Sedgewick. It has nothing to do with Sedgewick itself. It's only about ninety miles from here. I know – it seems strange that we moved so close after all that happened. But I was offered a job at the school here. And we suspected that in time I'd be able to bring Todd into the school, too. We should have gone to another state,' she flared. 'But we never expected lightning to strike twice.'

'I can drive there and read up on the trial.' Karen's mind charged ahead. 'Tiffany still lives there? But you wouldn't know that—'

'She and her mother went away right after the trial. Her mother sold the story to some tabloid – for a lot of money, people said. Then two years later – when my family was still there and I was away at college – they returned and bought a little house. Her mother gave up being a cocktail waitress and worked as a cashier at a supermarket. But that was years ago—'

'I'll drive over to East Sedgewick and go over newspaper microfilm,' Karen decided. 'First thing tomorrow morning.'

10.15 p.m., Friday, September 5, 1997

Neil returned to the TV station to wind up some of the day's work, despite the hour. He found Hank Graham waiting for him.

'I called you at home. Your mother said you were at the

station,' Hank said, explaining his presence. 'I phoned you at the station, and the night receptionist said you'd be back in ten minutes.'

'Yeah—' He'd checked with the station from Cindy's house to say he was on the way there.

'My rag back in the city is getting nervous about my hanging around here. They figure the guy is sure to be held for trial so why run up an expense account waiting for the grand jury?' Hank walked with him to the small office that was his private territory. 'So what's the scoop?'

'He'll be held for trial.' Neil tried not to show his irritation at Hank's invasion. 'No need for you to stay until then.'

'Has a date been set?' Hank's eyes were bright. 'You know I've got a special interest in that trial. A fifty-thousand-dollar interest.'

'Hank, he hasn't been indicted yet. The judge won't set a trial date before that happens.' God, this character was getting on his nerves.

'You think there's a chance he won't be indicted?' Hank's eyebrows shot up in disbelief. A hint of alarm in his eyes.

'We won't know until a jury comes in.' Neil reached for the memos the station secretary had left on his desk.

'Look, I'll give you a buzz now and then to check out the situation.' Hank recognized – reluctantly – that Neil wished to get on with station business. 'OK?'

'Sure. If I seem preoccupied, it's because I'm running behind schedule today. You understand.' His smile was perfunctory. Why didn't the creep get out of here?

'Yeah.' Hank rose leisurely to his feet. 'This guy Jake Rhodes – he's good for the reward? I mean, he's not some flake with nothing in the bank?'

'He's a rich man, Hank. One of the richest in the state. He'll be good for the reward – if it's coming.'

'I'll be here for the trial.' Hank's smile was cocky. 'And, meanwhile, I'll keep in touch.'

Neil sat in somber contemplation. *Was* Todd Simmons guilty? Was he allowing himself to believe Todd was innocent because Karen was so sure of that? He was reacting like a lovesick teenager, damn it! But he'd never met a woman who seemed to fit perfectly into his life the way Karen did. Three times he'd thought he might be getting serious – and each time bailed out. Karen was different. A woman for the long haul.

But he mustn't let his judgment rest on how Karen felt about a case. Sure, Mom and Dad, too, were convinced Todd was innocent – but they liked the guy. No doubt about it – Todd's conviction in that earlier case was hard to ignore. How many people believed Todd had been wrongfully convicted?

The first crime was rotten – but this was rape *plus* murder. A little girl was dead – and the town was screaming for a conviction. So far the meager evidence was circumstantial. Would the police come up with more against Todd? Was *he* allowing his feelings for Karen to dictate his own belief?

Sixteen

8.05 a.m., Saturday, September 6, 1997

K aren arose early this Saturday morning, prepared for the day. Now she lingered over a second cup of coffee with Helen before leaving for the long drive to East Sedgewick. A robe over her ballerina-length nightie because there was an unseasonable chill in the air.

'It looks like it'll rain any minute – and last all day. Are you sure you want to go all the way to East Sedgewick?'

'It could be important, Mom. I know – it's a long shot. But I've got so little to run with at this point.' *What is Morrison coming up with that I haven't been told about yet? How am I going to break down Matt Somers and Marie Bingham? Both are lying. I need something substantial to grasp hold of – but where is it?*

'Cindy is trying not to isolate herself in the house, but everybody is so nasty. Almost everybody—'

The phone rang. Karen leaned forward to pick up the receiver.

'Hello—'

'It's a rotten morning.' Neil stifled a yawn.

'Maybe you should have stayed in bed.'

'Too much on my mind. Anyhow, this is my day off. You were talking last night about going to East Sedgewick this morning for some digging. Is that still on?'

'Yes.' She felt a stir of anticipation. *This is so irrational! How can I emerge from that long stretch with Bob to feel this way about somebody else so quickly?*

Julie Ellis

'Like company? I can justify the time as following up a possible great story for the station.'

'I'd love company.' She was conscious of Helen's sudden alertness, her pleased smile. *Mom, no!* 'I'd planned on leaving in about half an hour—' *Why don't I brush him off?*

'Fine. I'll pick you up in thirty minutes.'

'You'd better take along a light sweater,' Helen advised. 'The temperature is supposed to take a steep drop.'

'I will.' Karen reached for the two empty mugs and headed for the kitchen sink. *Mom's entertaining romantic thoughts about me and Neil. I'll be here for a while, yes. Probably for months because of Todd's trial. But I don't know where I'm going with my life.*

'I'd swear that some of my regular customers are staying out of the shop because they know how I feel about Todd.' Helen's eyes were defiant. 'But I won't have my life dictated by a bunch of narrow-minded characters.'

'My being his attorney isn't helping. Already everybody seems to know.' Small towns could be so warm and friendly – but suddenly turn so intimidating.

'Stop by the shop if you get back early. A batch of early fall sportswear just arrived. You might want to pick out a few things.'

'Mom, you're spoiling me again—' She leaned forward to hug her. 'I'd better get dressed now.'

Neil arrived with directions to East Sedgewick that followed what he called 'the scenic route'. As they left town, Karen outlined her approach. First, a trip to the local library to read newspaper accounts of the case. Cindy had given her the pertinent dates.

'Then I must track down Tiffany Rollins' whereabouts. Does she still live in East Sedgewick?'

'That could be a problem.'

'If she's still living there and is married, I must ferret out her name—' She'd be about twenty-eight, Karen computed.

'Slow down, honey,' Neil chided. 'Don't expect to accomplish everything in one day.'

'Even if we locate her, I know the odds on her having a change of heart. But I have to make every effort to clear Todd. He's my only client—' She tried for a laugh. 'He can command my time every waking hour. I'm set for the grand jury hearing on Wednesday. Nothing complicated about that.' She sighed. 'We know the outcome of the hearing.' She couldn't erase from her mind the knowledge that Neil's TV station was presenting George Morrison on a nightly briefing of the prosecution's efforts. Morrison was so bloody confident of a conviction! 'I have to explore every avenue that might be of help to him.'

'What about Todd's little girl? Couldn't she testify that her father picked her up in Debbie's bedroom that day?'

'It looks like the trial will be some time in late November,' Karen reminded. 'The prosecution will point out that's a long time for a six-year-old to remember something like that, would claim she'd been coached. I wouldn't even try to put her on the stand. I've gone over every fragment of evidence. The towel wrapped around Debbie's body – it could have belonged to anybody. I—'

'That cologne still haunts me,' Neil broke in. 'I keep feeling it could tell us something—'

Karen shrugged in doubt. 'Then there's the rope about her throat. Tied in a boy scout knot. Todd has been a scout master for the last two years—'

'He's not the only one in town. And every kid in Paradise was a boy scout at one time. I know,' he forestalled her retort. 'We can't go around accusing every past or present boy scout.'

'I studied the police photos for hours – hoping the knot would lead me somewhere—'

'To a boy scout,' Neil reminded ruefully. 'Which goes nowhere.'

'I was hoping for something special – a knot that would indicate a profession. You know, something common to sailors or fishermen or whatever—' She gestured in defeat.

'I doubt there's a knot specialist in the Paradise forensic department – but this would come under consideration.'

'And meanwhile, somewhere out there Debbie's murderer is on the loose.' Neil sighed. 'Every parent here in town – almost every parent,' he amended, 'feels safe now. But how do we know that murderer won't strike again?'

'We don't.' Karen uttered a grunt of frustration. 'My job as Todd's attorney is to prove that he didn't rape and murder Debbie, but I keep arriving at the conclusion that I'll have to dig up the real perpetrator before I can do this. Where do I start? It could be anybody in Paradise.'

'The district attorney's case against Todd is very shaky. He—'

'But Todd is coming to trial,' Karen interrupted, 'and every prospective juror in the county knows about Tiffany Rollins and his conviction in that case. How is he to get a fair trial? And his fingerprints on the windowsill – that's damaging. I could wipe that out if Marie Bingham would tell the truth. But she won't.'

'We're taking a turn to the left just ahead. My mother tells me there's a pond here that's home to a family of ducks. I brought along a loaf of bread. If you like, we'll stop and feed them.'

'Let's.' Never in a million years, Karen thought, would Bob have considered such a pastime.

They parked beside the pond, coaxed the pair of adult ducks and the parade of ducklings to the edge to be fed. This was a precious pocket of serenity in a day that was bound to be tense and demanding.

She remembered driving past a tiny pond in East Hampton last summer and admiring a pair of ducks and a cluster of ducklings. Bob hadn't given them even a glance. He'd been spouting stock quotations at her – though neither of them owned a single share.

Back in the car, Karen listened to Neil reminisce about his years in the war-torn Balkans. He had such a wealth of compassion for ordinary people.

'I was reaching burnout—' Neil's voice brought her back to the present. 'It was time to come home.'

And time, she thought, for her to come home. But what next? For now she must focus on Todd's case. After that, what?

They drove into East Sedgewick with definite plans. First, they would go to the public library, acquire back issues of the local newspapers on the dates furnished by Cindy. They'd divide up the papers, make copies of every pertinent article, no matter how brief.

'They may not have back issues of newspapers,' Neil warned. 'In which case we'll head for the newspaper offices. But we'll get them.'

'Right.' Karen was determined to be optimistic. 'After that we'll try to discover if Tiffany Rollins and her mother are still living here.' The telephone directory would tell them this. Don't even consider that the two of them might have moved away – possibly without a trace.

The local library was surprisingly large for such a small town. The sprawling room to the left of the entrance contained newspapers, periodicals, and a call desk for back issues on microfilm. Attendance this morning was light. Karen filled out call slips, waited with Neil for the microfilm to be brought to her, grateful that the library offered this service. She had rolls of quarters in her purse to pay for print-outs of desired pages.

She and Neil divided the microfilm between them, settled at adjoining machines. Her heart pounding, she began to read. Demure photos of Tiffany Rollins – totally unlike Todd's descriptions – stared back at her. *But she believed Todd.* She smiled with unexpected tenderness as occasional grunts of approval emerged from Neil. He wasn't just following this out of hope for a great news break for the station. He wanted to see justice done.

At long last they rewound the final reels of microfilm, returned the cartons to the desk, and left the library.

'Todd was dealing with a sleazy mother and a devious

twelve-year-old,' Neil said softly when they'd settled themselves in the car.

'I'll go over these until every word is etched on my
memory.' Karen was grim. 'I'll be looking for some tech-
nicality that might be used to re-open the case. I know,' she
forestalled his next statement. 'That doesn't mean Tiffany or
her mother – or both – will cave. We don't even know if
Tiffany still lives here.'

'Let's find out,' he ordered briskly. 'We'll go in for lunch
and look for a public phone and a local directory.'

Neil's attitude was casual – yet his eyes were guarded, she
suddenly realized. He thought she was spinning her wheels.
That was a favorite phrase of Bob's when she dug in her
heels and tried to dig up evidence in a case. But often when
you dug hard enough, you found.

They parked on Main Street, scouted for a restaurant that
indicated telephone facilities were available.

'Here.' Neil indicated a white clapboard structure that was
inviting and offered a public telephone.

At shortly before noon the spacious, charming restaurant
was lightly populated. Karen and Neil headed for a rear table,
close to a pair of public telephones, a stand with a local
directory nearby. A smiling, middle-aged waitress came over
to take their orders.

'We're strangers in town,' Neil told her with an ingratiating
grin. 'What's the best sandwich on the menu?'

'I like the turkey.' She picked up his bantering mood. 'You
can have it all white meat, mixed white and dark, or—'

'That's what I want. A mixture, on rye toast. With a little
mustard on the side. And a tall glass of iced coffee, black.'

'Mustard with turkey?' The waitress considered it. 'I've
never tried that.'

'It's great.' Neil nodded in approval.

'Isn't this town well-known for something?' He pretended
to be searching his memory.

'Not much ever happens here.' The waitress chuckled.

'Oh, around sixteen years ago we had a rape case that hit the tabloids. This eleven- or twelve-year-old girl was raped by an overheated seventeen-year-old.' She lifted an eyebrow. 'I guess she liked it. She's been giving it away ever since.'

'She still lives here?' Karen felt a surge of excitement.

'Yeah—' The other woman seemed surprised at the question. 'Oh, nothing shy about Tiffany Rollins and her mother. Tiffany's a cocktail waitress at some dumpy gin mill at the edge of town. That's what her mother used to do – when she was younger. Before she got sick. So,' she wound up crisply because more diners were arriving, 'what'll you have?'

'The same. Also with mustard.'

Neil waited until the waitress was out of earshot. 'I could sense your antennae hurtling up. Tiffany's being promiscuous isn't going to imbue her with a guilty conscience.'

'She's here in town. I have to talk to her, Neil.'

'She's probably heard about Todd's new troubles.' Karen sensed his ambivalence about their approaching Tiffany. 'The newspapers have been full of it—'

'I know, we're probably hitting our heads against a brick wall,' Karen conceded. 'But more than ever, I want to talk with her.'

They left the restaurant and sought the house where Tiffany Rollins lived with her mother. As they had suspected, it was located in a rundown neighborhood, its tiny patches of lawns devoid of care. Here and there efforts had been made to upgrade the miniscule structures that lined the streets. The cars that sat in driveways or at the curbs were in varied states of dilapidation. Neil drove slowly. He and Karen watched for numbers – missing from some houses.

'There it is.' Karen pointed to a piece of driftwood stuck in the sun-parched lawn and bearing the legend, 'Rollins'.

They parked before the house – once a garish pink, with green trim, but now faded and peeling at intervals. Drapes were drawn. The once jaunty car that flanked the house was at least a dozen years old and bore the evidence of past collisions.

'Either Tiffany or her mother is home.' Karen tried for flipness. 'We're in luck.'

They left the car, walked up onto the tiny porch, rang the doorbell. Karen gazed uncomfortably through the screen door into the garishly wallpapered hall.

'Let me start the ball rolling,' Neil whispered. 'Judging from what the waitress said, they might be impressed that a rep from the Paradise television station is calling on them.'

'Right.'

They heard the clack of high heels on wooden floor. A tall heavily made-up platinum blonde in a short, red robe – tied tightly about the waist and revealing bosomy cleavage – sauntered into view.

'Yeah?' Her eyes dismissed Karen, focused in obvious approval on Neil.

'We're from Paradise.' Neil smiled ingratiatingly.

'Well, bully for you,' Tiffany drawled – without inviting them into the tiny, disheveled living room, whose decor featured a dizzying display of zebra slipcovers and drapes.

Neil chuckled. 'Paradise, New York. I'm Neil Bradford – from the TV station there. This is Karen Mitchell.'

'So?' But it was clear she was intrigued by Neil.

'You've probably heard about the murder in Paradise.' He was almost casual. 'We're doing some legwork on the case for the station.' All at once her eyes were wary. 'Are you Tiffany Rollins?'

'The last I heard.' Her eyes swung from Neil to Karen, back to Neil again. 'So what about it?' All at once she was defensive.

'The man being held as a suspect is the same one who was convicted here some years ago,' Karen picked up. 'You were very young then, of course.' She tried for a gentle, sympathetic approach. 'It would be helpful to his case if the defense could introduce the fact that he thought – at the time of your case – that you were seventeen rather than twelve.' She saw the fury welling in Tiffany. Damn, she was bungling this!

'He knew I was twelve,' she said viciously. 'And I'm sure he's guilty as hell this time, too. Hey, I'm lucky he didn't kill me!'

'He said you were attractive—' Karen struggled to be cajoling. 'He said you were – were—' She fought for words but Neil jumped in.

'He said you had a gorgeous figure already – like a young Marilyn Monroe. And nobody at the party was under seventeen.'

'You don't drag me into his new mess!' Tiffany's voice was shrill. 'I don't want to talk about this—'

'Tiffany—' A petulant intrusion from another room. 'Who's there? It's time for my medicine—'

'Get away from here,' Tiffany hissed. 'My mother's very sick – we don't want to hear nothin' you have to say!' She reached to slam the front door shut, despite the heat of the early afternoon.

Karen and Neil walked slowly away from the house.

'I suppose it was stupid of me to expect anything else.' She sighed in defeat as they settled themselves in the car.

'I thought – just possibly – she might want to be brought back into the limelight,' Neil admitted. 'So it didn't work out.'

'Todd knows the grand jury is sure to indict him. He's so depressed. And life's a nightmare for Cindy. She says the kids are bewildered. Mothers in town don't want their children playing with Laurie and Zachary.'

'They're all so sure that the rapist/murderer who hit this town is behind bars now.' Exasperation lent harshness to his voice. 'They don't understand that what happened to Debbie Norris could happen to one of their children. He's out there – whoever he is. I hope they have the sense to lock their doors, watch their kids.'

'Mom says that people who come into the shop are still

stunned that something so awful could happen in a town like this.'

'It's happening all over the world. In France and in Belgium recently. No country is immune. Let's pray this guy isn't a serial killer. That – right here in Paradise – he won't strike again.'

Seventeen

K aren and Helen sat down to dinner with the TV set rolled around so that they could watch the 7 p.m. news – when that time arrived.

'I don't know why you want to watch,' Helen scolded tenderly when midway through dinner Karen switched on the local channel. 'You only get upset.'

'Why does George Morrison have to appear every night when he just says the same things?'

'He's priming himself to run for the State Assembly,' Helen drawled. 'He's getting great exposure.'

'At Todd's expense,' Karen flared.

'It'll be a long time before this town returns to normal. Long after the trial—'

'Here's George—' Karen abandoned eating to focus on the television screen.

'Pompous ass,' said Helen.

'We're prepared for the grand jury hearing on Thursday of next week,' Morrison reported. 'In addition to the evidence we've given to the public, let me add something new.' He paused with an air of high drama. Karen tensed. *What now? He was supposed to share all new evidence with her.* 'Todd Anderson – known locally by the alias of Todd Simmons – has admitted to a guard and to the assistant prosecutor that he raped and murdered Debbie Norris. He gave details that only the police, the pair who discovered the body – and the perpetrator – could know. They—'

105

The rest of Morrison's speech was drowned out by Karen's outraged rebuttal.

'How dare he make a statement like that! There's no way that Todd would have made any such admission!' Her eyes blazed in a face drained of color. 'What are they trying to pull off? No way did Todd confess to anybody! And why wasn't I told before it became public knowledge?' But in her mind she could hear George's excuse: *'I tried to reach you all afternoon – but I kept getting your answering machine. I couldn't leave a message like that on the machine.'*

Helen strode to switch off the television set. 'This case is moving into a new arena. Again, somebody's out to frame Todd!'

'I'm going over to talk with Todd.' Karen pushed back her chair, rose to her feet. 'I *know* he made no such confession – but I want to hear it from him.'

Driving over to the jail – where Todd would be held until he was indicted – Karen re-ran Morrison's statement in her mind. Here was proof positive that Todd was being set up. There was a clique in this town out to protect the real murderer by fighting for Todd's conviction – and directions came from somebody high up. *Was George Morrison part of this?*

In the bare, closet-sized room allotted for attorney/client conferences, Karen briefed Todd on the latest development. He stared at her in dazed disbelief. He knew nothing of this new accusation.

'Who was the guard?' he asked, emerging from disbelief into rage. 'Which assistant prosecutor?'

Karen consulted her notes. 'The guard is Amos Rogers, the assistant prosecutor Jim Drake.'

Todd shook his head as though to brush away incredulity. 'Rogers' son is in my Little League group. Drake's daughter was in my class last year. They're lying! I never made such a statement!'

'I know they're lying,' Karen said gently. 'But in a way it's good that everything is out on the table this way. We know what we're dealing with now – we just don't know

106

who's behind this. But we *will*, Todd. We won't allow them to pull this off.' How confident she sounded, she taunted herself silently.

She returned to the house. Unlocking the front door, she heard the phone ringing, rushed to pick up.

'Hello—' Faintly breathless in her effort to out-race the answering machine.

'You heard Morrison on the 7 p.m. news?' Neil asked.

'We heard. You know it's a lie.'

'Somebody high up in this town raped and murdered Debbie Norris – and is trying to beat the rap. The guard and the assistant prosecutor were paid off – or blackmailed – to come up with that lie.' He hesitated. 'Shall I come over and share your fury?'

'Come and have coffee with us.' Her head reeled from this latest maneuver. 'Have you had dinner yet?'

'We eat early so Dad can get back to the station for his last shift. You know these entrepreneurs.' He tried for a touch of humor. 'Seven-day work week and long hours.'

'This is a conspiracy – nobody can tell me otherwise. And George Morrison will run with it as hard as he can. Come on over, Neil – we need to talk.'

Helen pushed back her chair, rose to her feet. 'I'm going over to Cindy – she must be a nervous wreck. There's more coffee for you and Neil. If he's hungry, there's cold salmon from last night.'

'Tell Cindy we all know now that there's some rotten plot underfoot to convict him – but the game's not over.'

Restless while she waited for Neil to arrive, Karen went to her new office – the guest room – brought out her laptop, and began to make brief notes on local people involved in the current political scene. Including George Morrison. One of them was desperate to pin Debbie's murder on Todd – to take the heat off himself. It was a broad field. But the guard and the assistant prosecutor were part of the conspiracy.

She heard a car pull up out front. That would be Neil. She

saved the document, exited the program and put away the laptop. She was at the door as Neil approached.

'Isn't this a bitch?' Neil was grim. 'They want to be damn sure that Todd's held for trial. Not that there was any doubt about that even before this new craziness.'

'Mom left fresh coffee. And if you're hungry, she says there's cold salmon in the fridge.'

Neil grinned. 'Honest, I'm not always hungry.'

Karen poured coffee for the two of them, brought the mugs to the table.

'This lovely little town, where people care about one another, and nothing bad ever happens.' Bitterness blended with hurt and dismay in her voice. 'I wish the station wouldn't allow Morrison to keep stirring up heated emotions every night this way!'

'I griped about that to Dad. He says he has no choice except to provide the time. It's a public service. People want to hear what's happening. They—'

'They're crucifying Todd! Even before he goes to trial!'

'I'll talk to Dad and Mom about our offering a flip side of the story.'

'Todd's side deserves to be heard.'

'The case can't be tried on television—'

'But that's happening! With only the prosecution's side being reported. I know—' Karen sighed. 'If I start making noises, the judge is going to lay down a gag rule. And maybe that's what I should do – to shut up George Morrison.'

'He'll claim he's only reporting what the public has a right to know. Morrison is convinced he's nailed the perpetrator. He'll never swallow a conspiracy theory.'

'We don't know that he isn't part of it.' Her eyes challenged Neil. 'He's dying to move up the political ladder.'

'There's not much we do know.' Exasperation crept into Neil's voice. 'You know what keeps bugging me? That damn cologne on the bath towel wrapped around Debbie's body. A man's cologne— I keep asking myself if Morrison and his crew have picked up that angle.'

'No.' She shook her head in dismissal. 'We would have heard. Morrison wants everything possible to present to the grand jury – because he has no real case. Until this phoney confession story. If Marie Bingham came forth with the truth, he'd have *nothing* except that. So Todd was driving through town around the time Debbie was murdered. That means nothing.'

'I still can't shake off the feeling that the cologne should tell us something.'

'You figure if we can track down the owner of the cologne, we'll take a giant step forward. You're right – that could be a major lead.'

'Our only lead at the moment – other than that we know Rogers and Drake are part of a conspiracy.' Neil checked his watch. 'The drugstores in town are back to their usual hours – they're closed now. What do you say we start sniffing scents tomorrow?'

'First thing.' Her mind leapt into high gear. 'We're checking for a cologne your uncle favors – you can't remember the name. But you want to buy a bottle for his birthday,' Karen plotted. 'What time will you be clear tomorrow?'

9.46 a.m., Sunday, September 7, 1997

Karen stacked breakfast dishes in the dishwasher while Helen talked with defiant lightness about attending church services that morning.

'So I'm getting the cold shoulder from some people in town. Haven't they heard that we live in a democracy?'

'How can people turn on Todd this way, after all he's done for this town?' Karen felt a recurrent surge of anger.

'Honey, you know. If you haven't lived here for forty years, you're a newcomer. But the local papers – and the local radio station – shouldn't pick up the tabloids' hysteria.'

'Cindy stuck with Todd all through that first trial. Her parents believed in him. But I'm furious,' her voice soared, 'at the way Laurie and Zachie are being ostracized. How can people treat innocent children that way? How can Cindy explain to them why the other kids aren't allowed to play with them?' The cloud of rage that darkened her face suddenly lightened. A car was pulling up in front of the house. 'There's Neil.'

'Let me get to church and pretend I don't know I'm being brushed off by people who should know better.' Helen rose to her feet. 'But my patience is wearing thin.'

Karen heard Neil exchanging greetings with Helen.

'Karen's out in the dining area,' Helen told him. 'There's fresh coffee if you're in the mood.'

'Another cup and I'll float. But thanks.'

'I'll give you a life-preserver,' Karen called.

'Hi.' Neil sauntered into view. 'I checked with drugstore hours for Sunday. Two places will be opening in about two minutes. Let's go sniff.'

Despite the fact that church-going was a major occupation on Sunday mornings, Wheat's Drugstore was doing a lively business. Determinedly casual, Karen and Neil strolled to the rear of the store – the habitat of cosmetics and scents, both delicate and sultry. An exotic oasis in the midst of mundane health supplies and household necessities.

'You don't need to sniff at Chanel No 5 or White Diamonds or Trésor,' Karen joshed. 'That's not what your uncle would wear.'

'It's kind of heavy,' Neil recalled and Karen nodded. 'Very distinctive.'

For an agonizing moment Karen was swept back into the woods again as a police officer shoveled dirt away to reveal the towel-wrapped tiny body – the towel reeking of a pungent cologne. Now she sprayed from an atomizer for Neil's benefit. He drew in a breath, shook his head. 'That's not it.' Karen nodded in covert agreement.

A saleswoman came down the length of the counter to help them. Karen saw – for a moment – a glint of recognition in her eyes. Nobody she knew, Karen realized – but people were beginning to recognize her as Todd's

110

attorney. She'd win no popularity contest in this town right now.

'I'm looking for a cologne to buy for my uncle's birthday,' Neil fabricated. 'I can't remember the name of the one he likes. It's quite strong and distinctive.'

'Perhaps it's Obsession by Calvin Klein.' The saleswoman sprayed. Neil dutifully sniffed.

'Nope, that's not it.' His smile hid his disappointment.

Karen's smile became fixed as the saleswoman persisted. She sprayed. Neil sniffed. He shook his head. Over and over again, this was repeated.

'That's everything we have.' The saleswoman tried to conceal her annoyance. 'Our stock covers the field.'

'Perhaps he picked it up when he was down in the Caribbean last spring,' Neil apologized. 'Thank you for your trouble.'

As they walked through the aisles to the entrance, Karen was conscious of stares. Oh, yes. She was becoming a marked woman in Paradise. To most she was a traitor for daring to defend Todd.

'I should get back to the station.' Neil broke into her introspection. 'Hey, how about coming up and receiving the grand tour?'

'I should go back and talk with Cindy.' To go to the station with Neil was to meet one or both of his parents. She wasn't ready for that. Mom had invited them to dinner next Sunday. She'd contrive to be with Cindy.

'I'll drive you home.' Neil pulled the door wide, and they walked out into the serenity of Sunday morning in a small town.

'We're getting nowhere,' she burst out in frustration while they settled themselves in the car. 'Everywhere a dead-end!'

'I wish to hell I could remember where I ran into that cologne before. It *exists*. You smelled it. Nothing like what we found in the drugstore.'

'It's being so elusive could narrow the field.'

'Tomorrow let's drive over to one of the shopping malls

111

outside of Albany. You know, one with major department store branches. There must be some brands that Wheat's doesn't carry.'

'Let's do it.'

Neil paused in some inner debate. 'I know you can't go out and hire fancy investigators. Cindy and Todd don't have that kind of bankroll.' His smile was sympathetic. 'So we'll be their investigators. Of course, we haven't done great so far.'

'Todd and Cindy are very grateful.'

'I'll confess – now – that there have been moments when I asked myself if we were all wrong. That maybe Todd *was* involved. But no more,' he said before she could protest. 'I count a lot on instinct. And when I saw Tiffany Rollins, I was sure he was right, that he was framed that time. And I'm convinced he's being framed again. By somebody with an important position in this town. Who else could pay off – or blackmail – a jail guard and an assistant prosecutor except somebody with standing in Paradise?'

'I've got notes set up, a lot of questions.' Karen was somber. 'But not a lot of time. Even though Todd hasn't even appeared before the grand jury, I know George Morrison is bucking for an early trial. I'm after a late November date. With a little luck I may be able to swing it.'

9.10 a.m., Monday, September 8, 1997

On Monday morning Karen and Neil left for the long drive to the mall just outside of Albany. In the afternoon, Karen told Neil, she'd be holed up in the library and reading back issues of the two local papers.

'I'll look for anything I can find on Amos Rogers and Jim Drake. We have to discover why they're lying this way. Either somebody has grounds for blackmail – or they're terribly greedy. In fact,' she said with grim determination, 'I mean to check on everybody of any importance in this town. Whoever killed Debbie is in a position to manipulate others.'

'What about Jake Rhodes?' Neil grinned at her stare of astonishment. 'He's the most influential person in town. And his big fancy house is just on the other side of the woods where we found the body. Hey, we have to start somewhere.'

'Let's find out where he was the night Debbie was killed.' Karen's mind charged ahead. Nobody in this town really knew Jake Rhodes, Mom always said. He was something of an enigma. Could it be as simple as this?

'It shouldn't be too hard to nail down.' Neil, too, seemed to exude fresh hope.

Realizing that the mall shops wouldn't open until 10 a.m., Neil suggested they stop en route for coffee. They turned in at a diner that was clearly a stop for long-haul truck drivers – a sure sign the coffee would be good, Neil told Karen. Over freshly brewed coffee in a booth at the far end of the diner, Karen admitted yet again to a fear of inadequacy.

'Todd needs a top-drawer criminal attorney. That's not me. It's scary – knowing his life is in my hands.' Why did Morrison keep yapping about demanding the death penalty?

'You told me you enjoyed your summer handling criminal cases for that legal aid group.'

'Neil, those were petty cases – not a trial for murder.'

'You're focusing on the one case – you believe in Todd's innocence.' He paused, staring into his coffee for a moment. 'After we finish up at the mall, I'll take you back to the station with me. Let's talk with my parents about doing a one-shot program on "the Todd Simmons this town has known". You know, to counteract the tabloid hysteria.'

'Not just the tabloids,' Karen raged. 'The local papers are no better.' *The media was infecting their jury pool.*

'We'll sit down and talk with Mom and Dad,' he soothed. 'In their five years here Todd and Cindy did a lot of good in this town. We'll try to find some people brave enough to come on and talk about Todd's work with local children.'

Karen's face was luminous. 'Neil, that would be wonderful.'

'Don't jump,' he cautioned. 'It's something we'll try to work out. There's no guarantee we can bring it off.'

They left the diner and proceeded to the mall. They sought out the perfume section of the department store, explained their mission. Again, the saleswoman so eager to locate their objective soon grew testy when each new scent was discarded.

'Perhaps it's not an American cologne,' she said at last. 'Not every foreign perfume company distributes in this country.'

'Thank you for being so helpful,' Karen said in sweet apology – with a warning glance at Neil. Why was he looking so strange?

'Let's get out of here.' He reached for her arm, prodded her towards the line-up of doors.

'Neil, what's bothering you?' she asked when they were out of the store.

'That woman was right.' He was brusque with excitement. 'It's a cologne from somewhere in Europe. There was this weird French photographer in Sarajevo who used to drown himself in it because showers were at a premium. Whoever murdered Debbie Norris spent time out of this country.'

'Let's drive over to the shop and talk to Mom.' Karen's mind moved into high gear. 'Somebody from Paradise bought cologne out of the country. Somewhere in Europe,' she pinpointed. 'Probably within the past few months. Mom will know who's been traveling recently.'

'It may not have been recently,' Neil warned.

'Then it'll take us a little longer to track down.' Karen refused to relinquish this fresh hope. They were on the right track.

'He – or she,' Neil amended, and Karen lifted an eyebrow in skepticism, 'could have bought the cologne a year or two ago. Still, the field is narrow. Not a lot of people from Paradise play the European travel scene.'

They drove back to Paradise, left the car in the municipal parking lot, and walked to The Oasis. Della was showing

114

sweaters to a woman Karen recognized as a member of the town council. Frances was arranging a display table. No other customer in the shop. Mom admitted business was way off. Because she was acting as Todd's attorney, Karen understood and felt a fresh attack of guilt.

'Hi, Karen.' Della inspected Neil with interest. 'Helen's in the office.' A sure indication that business was slow. Her defending Todd was costing Mom money.

Helen looked up with a lively smile when Karen and Neil appeared in the doorway of her office. Instinctively she knew this wasn't a casual visit. Karen closed the door behind herself and Neil, explained their mission.

'Not a lot of people from Paradise are bigtime travelers,' Helen conceded. 'Some of our retirees save up and make one major trip every year or two. Bill and Charlotte McBride went to Alaska for ten days in July—' She paused, squinted in thought.

'Mom, who went to Europe?' Karen emphasized.

'Lila and Stewart Allen went to the Greek Isles on their honeymoon in June. You remember Lila. You were in the same dance class when you were about ten—'

'Anybody else?' Neil probed.

'This isn't an affluent town,' Helen reminded, but she was searching her memory. 'Oh, Jake Rhodes went to some city in England – I don't remember just where – this past spring. A business trip – something to do with factory equipment.' She gazed from Karen to Neil, astonished by their sudden air of excitement. 'You don't suspect Jake Rhodes?'

'He fits the profile we've drawn together.' Karen exchanged a swift glance with Neil. 'He's rich. He's important in this town. He probably has more influence than anybody else. He could easily manipulate the prison guard and the assistant prosecutor into lying about Todd's confessing. And I gather nobody gets elected in Paradise without Jake Rhodes's support.'

'That includes George Morrison,' Neil added. 'Let's find out where Jake Rhodes was the night Debbie was murdered.'

'His housekeeper – Althea Jackson – belongs to my reading group,' Helen said after a moment's hesitation. 'There's a meeting tonight. I hadn't planned on going. We're both mystery fans,' she told Neil and Karen, and chuckled. 'Jeannie told me once it was a toss-up who bought the most mystery and suspense novels at the bookstore where she works – Jake Rhodes or me. Not that he reads them. I doubt he reads anything but stock reports. Althea told me he sends them to his son at boarding school.'

'Mom, go to that meeting tonight. Talk to the housekeeper,' Karen said urgently. 'Try to find out what Rhodes was doing the night Debbie was murdered. That might be a lead.'

'Jake Rhodes? No way.' Helen grunted in rejection. 'But I'll see what I can come up with tonight.'

Back in the car Karen and Neil sat for a few moments to dissect their progress. Both were jubilant, convinced they were approaching a breakthrough.

'I'll take you home and head back for the station.' Neil reached for the ignition key. 'My presence is expected there at regular intervals.'

'What about the one-shot you talked about? You know, "the Todd Simmons this town has known".'

'I'll take it up with my folks tomorrow morning,' he said after an indecisive moment. 'Let's get that show on the road.'

Eighteen

K aren was conscious of the intense curiosity of the librarians as she requested reel after reel of back issues of the *Enquirer* and the *Evening News*. They were too polite to show open hostility, but she was sure they looked upon her as the enemy. They forgot about the Saturday morning story hours Cindy had conducted here for enthralled pre-schoolers. They forgot about Todd's theater group, held here after school for fifth and sixth graders. They *believed* that Todd had raped Tiffany Rollins. They *believed* he'd raped and murdered Debbie Norris.

Trying to ignore the overheated atmosphere, she focused on reading. Nothing helpful so far, she conceded in frustration at close to 5 p.m. Head home now and start dinner. Mom's reading group met at eight tonight. Please God, let Mom come up with something useful. She returned the reels of microfilm to the desk and left the library.

Arriving at the house she checked the mailbox. She reached inside and pulled out a pair of bills, the usual array of catalogues. And an envelope addressed to her. Not through the mail, she noted – it had been dropped off by hand. She ripped open the envelope, pulled out a sheet of lined notepaper. The message was scrawled in large block letters with a red magic marker.

'You can be Todd Simmons's lawyer because we know he'll fry. But don't think you can practice law in this town after this. We don't want the likes of you here.'

Churning with anger, Karen ripped the hand-delivered message to shreds as she walked up to the house. Nothing like this ever happened in Paradise. But then no six-year-old was ever raped and murdered in the history of Paradise. Its innocence was forever destroyed.

She should have expected this, she taunted herself. She would encounter more such incidents before the trial was over. *Learn to deal with them.* But the warning against practicing law in Paradise thrust her into disturbing contemplation. What did she plan to do with her life after the trial?

No way would she go back to Bob and the firm. That was untenable. But would she want to make Paradise her permanent home? Growing up she'd always been so relieved to come back to Mom. To Paula and her Paradise had been home. Right now she was living in a vacuum. Mom was so happy that she was here, wouldn't allow her to contribute anything to the household expenses – which allowed her to handle Todd's case on what he and Cindy could afford to pay.

She didn't want to be like Eve – roaming from man to man. She needed roots. Could she find that with Neil? *How can I feel this way about him when I've known him such a little while? It's unrealistic.*

Karen changed from her crisp, mint-green summer shift into pale yellow shorts and T-shirt, phoned Cindy to see if she needed groceries.

'I'm stocked for the next two or three days,' Cindy reported, sounding exhausted. 'My major problem – other than worrying about Todd – is keeping the kids amused. We have "school" for several hours each day – but it's the old story. *"Why can't we go play with somebody?"*'

'Tomorrow afternoon let's you and I take them over to that new petting zoo that opened up this summer. Mom says the kids all love it.'

'Would you go with us?' A wistful hope in Cindy's voice. 'I – I still can't bring myself to go out alone.'

'We'll leave around two o'clock,' Karen promised.

'We miss Todd so much,' Cindy whispered. 'Every minute of each day I think about him sitting there behind bars. I ask myself, how can it happen again this way? He spent three and a half years in prison for something he didn't commit – and now this. I can't believe the way most people have turned against us. People we considered our friends.'

'I blame the media.' *How many times have I said that?* 'They're letting rumors replace facts. We see it over and over again. Every time we pick up a newspaper or magazine. We see it on television and hear it on the radio.' But that was of little comfort to Cindy and Todd.

'I'm so scared. The way George Morrison talks about asking for the death penalty – and the newspapers are backing him up—'

'Cindy, you hang in there,' Karen ordered. 'We know Todd is innocent—'

'But what does that mean?' Cindy's voice was a high, thin wail. 'George Morrison's daughter was in Todd's class last year. She was having attention problems – he worked with her after class to help her catch up. He talked to her parents about her begging for more attention at home. He helped that little girl, Karen – and now her father is out to crucify Todd. Doesn't he realize those two men who said Todd confessed are lying?'

'I don't know— But I'm fighting to find out, Cindy. And Neil Bradford is working with me. He's—'

'Something sick happened last night,' Cindy broke in. 'I'd told myself I wouldn't tell you—'

'What happened?' Karen tensed in anticipation.

'Some young hooligans – I heard them giggling, several teenagers – dumped garbage all over our front lawn. I knew everybody was asleep – I went out and piled it into plastic bags and put it in the garage for now. I keep telling myself, not everybody in town is rotten like that. Earlier in the evening one of the mothers from the school came over.' Cindy was struggling for poise. 'I was scared to open the door at first – then I recognized her voice. She'd brought over a batch of cookies. She said she didn't believe Todd could do something so awful. She didn't believe he'd raped Tiffany Rollins. She told me her grandmother grew up in Atlanta and talked about something called the Leo Frank case down there—'

'It was a case that hit the national headlines, back in 1913. Leo Frank was accused of murdering a thirteen-year-old girl named Mary Phagan. She worked in the factory he owned. There was much sensational newspaper coverage before and during the trial.'

'They did to him what they're doing to Todd—'

'Exactly.' Karen paused, reluctant to continue – knowing the tragic fate of Leo Frank.

'Go on,' Cindy urged. 'I want to know what happened to him.'

'He was convicted and sentenced to death. A janitor claimed Leo Frank had killed her and paid him two hundred dollars to carry the body to the factory basement. The public assumed she'd been raped before she was killed – though there was no real indication of this. There was no other evidence against him – and the janitor gave several different versions of his story. The governor took a courageous stand despite the public feelings and commuted the sentence – at which point a mob kidnapped Frank from jail and lynched him. Cindy, you insisted I tell you,' she whispered, unnerved by Cindy's sudden silence.

'I wanted to know.'

'Then sixty-nine years later – in 1982 – an eighty-three-year-old man broke into the news with the confession that he knew who killed Mary Phagan – and it wasn't Leo Frank. He'd been fourteen years old at the time he inadvertently witnessed the murder – and the janitor threatened to kill him, too, if he ever told what he saw. Near death, he felt obliged to come forth with the truth. And there've been other cases. How many times have we picked up a newspaper and read how men who've served years for rape had just been exonerated on the basis of DNA reports?'

'That wouldn't have helped Todd – either time. He admitted having sex with Tiffany. Debbie's body had been washed clean. The murderer knew not to leave a calling card. I keep asking myself – what did Todd and I ever do to deserve such punishment?'

'You're two very good people,' Karen said gently. 'Better times are coming. I refuse to believe anything else.'

'It hurts so to see people turning against Todd.' Cindy paused at explosive sounds from somewhere else in the house. 'Laurie, you and Zachie stop fighting! Karen, I've got to go to the kids.'

'We've got a date tomorrow at 2 p.m. Laurie and Zachie will love the petting zoo.'

6.50 p.m., Monday, September 8, 1997

Doug glanced at his watch as he prepared to leave the office. Jeannie kept complaining about his working so late, but he was grateful for the overtime. Without her paycheck each week they were tight on money. Property taxes just went up. Their adjustable mortgage went up a quarter percent. He wished she'd go back to the bookstore instead of moping around the house. She'd feel better. How much longer would they hold her job open?

He went out to the factory floor for a last-minute check. Everybody was gone for the night. He turned off the lights, headed down the empty hall. He heard Jake talking in his office with someone, then realized it was his father-in-law.

'It hasn't been officially announced yet, but the trial will begin on Monday, December eighth,' Clay said. 'I got the word this afternoon.'

'Hell, why so late?' Jake was annoyed. 'Push the old bastard to set it for an earlier date.'

'I tried. No dice. I want it to be over with so Jeannie can get her life back. Not that things will ever be the same for us again—'

Doug hurried out into the early dusk. For Tommy's sake,

he and Jeannie had to look ahead. She alternated between smothering him to death and ignoring him. Poor little guy, he couldn't figure out what was going on.

He climbed behind the wheel of his beat-up pick-up and headed home. Steeling himself for another somber scene with Jean. He tried so hard to get her into therapy. It was useless. Clay was no help – he thought therapy was for nutcases.

He parked in the driveway and strode to the house. Opening the door he heard the VCR blasting. That meant Tommy was watching one of the cartoon videos Jeannie bought for the kids on Tommy's birthday in May. Once Marie left for the day, Jeannie parked him in front of the VCR.

'Jeannie, I'm home!'

'Hi.' Moments later Jeannie trailed into the living room, where Doug was hoisting Tommy into his arms for their nightly ritual. The VCR was switched off. 'You're late again.' Reproach blended with resignation in her voice.

'Hey, that overtime helps with the mortgage.' He leaned forward for a perfunctory kiss. Not only had he lost his daughter – he'd lost his wife. He felt like a monk these days.

'I can't go back to work yet,' she said quickly. 'Not until that monster is put away for good.'

'It hasn't been announced, but I overheard your father and Jake talking. The trials set to start December eighth.'

'Why so late? They know he's guilty!'

'I'm not so sure,' Doug said without thinking and was instantly sorry.

'What do you mean, you don't know?' she blazed. 'He confessed! I hope he rots in hell for what he did to my baby!'

'Karen claims he was framed – that those two guys are lying. Todd vows he never confessed.'

'After he raped that little girl in East Sedgewick, they should have put him away for life. And you're going to say that was a frame-up, too?'

'It was his word against hers. I don't know, Jeannie—' He'd been agonizing over this since the day the police announced Todd was a suspect.

'Oh, you make me sick! Except for your damn allergies, we would have had a dog. Nobody could have walked off with Debbie if we had a dog in the house. Why didn't you take care of the air-conditioning system? Then the windows in the bedrooms would have been locked.'

'Jeannie, let's don't go into that again.' How many times had she thrown those things in his face? And no windows in this house were ever locked. 'Tommy, you're wet,' he discovered.

'You change him. I'll get dinner on the table.' Usually they had a roast or a chicken – each of which lasted for at least two nights. Marie cleaned the house and put up dinner as well as watching Tommy.

Doug carried Tommy off to his bedroom. Damn, why did Jeannie keep Debbie's bed piled up with all her stuffed animals and dolls, as though waiting for her to come back to them? Tommy was paddled if he made a move to take any of the animals. He kept up a running conversation with Tommy while he changed his diaper. He was conscious of the dust on the night table beside Debbie's bed, on Tommy's crib.

God, Marie was a slob, he thought distastefully as he bent to pick up Tommy's pajamas which lay half-concealed beneath the crib. But Jeannie insisted it was hard to get help these days. '*So she's not the greatest. At least, she shows up.*'

What was this? He frowned, picked up a tiny object that he'd pulled out along with the pajamas. It was one of the pins awarded to the volunteer fireman last winter, he recognized.

'Daddy!' Tommy reproached querulously. 'Play with me!'

'You bet, Tommy—' He lifted his son from the crib and began their usual pre-dinner roughhousing.

His mind dwelt on the pin he'd discovered under the crib. Todd wore his pin all the time – he was proud of being a volunteer fireman. Todd said he'd been here to pick up Laurie – that accounted for his fingerprints on the windowsill. He'd opened the window wider because the afternoon was so hot. Todd had been in this room – the way he said.

But if he took the pin to the police and told them about finding it here, Jeannie would never forgive him. He broke into a sweat as he visualized her rage.

'What difference does it make if he alibis his fingerprints? He confessed to two men! He can't deny that! He'll get the death penalty. George will see to that!'

Nineteen

7.20 p.m., Monday, September 8, 1997

Karen and Helen were hurrying through dinner this evening. Helen's reading group was to meet at 8 p.m.

'We kind of settled on Monday nights because that's Althea's evening off,' Helen explained. 'She's been working for Jake Rhodes for almost five years. On Monday nights like clockwork he has dinner out with Mayor Gilbert and whoever they round up for that night. She says it's not a bad job – just him at home, and maybe four or five times a year his daughter and her family come over for the weekend. Once a year his other daughter who lives out west comes home for a visit.'

'What are you reading now? A suspense novel, of course,' Karen joshed affectionately.

'What else?' Helen chuckled. 'It was my turn to choose. We're reading Seymour Shubin's new psychological suspense, *Fury's Children*. It's about a pair of teenagers who do horrible things.' Her face was suddenly somber. 'And in a year or two we'll probably be reading a new novel based on what's happening right here in Paradise.'

Karen leaned forward with an air of urgency. 'Mom, try to find out where Jake Rhodes was the night Debbie was murdered.' She searched her mind for a way to handle this. 'Maybe all of you could reminisce about where each of you were that night – then expand it—'

'I'll work on it,' Helen promised.

'Remember, tomorrow evening we're having dinner out. We have to celebrate your birthday in style.'

'Sure. How often do I arrive at this threshold? Eligible for Social Security and Medicare?' Her smile was besmirched with cynicism. 'I can join those other senior citizens who are shocked by the shenanigans of doctors playing larcenous games with Medicare.'

'Mom, why don't more of them report these frauds?'

'Darling, you're young enough to be outraged – and that's right.' Helen paused a moment. 'Like Kate Reardon, who rails against her doctor. But he's been her doctor for eighteen years. She trusts him to handle her health problems. She doesn't want to lose him. And some are just fearful of having it backfire on them if they report their doctors. It's as though doctors – ethical in every way – feel they have a God-given right to screw the government.' She laughed. 'I get so riled up myself my language gets ugly.'

'You remembered to invite Della and Frances, didn't you?'

'Sure thing.' She sighed. 'It feels wrong that we're having out little party when Todd is rotting in jail. And Cindy won't be with us—'

'Mom, life has to go on. We both know we couldn't ask Cindy to join us.'

'Even if we did, who would sit with the kids?' Helen's voice was acerbic. 'They're pariahs.'

The nine members of the reading group sat in the small conference room that the public library provided for their meetings and discussed the new Shubin psychological suspense novel with gusto, dissected every aspect of the plot. It was easy, Helen congratulated herself, to switch the conversation over to their own chilling mystery. Still, she was disconcerted that of the eight others present only Althea agreed with her that the tabloid press was trying Todd Simmons on their front pages – even though his grand jury hearing wouldn't take place until the day after tomorrow.

As she'd told Karen at dinner, her pet supermarket hate – even more than the frustration of trying to open up those plastic bags in the produce department – was watching people in line at the checkout counter as they read the tabloid paper headlines.

'Come on, Helen, he's guilty as sin,' one member exhorted with an arrogance that warned her to tread carefully. 'If they'd kept Todd Simmons – excuse me, Todd Anderson – locked up after that last trial instead of letting him out, Debbie Norris would be alive today.'

'He was framed in the Rollins case,' Helen began, and the others hushed her with derisive laughter. 'Damn it, that happens!'

'Twice?' Another of the dissenters shook her head. 'No way.'

'It could have been anybody in this town.' Helen was doggedly determined to pursue this. Plotting her route. 'All right, any man,' she conceded. 'Peggy, can you prove where your brother was that night? Sylvia, what about your husband?'

'Hey, they can't go around asking every man in town where he was between midnight and 1 a.m. that night,' Sylvia protested. 'Anyhow, most of them were in bed asleep – which Todd Simmons wasn't. Witnesses have testified to that.'

She was getting nowhere, Helen scolded herself. It would be indelicate to ask Althea if she knew where Jake Rhodes was that night. It would be like suggesting that maybe he was in bed with her. All right, go out for coffee with Althea after the meeting. She was an insomniac – she'd like that. The Mimosa was open until midnight. And they had low-fat muffins. Althea was always fighting to take off twenty pounds.

The night air was mild and fragrant when Helen and Althea left their cars in front of the Mimosa Diner at close to 10 p.m. Only a handful of patrons were scattered about the booths. Helen and Althea headed for a booth at the far end. The nearest patrons were three middle-aged men arguing vociferously about the handling of political campaign contributions. Too involved in their own battling to eavesdrop on Althea and herself, Helen decided with satisfaction.

'You know somebody's going to write a gory novel based on what's happening here,' Helen picked up after a waitress had taken their orders. 'It's natural.'

Deviously she wove a possible story line. Althea jumped into the project.

'Maybe – like you just said – some bigshot in town has this secret vice that he's managed to hide all these years. He has a thing for very young girls and—'

'Let's make it somebody like Jake Rhodes,' Helen broke in. 'He's the most important man in this town. Where was he the night Debbie was murdered? I'll bet you don't remember,' she challenged.

'Oh, sure I remember.' Althea waved a hand in dismissal. 'That was the night I drove over to Albany for dinner with my niece – and I slept over. Mr Rhodes had gone to the town where his daughter Olivia lives. He addressed some business group there that night and slept over at Olivia's house.'

So much for Jake Rhodes as a suspect. Helen masked her disappointment, continued with the little game she had launched with Althea.

Who else was out of the country in the last year or two? Again, she searched her mind.

10.42 p.m., Monday September 8, 1997

Suppressing a yawn, Neil reached for the TV remote and switched off the national news. How many times could he watch the same stories? Occasionally he felt a surge of restlessness when he viewed Third World areas in Asia or Africa where troubles were erupting. His mind told him there were great opportunities out there – but his enthusiasm was fleeting. He was growing too accustomed to easy living.

Now he became aware of enticing aromas drifting in from the kitchen. A moment later his mother strolled into the den.

'In the mood for coffee? Decaf, of course.'

'I'm in the mood.' He grinned. 'What goes with it?'

'No cake tonight.' Mom had joined the health-conscious. She read labels, counted calories, fat and cholesterol content. 'Hot apple slices topped with rum raisin frozen yogurt. Low fat.'

'Is there any other kind?' His eyes were teasing but his affection obvious.

They heard a key in the front door. 'There's Dad. Apple slices for three coming up.'

It was great being here at home this way – but he had to look ahead, he thought uneasily. Was he willing to settle here, stay with the station, forget the old lifestyle? Would it be enough?

Maybe I want to live Dad's dream. To give back a little to my space on earth. Make a contribution. Todd was doing that before the second frame-up. Dad and Mom will give me a lot of leeway if I stay with the station. I'd have a chance to accomplish small – good – things. If all the everyday people in this world did just a bit to make it a better place, what changes to the good we could make!

Will Mom and Dad be upset if I look around for a place of my own? Hell, they know that at thirty – and after my years of roaming – I'll eventually want my own place. Will Karen stay here in Paradise after the trial is over – or will she head for New York? Is there a future for the two of us? I told her the truth – she's the first woman who brought out homing instincts in me. But will she settle for the life of a small town attorney? Am I jumping too fast? Cool it, old man.

Neil joined his mother and father in the large country kitchen. They settled themselves in comfortable captain's chairs about the oak table. A serenity here that he relished after the years of chasing about the globe.

'Did you talk to Neil about Janice?' Frank asked Arline.

'Not yet. I thought you ought to explain about the new program you have in mind for her.'

'Talking about new programs,' Neil jumped in, grateful for this springboard, 'Karen and I were bitching the way most people are forgetting all the good Todd has done in

129

this town. We were thinking that maybe the station could do a "one-shot" showing this.' He tried to appear enthusiastic despite negative vibes he was receiving. 'It's only fair to Todd—' His voice trailed off.

'People will say we're trying to influence possible jurors,' Frank said unhappily.

'Damn it, Dad, that's what the tabloids are doing – in a rotten, misleading way!'

'Frank, this is our station,' Arline chided. 'We can express our opinions. Neil's right – the media's unfairly stacking the cards against Todd.'

'But advertisers may complain—' Frank was ambivalent. 'We can't afford to lose business.'

'A "one-shot", Dad,' Neil pushed. 'They complain – you tell them there'll be no more. And it'll be over long before the trial begins. Look at the way George Morrison insists on coming on every bloody night to report on his so-called "latest word on the case". He wants to keep his face out there. He's using the station to promote his own political career.'

Frank paused in thought. 'All right, we'll do it. Work out the time slot. Let me know what you're setting up. We'll take a chance.'

'Tell him about Janice now,' Arline prodded.

'Who's Janice?' Neil was wary.

'Janice Hilton. She's the society editor at the *Enquirer*,' his father began. 'Her mother and your mother are friends. Janice is bored with her job at the newspaper. She's talking about taking a job as foreign correspondent for some schlocky publication she's been exchanging E-mail with. She's got a bunch of romantic notions about how exciting that could be.'

'Her mother would like you to give her the real nitty-gritty picture of what it's like to live in war-torn Third-World nations.'

'I like the idea of giving her a once-a-week spot to talk about local social affairs,' his father picked up. 'She's very pretty, handles herself well. Call her up tomorrow, take her out to dinner, and offer her this spot on the station. No salary until a sponsor comes through, but she'll understand that. And, meanwhile, slip in a realistic picture of what a foreign correspondent's life is actually like these days. She visualizes herself holed up in some swanky hotel and hobnobbing every night with fascinating newspaper people.'

'She's twenty-three years old,' his mother derided indulgently. 'The roughest life she's experienced is a month at some summer camp.'

'I've been to camp,' Neil recalled. 'That's not what she'll find in hot spots in Asia or Africa.'

'Take her to dinner tomorrow night,' his mother urged. 'Give her the unglamorous details of being a foreign correspondent – then offer her fifteen minutes once a week as "the eyes and ears of Paradise". Let my friend stop chewing her fingernails every waking minute. Call it your good deed for the week.'

'I'll talk to her,' Neil promised and grinned. 'I'll even show her my battle scars.'

'You're taking her out to discuss an assignment,' Frank pinpointed. 'The rest you shoe-horn in at opportune moments.'

7.42 a.m., Tuesday, September 9, 1997

Karen awoke that morning with an instant realization that today was her grandmother's birthday. Sometime within the next hour and a half, she predicted inwardly, Paula would call. Whenever she and Paula were away from Mom on this day, they always managed to phone. Eve never remembered. They did. But more often than not, they were right here in Paradise – with Mom.

She felt a rush of tenderness as she recalled Mom's show of delighted astonishment when she and Paula – as little girls – produced the 'surprise' birthday cake.

'Whenever did you two manage to make this cake? And it's so beautiful!'

The cake was always pink – and, of course, a 'mix'. Their current sitter their co-conspirator. Mom always made sure there was somebody at home when they came home from school. She was always at the shop, as long as they could remember. Mom never let on that she knew they were plotting a birthday surprise. In every way except giving birth, *she* was their mother.

Karen heard sounds in the kitchen. Mom was up already, though they'd gone to sleep later than normal because of what Mom called her half-baked detective work. It *was* a disappointment that Jake Rhodes was ruled out as a suspect.

She'd call Neil later at the office and tell him. She shied away from phoning him at home – as though this put their relationship on a personal basis. So she was weird – she didn't want to have even a brief encounter with his mother or father – if either of them should pick up the phone. Mom was having them over for dinner Sunday night, she reminded herself. Contrive not to be here. She didn't want pressure from either side.

Neil had been so sure that the cologne angle would lead them to the real murderer. But they still shouldn't rule out that lead. She'd go back to the microfilm – check on local society news. Perhaps someone Mom didn't know had traveled to Europe in the last year or two. They couldn't afford to overlook any possible lead.

She left the bed, hurried into the shower. By the time she'd emerged and was dressing, she heard the phone ring. That would be Paula. It was barely 5 a.m. in Berkeley – but Paula was determined to wish Mom 'happy birthday' first thing in the morning.

She reached into a dresser drawer, fished out Mom's birthday present hidden beneath a pile of lingerie. She'd gone to the bookshop where Jeannie worked – comfortable in the knowledge that Jeannie had not yet returned to her job there, so there would be no uncomfortable encounter. She knew Florence Matthews – the owner – slightly, but Mom and Florence were longtime friends. Florence would know what new suspense novels Mom hadn't bought yet.

Mom was talking on the phone when she walked into the

kitchen, paused to pantomime that Paula was on the other end. Karen placed the gift-wrapped parcel of three suspense hardcovers at Mom's place at the table and waited for her turn to speak to her sister. She'd written Paula to alert her to the break with Bob, to let Paula know that she was here at home for the present and not to write her at the New York address.

'Oh, honey, it would be wonderful if you all could come home for Christmas!' Helen's face was luminous. 'I haven't seen my little angel since April – and she must be learning so many new things.' She listened to Paula for a few moments more. 'Darling, this is costing you a fortune – let me put Karen on now.' She extended the phone to Karen.

'Hi, Paula. How's everything in your neck of the woods?'

She steeled herself for a barrage of questions from Paula. They came at her in torrents. How could she have given up such a marvelous job? Why had she broken up with Bob, who was supposed to be the love of her life? Had she heard from him? How much longer would she be in Paradise? One by one she replied in succinct sentences.

'Paula, enough about me,' she interrupted at last. 'How's life at Berkeley?'

'Oh, God, I'm bored to death most of the time.' Paula's earlier ebullience evaporated. 'Ron works two or three nights every week. He goes in to the lab over weekends. He's fascinated by his work. But I'm alone so much.' A familiar lament.

'What about your job?' Paula was an administrative assistant for some small press.

'Dull, dull, dull. And I always worry about leaving Jill with the nanny. You know. I live with guilt. Is she happy? Am I being neglectful, going off to work five days a week? Will I regret it later?'

'Suppose you quit your job and stayed home?'

'With a huge mortgage and two car loans?' Paula scoffed. 'Get real. But don't repeat any of this to Mom.' Alarm crept into Paula's voice. 'I don't want her worrying about me.'

'I'm glad everything's so well,' Karen dutifully said, for Mom's ears. 'Give Jill a big hug and a kiss for me.'

'Write!' Paula ordered. 'Oh, have you heard from Eve?'

'Not for weeks.'

'That figures. Hang around there until Christmas,' she ordered. 'Ron thinks we can manage the air fare for a trip home at the Christmas break.'

Off the phone Karen turned to Helen. 'Open your present while I fix breakfast. You don't cook on your birthday—'

Bustling about the kitchen, Karen enjoyed Helen's making a major production of opening her birthday present.

'Such lovely wrappings. I almost hate to open this. But I can't figure out what it is.' Florence had placed the books in a box. Slowly Helen untied the festive bow, peeled away the colorful paper, lifted the lid of the box and brought out the books. 'Oh, Karen, I've been dying to read these! All three,' she marveled, inspecting the titles. 'How on earth did you know what I wanted?'

'One guess.' Karen laughed. 'I asked Florence what you hadn't picked up yet.'

'Did I ever tell you who started me reading mysteries? It was your grandfather. So long ago—' A wistful glow in her eyes now. 'Before Eve was born. He brought me a copy of *Cry Hard, Cry Fast*, by John D. MacDonald. Money was tight in those days – it was the paperback edition, cost sixty cents.'

'Times have changed.' As a teenager she'd always wondered why prices always went up. It was just a change in figures, Mom said. Everything cost more – but salaries went up, too.

'Neil's going to be disappointed that Jake Rhodes is in the clear—'

'It was a great try, Mom.' Karen forced a smile. 'I'm going to dig around in newspaper back issues, see if I can come up with someone unknown to you who traveled to Europe. We can't afford to let any lead slip past us.' Because she was hitting stone walls trying to prove Todd's innocence.

Now talk turned to the restaurant where they were to have

dinner that night. The new place in town – The Colonial – where Neil had taken her for dinner. It had become so popular reservations were essential even midweek.

'The girls want to dress up a bit for dinner,' Helen warned. 'That makes it an occasion.' She chuckled. 'I'll dig out my double strand of pearls.'

'That's why you told me to make the reservations for seven thirty.' Karen understood now. 'Why I'm not to pick the three of you up at the shop.'

'I feel bad about not inviting Cindy.' Helen was somber now.

'Mom, you know she wouldn't feel up to going – even if she could find a sitter,' Karen consoled. 'Not under the present circumstances.' But she understood Mom felt guilty at celebrating a birthday when Cindy and Todd were in such pain. 'Cindy and I are taking the kids to the petting zoo this afternoon. At least I'll be getting her out of the house.' The only time she left was to visit Todd – when either she or Mom stayed with Laurie and Zachary.

'I'd better get moving,' Helen said at last. 'And I love the books. They're a great present, honey.'

Karen checked the kitchen clock. Neil would be at the office by now. Call him. She reached for the phone.

'Neil Bradford—' His voice – brisk yet warm – came to her on the first ring.

'Mom did her detective work last night,' Karen reported. 'Jake Rhodes is in the clear. He was out of town that night.'

'That would have been too easy,' he conceded and sighed. 'But let's not give up yet on the cologne lead.'

'No way,' she agreed. 'I'm heading for the library in a bit. It doesn't open till ten. Somewhere in the local papers there must be a line about a local visitor out of the country. Maybe on a business deal. Whatever, I aim to find it.' She hesitated. She didn't want to seem to be pressuring Neil. 'You'll be talking to your parents about the one-shot this morning?'

'We did last night. I've got the go-ahead.'

'Great!'

'Oh, I have another call coming in – I'll get back to you in a few minutes.'

'I'm leaving for the library. We'll talk later,' she said quickly.

She sat in thought for a few moments. Her mind reverting to the conversation with Paula. She hadn't expected that Bob would call her. He must know she was here – but so what? Yes, she admitted with painful candor, she'd half-expected some word from him. But it would be wrong to start up with Bob again. It was wrong from the beginning.

Unwarily her thoughts turned to Neil. This wasn't a rebound situation – there was real chemistry between them. *Will Neil ever be satisfied to settle in one place? Put down roots, raise a family? He's spent close to eight years roaming the globe. He loved it. How much longer will he be content in this kind of life? He was building a reputation. So I didn't know him by name – lots of people do. He came right out and said he wants something more than a casual relationship with me. In time. And be honest – I want that, too.*

Neil sighed with relief as he put down the phone. After four frustrating calls, he'd finally talked to somebody willing to go on the 'one-shot' program for Todd. Karen was right – people were scared shitless to come out in Todd's defense. He scowled at the jarring intrusion of another call. He wanted to pursue this deal.

'Hello.'

'Is this Neil Bradford?' A light feminine voice, faintly breathless.

'Yes, it is.'

'I'm Janice Hilton. You left a message on my machine last night. I didn't get home till very late. I was covering a charity event that went on till all hours.'

'I understand that.' Hell, he hadn't realized until after he'd called that it was so late – but then he hadn't mentioned the time of his call. 'We've been discussing a new program for the station, and we thought it was something that you could handle well.'

'That sounds exciting!'

'Suppose we talk about it over dinner tonight – if you're not going to be tied up on an assignment.'

'No, I'm free,' she said eagerly. Was she envisioning herself as some future Barbara Walters?

'What about meeting at The Colonial about seven tonight?' Don't pick her up and drive her there – that would look like a date. This is business – plus a boy scout deal for Mom. 'Is that OK?'

'That'll be fine.' Her voice crackled with elation. 'See you at seven. At The Colonial.'

6.48 p.m., Tuesday, September 9, 1997

Karen inspected her reflection in the mirror on the door of her bedroom closet. She'd bought this Donna Karan dress for her interview at the firm. Bob insisted she wear something expensive and smart – and this was both.

Don't let bad memories spoil it for me. Heaven knows when I can afford something like this again. Wear the jacket, too – though the evening is humid. Restaurants are usually air-conditioned for men in summer-wool suits. Women are second-class patrons.

Her mind shot back to the evening she had dinner with Neil at The Colonial. It seemed so long ago. In truth, it was about two weeks ago. She'd been disconcerted to find herself drawn to another man when she was still stunned from the break with Bob.

'Karen?' Helen hovered in the doorway. 'We should be leaving to pick up the others.'

'I'm ready, Mom.' She reached into the closet for her jacket.

'That's a gorgeous outfit.'

'Part of the business wardrobe.'

'Were Laurie and Zachie excited about the trip to the petting zoo?' Helen asked tenderly.

'Oh, they loved it! So did I—' Oddly, her mind darted back to the morning she and Neil had fed the ducks at the pond midway between Paradise and East Sedgewick. She'd known then that Neil was special.

She was amazed that she had so enjoyed the afternoon with Cindy and the kids at the petting zoo. Oh, she wished Paula and Ron and Jill lived close by. Her only niece and she'd only seen Jill three times since she was born. For both Paula and her, family was something to be cherished.

She was glad that she'd been able to lure Cindy from the house. She seemed so depressed, so exhausted – and there was such a long haul ahead. Even though Cindy knew about the likely outcome of Thursday's grand jury hearing, she clung to some wild hope that Todd would be released. There'd be no bail set – the judge was sure to rule that out.

'Della and Frances have never been to The Colonial,' Helen said while she settled herself behind the wheel of her nine-year-old Dodge. 'They're so pleased that you chose that.'

'It's a lovely room.'

'You went there with Neil, didn't you?'

'When he asked me for help about doing a human interest report on Jeannie and Doug.' Oh, God. Mom had that look in her eyes again. Ten to one she was talking with Neil's parents about what they'd call a 'blossoming friendship'. This thing between them was soaring too fast. Yet she felt exhilarated at the prospect of a real relationship with Neil.

It can happen this way. So it's a storybook romance. It happens outside of novels, too – in the real world.

'What's with that "one-shot" you talked about for Todd?' Helen asked as she pulled up before Frances's modest ranch house.

'I should have told you – it's in the works.'

'Remember, I'm available for a solid plug. That's like getting a free TV commercial.' But Mom knew, Karen thought, that it could also turn away customers.

Frances emerged from her house, hurried to join them in the car.

'I'm glad for your birthday, Helen.' She slid into the rear seat. 'So we have a reason for a little celebrating. This town has been so grim since that awful night. And it'll just get worse when the trial comes up.'

'The hotels will be happy,' Helen jeered. 'There won't be a vacant room in town with the media people pouring in.'

'I don't dare say it to anybody else,' Frances subconsciously lowered her voice to a whisper, 'but I just can't believe Todd's guilty. Though it is hard to explain that earlier rape conviction. Of course, he was just seventeen then—'

'Let's don't talk about the case tonight,' Karen decreed. 'Everybody needs a little respite.' She was silent for a moment. 'Todd wasn't guilty then. He isn't guilty now.'

But how do I convince a jury of that? A jury sure to be tainted by the news media. Will I be able to get a change of venue? Is there any place in this country that hasn't heard about the earlier conviction? How do I convince a jury that there's a conspiracy in this town to make Todd appear guilty? Who's behind that conspiracy?

A few minutes later they picked up Della and headed for the restaurant. The parking area before The Colonial indicated that others in Paradise were in a dining-out mood. They left the car and walked to the entrance.

'Tuesday night used to be a slow night in this town,' Frances said as they walked from the sticky night into the comfort of air-conditioning. From the spacious foyer, they saw that many of the tables in the flower-scented, softly illuminated dining room were already occupied.

A hostess led them to their table – in a private corner of the room, as Karen had requested. A small birthday cake would arrive with their coffee.

'Oh, this is a lovely room,' Della effervesced.

'We've become a dining-out society,' Frances added. 'But most of the time for me it's Wendy's or that new pizza place that opened up last winter. Tonight we're living it up.'

'With so many women working, it's natural.' All at once Helen seemed startled, her eyes focused on a table across the room.

While the other two began a lively discussion about the menu, Karen allowed her gaze to follow Helen's. Across the room – in animated conversation – Neil sat with a very pretty young blonde. The Neil Bradford charm turned on full wattage, she thought in bitter recognition. Was he telling her, too, how he'd never had time for a real relationship? How he'd never met anyone that felt right? Until now?

How could she have been so gullible, so naive? Hadn't she learned anything from the bad scene with Bob?

Twenty

Neil felt a thunderbolt of shock, though he managed a façade of interest as Janice Hilton avidly related her college campus experience as a TV commentator. Did Karen think he was here on a dinner date with Janice? He hadn't picked Janice up, had met her here at the restaurant to set this as a *business* meeting. He'd have to be stupid not to realize he was the object of pursuit by several local twenty-something women.

Now he forced a bright smile of recognition, returned Karen's wave. Should he go over and say 'hi'? No, that would just emphasize this weird sense of guilt that was inundating him.

Karen's bright – she'll understand when I explain why I'm here with Janice. Won't she? Explain tomorrow. Casually.

Still, he was relieved when he could bring the dinner meeting with Janice to a close. He debated for a moment about circling around to stop at Karen's table on their way out. No, don't make a big deal of this. Explain tomorrow. Don't phone tonight.

He had a sudden, absurd hope that Karen would glance out the window, see that he and Janice were leaving separately. But that wasn't likely. Hell, Karen knew how he felt about her, he consoled himself as he drove from the parking area. He respected her wish to take this slowly. But even Mom and Dad were getting wise glints in their eyes each time he mentioned Karen. Of course, in this town when you were seen twice with anybody, it was considered serious.

Arriving home he heard sounds from the TV in the den.

141

Mom was home. She'd be eager to hear about his dinner with Janice.

'This time of year TV programming does wonders for the library circulation.' Arline switched off the remote with a grunt of distaste, turned to Neil. 'So? Do we start the local society segment in a couple of weeks?'

'We do.' He dropped into a chair.

'You'd like coffee?'

'No.' He brushed this aside. 'Janice is enthralled at the prospect of a weekly TV spot.'

Arline nodded. 'I figured. And you de-glamorized the foreign correspondent scene?'

'I disillusioned her. I made her realize that while Christiana Ammanpour may lead a exciting life and make bundles of money, she had to endure much physical discomfort and definite danger. Tell Janice's mother to relax.'

Arline glowed. 'Did you have dessert?'

'No, we refrained.' He chuckled. 'Janice has been watching our "Your Good Health" series.'

'OK, then you can have a piece of my carrot cake. It's low fat – I replaced most of the oil with prune purée – and it has carrots and pineapple and raisins. Things that are good for you.'

'Then make it a big piece,' he ordered. 'After all, I accomplished your mission.'

'How are you doing with the "ode to Todd" segment?' she asked with an effort at lightness.

'Not too well so far.' All at once he was serious. 'Your friend Althea Jackson agreed to appear – and one of the teachers at the school where Todd teaches. Where he taught—' Neil amended. 'Though she's nervous about being fired by the school.'

'It's something we have to do,' Arline said after a moment. 'Though I know Dad's worried about public reaction.'

'It's a free country, Mom. Remember the First Amendment.'

'I hope our viewers remember.'

142

7.10 a.m., Wednesday, September 10, 1997

Neil awoke with an instant recall of the previous evening's disturbing incident. It was absurd to be so upset that Karen had been at The Colonial. She was bright, down-to-earth – she'd understand he was there to talk business with Janice – that it wasn't a social occasion. How many times had she gone to dinner with a client – male – to discuss a case? *What's the matter with me? I'm acting like a lovesick fifteen-year-old!*

He'd feel less uneasy, he considered, if he could call Karen with something helpful to Todd's case. Not as a diversionary tactic, he alibied self-consciously – but he would win points with it. She was so uptight about the grand jury hearing tomorrow. Damn that pharmacist and Marie Bingham for lying.

Now his mind zeroed in on Marie. What could he do to make her admit that Todd was in Debbie's bedroom that afternoon? Or at least admit to some doubt about it, he pinpointed. '*I had to change Tommy – Mr Simmons may have gone to the bedroom with the girls. Debbie wanted to show him her new Barbie doll,*' he improvised her testimony.

Marie was unfinished business – in Karen's mind and in his. How could he scare her into a change of heart? Morrison was sure to call her as a witness.

He pulled himself up in bed – fully awake, churning for action. Go over to the Bingham house, remind Marie that to lie under oath was perjury. She could go to prison.

His mind charging ahead, he inspected the clock on his night table. Karen said that Marie still worked for Jeannie and Doug Norris. Be outside her house this morning when she left to go to the job. *Scare the hell out of her. Make her terrified to testify to a lie.*

He showered and dressed in record time. This was his late night at the station – he wasn't due in until 11 a.m. His mother lifted an eyebrow in surprise when he appeared in the kitchen as she was about to put up coffee. She'd expected him to sleep until nine. Most mornings – except when there was breaking news – the two of them had a leisurely breakfast together. After twenty-five years of heading for a classroom at 7.20 a.m., she relished sleeping till seven, dawdling over breakfast in nightwear and robe.

'I want to talk to Marie Bingham again,' he explained, reaching into the refrigerator for the orange juice container. 'Before she takes off for work.'

'You think she'll cave?' Arline was skeptical.

'I'll give it a strong try.' He poured juice, swigged it down. 'I'll see you later.'

'Stop somewhere for breakfast before you come to work,' Arline called after him.

The morning was pleasantly cool, though weathercasters predicted another hot day in the hours ahead. He lowered the car windows – no need for the air-conditioning this morning, he thought with satisfaction. He set up the cell phone – for any emergency call from the station – and headed for the rundown neighborhood where the Binghams lived.

Even a small town like this had its version of a slum, he mused. No homeless people – not so far, thank God. That was one of the comforting things about coming home – not to have to face each day the grief and anguish of thousands upon thousands of homeless refugees. His loyalties had wavered from one side to the other. It was the leaders he hated, he recalled – the people were helpless pawns.

He parked about forty feet past the Bingham driveway and waited for Marie to emerge from the house. Moments later her father ambled out, slid behind the wheel of a battered pick-up, drove away. Neil's mind framed ominous words to bounce off Marie while he waited for her to appear. Then he saw two women at the door – arguing loudly. He straightened into alertness, prepared to move.

'Will you knock it off, Ma? So I'll be five minutes late. Jeannie ain't goin' nowhere.'

He moved swiftly, arrived at the driveway as Marie approached her beat-up car.

'Marie, we need to talk,' he said briskly.

Marie stared at him. 'Who're you?'

'Neil Bradford – from the local TV station. We're doing some background checking for a story on the Todd Simmons case.'

'I talked to the cops.' The atmosphere was suddenly supercharged. 'I don't have to talk to you.'

'You'll be a witness at the grand jury hearing tomorrow.'

'So?' She exuded defiance.

'You'll be under oath. If you lie, you'll be committing perjury. A felony. You'll go to prison.'

'You're weird, you know? Who's to say I'm lyin'?' Her voice was shrill.

'Unexpected witnesses show up.' He was casual, yet a quiet menace crept into his voice. 'A couple were passing, happened to glance towards a bedroom window. They saw Todd there. Or maybe two or three kids were playing in the woods. Their ball rolled out into the Norrises' yard. They chased after it. It stopped right beneath the window that Todd was opening wider because the afternoon was steamy. They—'

'Get off our property!' She hurried into the car, reached for her ignition key. 'Beat it, or I'll call the cops!'

She backed out with a foot heavy on the gas. But she was shaken. He would talk to Karen about this encounter. Let her know he'd planted seeds of fear in Marie Bingham. Of course, he forced himself to acknowledge, there was no way to know how she would react in the witness chair.

From his cell phone he called Karen.

'Hello—'

'Hi.' He strived for a casual tone. 'I've got some news of sorts. May I drop by?'

'Sure.' But he sensed a reserve in her voice. *Damn, she was annoyed about last night.*

'I have time off this morning.' He managed a slight chuckle. 'I took over for Dad last night on a business dinner. I've signed up the *Enquirer*'s society editor for a

145

fifteen-minute spot once a week – you know, a rehash of what's been happening around town on the social scene.'

'What's with Todd's segment?' The reserve was disappearing, he noted. Karen understood dinner with Janice was a business deal.

'I'm moving ahead. Dad's about to write it into next week's programming schedule. Any ideas you or Cindy have about people to approach will be welcome.'

'What's this other news?' she probed.

'I'll be right over to explain. Five minutes.'

'Was that Neil?' Helen asked, an impish glint in her eyes.

'He wants to talk about something that's come up with Todd's case,' Karen explained.

'Who else but Neil would call this early in the morning?' Helen's smile was indulgent. Then with devious casualness she drained her coffee mug. 'I have to get to the shop. Clear up some crazy bookkeeping error on yesterday's shipment from a supplier.'

'Nobody will ever put anything over on you, Mom,' Karen joshed. Helen was determined to provide time alone with Neil. Her approval of him was blatant. But let her not rush to conclusions.

Karen glanced at her watch. Neil said he'd be here in five minutes. With morning traffic it could be longer. Go make notes for tomorrow's grand jury hearing. Did Neil have something of value – or was he feeling guilty about last night's encounter?

She settled herself at her laptop, stared at the screen without seeing. Neil said he'd taken over for his father at a 'business dinner' last night – '*I've signed up the* Enquirer's *society editor for a fifteen-minute spot once a week.*' She could accept that. Still, her mind ordered her to be cautious about jumping into a new relationship when, in truth, she was still hurting from the last one.

Don't be like Eve – so quick to move from an old love to a new one. I'm not like Eve – I can survive without a man in my life. It's time to learn to stand on my own two feet. To make my own decisions. I made a serious mistake, thinking I was in love with Bob. Don't make another mistake.

Too uptight for constructive thinking, she turned off the laptop, pushed back her chair. What was Neil's news? Was this a kind of peace offering because she'd caught him at dinner with another woman? Their relationship wasn't that serious. So they'd both made unwary statements – there was no commitment between them. She'd made that clear. Hadn't she?

In a burst of restlessness she left what Mom called her 'home office' – the closed-up guest room now designated for this purpose. To Mom, she thought with a flicker of unease, this indicated a kind of permanence in Paradise. She had made no decisions about her future.

She tensed at the sound of a car pulling up out front. Traffic was light. Neil was here already. She hurried to the front door, pulled it wide for him.

'Hi.' Her smile was almost normal.

'I got an early start this morning.' He grinned as he walked into the foyer. 'I had a talk with Marie Bingham.'

Karen's eyes lighted. 'She admitted Todd went into Debbie's bedroom?'

'No. But I scared the hell out of her. I warned her that if she was caught lying under oath, she'd go to prison. I gave her some scenarios that unnerved her.'

Disappointment welled in Karen. 'It's hot already – coffee or iced tea?'

'You know me. I'm always ready for coffee—'

'It's waiting in the kitchen.'

Did she know him? Was his whole romantic pitch motivated by Todd's situation and what a great story could do for his station? *How could she know?*

Over coffee he reported in detail on his meeting with Marie, his conviction that he'd set up doubts in her mind about how to handle herself.

'You're saying I should challenge her understanding of what happens when somebody lies on the witness stand?'

'There's a good chance she'll come up with some doubts about her recall. That'll wipe out Morrison's claim that Todd was *not* in Debbie's bedroom that afternoon – that his fingerprints were left late that night when he stole into the house.'

'I should have gone after her before this.' Karen frowned in self-reproach. 'I should do something about the pharmacist.'

'He'll be much tougher,' Neil warned.

'And it's important to make a jury understand that the guard and the assistant prosecutor are lying when they say Todd confessed.' But her eyes were bleak. 'It's two against one – and that's not good.'

11.52 a.m., Wednesday, September 10, 1997

Jake Rhodes waved the mayor to a chair across from his desk as he moved to his office door.

'Hold my calls,' he ordered his secretary and closed the door.

'What's got you so riled up, Jake?' Clay felt a surge of unease. It took a lot to upset Jake this way.

'I can't believe what I just learned.' He paused, with dramatic effect. 'Frank Bradford over at the TV station is preparing some dumb program about all the wonderful things that bastard Todd Simmons has done for this town! When he knows about the guy's past – plus what he did to Debbie!'

'How did you find out?'

'Clay, you know nothing happens in this town that isn't reported to me.'

'Why would Frank do something like that?' Clay was shaken. He'd always considered Frank Bradford a fine man.

'Trying to butter up prospective jurors, that's what.' Jake dropped into his chair, leaned forward with an air of urgency. 'Clay, what are you going to do about it?'

'Nobody will believe them,' Clay said after a moment.

'They can't whitewash a murderer. Look at the evidence against that son of a bitch.' Clay flushed with rage.

'We don't need upstarts coming to Paradise to defend a bad element. You're the mayor, Clay. You go over to the station and let them know local people don't want this program to be shown. Let them know you'll see to it that advertisers will pull out. Get them where it hurts—'

'Right, Jake.' Clay rose to his feet. 'Nobody's going to whitewash Todd Simmons. Morrison will get a conviction – and he'll demand the death penalty.'

Jeannie and Doug were fighting like crazy about that. Doug didn't believe in the death penalty for any crime. '*How many times do you read about somebody's being in jail for a dozen years when something comes up to prove them innocent? You can't undo the death penalty.*'

But Todd Simmons had confessed. He was guilty.

Twenty-One

K aren inspected her reflection in the door mirror in her bedroom. This was the fourth dress she'd considered this morning. Her outfit had to be just right. The dress conservative in length, conservative in style. Low heels, lest she appear taller than George Morrison, who was probably 5 feet 6 inches. Even though everybody knew the outcome of the grand jury hearing, she must present the best case possible.

All right, this timeless, turquoise shirtwaist would do. Low-heeled bone pumps with rounded toes – not the clunky platforms that were 'in' this year, nor the pointy toes that some fashion leaders still favored. After the hearing the grand jury would go out and talk about their reactions. Let her plant a subliminal seed of doubt in their minds about Todd's guilt. The grand jury wasn't labeling him guilty – just that he should be held for trial.

Let Neil be right about Marie. If Marie was scared to lie, then she'd score one point for Todd. And somehow – between now and the trial – she must dig up incontrovertible facts to convince a jury that Amos Rogers and Jim Drake were lying about that confession.

Mom knew she was edgy this morning, she realized gratefully when she arrived in the kitchen. The radio was silent. No doubt, the news revolved around the imminent hearing. Mom's conversation was casual, requiring little from her. The TV next door was loud – Laurie and Zachie listening

150

to cartoons, she guessed. Poor little kids, this was a rough period for them. Cindy was so upset that she couldn't be present, that grand jury hearings were closed affairs.

Karen made a pretense of eating breakfast, sipped at her strong black coffee as though seeking sustenance for the hours ahead. *Todd's life was in her hands.* Not only Todd's – Cindy's and Laurie's and Zachary's. Her corporate law experience meant nothing in this situation. Between now and the trial date she must cram like mad, try to compensate for her lack of experience in criminal law.

'You'll do fine,' Helen said with quiet confidence when Karen prepared to leave for court. 'You believe in Todd's innocence.'

'Pray,' she said, her smile insecure. 'We'll need a small miracle between now and the trial date.'

In the usual manner Karen questioned each of the prospective jurors. Each professed to be unbiased. Yet even before the judge took his seat in the small courtroom – the windows opened wide because the air-conditioning had broken down the previous evening – she sensed hostility in the jury. They'd come here with their minds already set. Her eyes searched the face of each of the jurors. Was there perhaps one among them who had doubts – or believed in Todd's innocence? But it wasn't this jury that would be the determining factor. She was prepared for Todd's being held for trial. She was prepared for the judge to refuse bail. It was the actual trial that terrified her. *Could she handle it properly?*

Morrison's first witnesses – as she'd anticipated – were the couple who reported seeing Todd drive through town shortly past midnight – 'hell bent for election', the man described it. She managed to elicit the fact that, no, he couldn't give proof positive that Todd was speeding. Then Morrison brought in the fingerprint expert. Karen knew Marie Bingham would be Morrison's next witness because he knew *she* would claim Todd had been in the bedroom hours before Debbie was taken.

Marie wore a garish, floral print dress, its hem barely reaching mid-thigh. She crossed her legs, and every male on the jury focused on that area. Karen's throat tightened as Morrison questioned Marie.

'Mr Simmons was in the livin' room,' Marie said. 'Debbie and Laurie were playin' on the floor – doin' a puzzle. He never went into the bedroom.' Still, Karen felt an unease in her. Neil had planted some alarm in Marie.

Now it was Karen's turn to question Marie. She approached the witness stand with a calm – almost ingratiating – air. Her voice soft when she spoke.

'Marie, you realize you're under oath?'

'Yeah—' Her eyes – outlined with pencil so darkly as to be almost grotesque – avoided contact with Karen's.

'And you understand that to lie under oath is a felony?'

Morrison leapt up and objected to this line of questioning. The judge concurred.

'Marie, I want you to think back very carefully,' Karen resumed gently. 'Were there a few moments when you were out of the room? When Debbie and Laurie could have taken Todd Simmons to the bedroom to show him Debbie's new Barbie doll, as he stated?'

'Well – I—' Marie hesitated, shifted in the chair. 'Tommy kept sayin' he wanted some apple juice. I went out to the kitchen to get his bottle.'

'That took a while, didn't it?' Karen was indulgent.

'Yeah— there wasn't much in the bottle. I filled it up – and then I went back to the livin' room. Mr Simmons was there with the two girls and Tommy.'

'But he could have gone the few feet down the hall to Debbie's bedroom while you were in the kitchen? You brought out the bottle, then went back to the refrigerator for more apple juice. You—'

'I guess so—' Marie broke in, seeming simultaneously reluctant and relieved.

But Karen could do nothing to soften the blow of the two witnesses who claimed to have heard Todd's confession –

other than to deny this. Todd tried to stare each of them down – but they avoided eye contact. *Their body language said they were lying.*

The judge announced the trial date would be the first Monday in December. For that Karen was grateful. Morrison had been battling for an early date. She'd asked for late November. He'd bypassed that to avoid the Thanksgiving week. Thank God for the delay. Every additional day was precious.

Karen was startled by the barrage of reporters and camera crews waiting outside the courthouse. She should have expected this! Still, it was unnerving.

'We'll prove Todd Simmon's innocence,' she said with conviction and brushed aside the volley of questions that followed. She was grateful when – moments later – Morrison appeared and attention was diverted to him. At the rear of the descending horde she spied Neil, along with the camera crew from the station. She gave no recognition, hurried towards her car.

Neil looked so uncomfortable in this scene, she thought as she drove away. Could he ever settle for life here in Paradise after the years of chasing around the globe on major stories? Could there ever be a life for them? She knew now that she wanted roots somewhere. Where that would be at this point was unclear.

4.10 p.m., Thursday, September 11, 1997

Neil looked up from his computer at the light knock on his office door.

'Come in—' He smiled as his mother appeared.

'This may be nothing, Neil – but I think you'll want to follow up on it—'

'Clue me in—' Instantly he was alert.

'You know I'm working with a group to raise funds for a permanent shelter for abused women here in town.' At the moment the group was using a large, rambling Victorian house that was up for sale. They were painfully conscious that this was a temporary deal.

'Right.' Mom was privy to every detail to do with Todd's case. She was eager to be helpful.

'You said you needed background on Amos Rogers. Daisy Ryan knows just about everybody in this town. I mentioned his name – and guess what? About four months ago he was dragged to the police station after neighbors called to report he was beating his wife. But she refused to sign a complaint, and the case was closed. Then ten days later he beat her again. This time she was ready to sign a complaint, Daisy said – but, somehow, the whole thing was hushed up.'

'He would have lost his job if it hadn't been.' Neil was thoughtful. 'Even if his wife did refuse to sign a complaint.' Often the wife or girlfriend was afraid to sign a complaint.

'The question is,' his mother pondered, 'who saved his hide?'

'Anyway, why?' Neil followed up. 'Somebody buying up favors? George Morrison? The police chief? Mayor Gilbert?'

'And this is pay-back time.'

'Mom, Nora Charles had nothing on you.'

'What's with your cologne theory?'

'It's on the back-burner for the moment. But we're not eliminating it as a lead.'

He tried to focus on the new line-up for their Sunday afternoon programming, but his mind insisted on zooming back to the scene at the courthouse when Karen and Morrison emerged from the grand jury hearing. In the eyes of the press Todd was guilty – and that was the message being flashed to the American public. In a surge of impatience he abandoned the project at hand, reached for the phone and hit Karen's number.

'Hello—' Karen's voice held a new wariness.

'I'm trying to focus on station work, but my mind won't cooperate. What about an early dinner tonight so you can fill me in on the grand jury hearing?'

'All right,' she said after a faint hesitation. 'What time?'
'Six o'clock OK? I have to be back at the station a few
minutes before nine.'

'Sure. No problem.'

'I'll pick you up at six.' So this *was* a date. 'I heard about
a new place just a dozen miles towards Albany. Shall we give
it a whirl? They're supposed to be great with seafood.'

'Fine. I love good seafood.'

'I have a little tidbit of news for you. I'll tell you at
dinner.'

He always did this, she thought with a flicker of exasperation. He never wanted to discuss anything like that over the
phone. Was it just a hangover from his 'cloak-and-dagger'
days? An indulgent smile escaped her. In his way Neil was
a romantic.

5.50 p.m., Thursday, September 11, 1997

Karen finished up the conversation with Helen – who was
leaving for a dinner meeting with one of her civic groups
tonight. She focused again on her computer notes. She'd
gone straight from the courthouse to report to Cindy about
what had happened at the hearing. Now she wanted to record
that. She was grateful that Neil had scared Marie into backing
down on her testimony today.

She still had the other two lying witnesses to beat down. If
she could prove they'd perjured themselves, then Morrison
would have no real case. Todd's earlier conviction wouldn't
be allowed to be presented at the new trial. But proving Amos
Rogers and Jim Drake had lied would be rough. She worried,
too, that the jury pool had been tainted by the media's sleazy
handling of the case.

She glanced at her watch. All right, enough for now. She
turned off the computer, went into her bedroom. She reached
into the closet for the lemon yellow silk-and-linen pantsuit
she would wear to dinner tonight.

She debated for a moment, dabbed a bit of the new scent by

Donna Karan in strategic spots. This wasn't a real date. Neil was dying for a firsthand report on the grand jury hearing. He was sincere in wanting to clear Todd. Was he sincere in what he inferred about the two of them?

Why am I letting myself put so much emphasis on his taking Janice whatever-her-name out to dinner? I'm glad that he did. It was a reminder to me not to jump impetuously into another relationship.

She was out the front door the moment Neil pulled up at the curb. Only now did she realize how tense she was. *Why?* Everybody had known the outcome: Todd would be held for trial. And the judge hadn't waited to announce the trial date. Todd would go on trial for his life – with Morrison vowing to exact the death penalty – on Monday, December 1st.

'You look marvelous in that outfit.' Neil took admiring inventory of Karen's favorite pantsuit as he held the car door open for her. 'Did you wear it at the trial?'

'Oh, no.' Karen lifted an eyebrow in self-mockery. 'I was ultra-conservative.' It was ridiculous to be so pleased that Neil approved of her pantsuit.

'OK, fill me in,' Neil ordered and reached for the ignition key. 'I was pissed that I couldn't be in there.'

'First your news—' She waited expectantly.

In a few brief sentences he told her about Amos Rogers's wife-beating history – which had no impact on his job at the local jail.

'You mean it was wiped off the books? No record at all?' Neil shook his head. 'I know they couldn't arrest him unless his wife filed a complaint, but you'd think his job would be in jeopardy. I mean, that kind of violence in a man dealing with prisoners?'

'Daisy Ryan told my mother the slate was wiped clean. Mrs Ryan's—'

'I know,' Karen interrupted. 'Mom works with the group trying to raise funds for the shelter, too. Somehow, you never think something like that is necessary in a quiet, small town like this.' Irony crept into her voice. 'But who in this town could pull that off?'

'Not a lot of people. And whoever did it was cagey enough to know that Amos Rogers owed him. I'm not sure how – but it's damned important to check this right back to its roots.'

'Yes—' Karen was somber.

'Now tell me about the grand jury hearing.'

Karen reported on the morning's proceedings – giving full value to his efforts to frighten Marie Bingham into sitting on the fence concerning Todd's appearance in the children's bedroom that fateful afternoon.

'It was almost as good as her admitting Todd was there,' Karen wound up. 'But we still have to convince a jury that Amos Rogers and Jim Drake are lying about Todd's confession.'

The restaurant was an immaculate, white shingled colonial, set on a quarter-acre of exquisitely tended lawn and garden, fragrant with late summer roses and first chrysanthemums. A plaque at the cornerstone identified it as circa 1791. The lower floor had been opened up to include a small reception area, a large dining room, and a kitchen. The owners, Karen assumed, lived on the upper floor.

'Oh, Neil, it's charming.'

The smiling hostess led them to a linen-covered corner table. Neil glanced about with approval as they sat. 'Let's hope the food lives up to the surroundings. I used to dream about places like this when we were sleeping in bombed-out hotels and eating Red Cross meals.'

'I'd forgotten how serene a small town could be – after the years in New York.'

'Serene on the surface.' Neil was serious now. 'There are enough women being abused here in Paradise for thinking people to realize we need a shelter. There's corruption in town government if a man known to beat his wife is kept on the payroll as a prison guard. And how much more is swept under the rug each day?'

'I want to know who's collecting favors from Rogers and

Drake.' Karen clenched a fist in frustration. 'That'll lead us to who murdered Debbie Norris.'

'A thousand to one that man owned a bottle of cologne bought out of this country.'

'I've been thinking a lot about that. Some time in the next few days I'll pay a visit to the travel agencies in town—' She smiled as she saw comprehension light his face. 'Yeah. I'll make some inquiries about an attractive spot for a late winter vacation. After the trial. Somewhere out of the country. And would they recall anybody who'd visited there in the last year or so?'

'Good move.'

A waiter arrived at their table. He was eager to be helpful, made suggestions. The atmosphere became convivial.

Why do I feel so comfortable with Neil? I even like the way he deals with waiters. With Bob I was always uneasy. He was so demanding. Supercilious sometimes. How could I have brushed aside all my misgivings about him each time we made love? He was my safety net – that was it. But that's not the basis for a lasting relationship.

'I gather nobody gets into office in Paradise without the support of Clay Gilbert and Jake Rhodes.' Neil paused. 'Particularly Jake Rhodes. And that includes George Morrison.'

'We can't consider Gilbert a suspect. And Jake Rhodes was out of town that night. No way he could have driven back here, murdered Debbie, then surreptitiously returned to his daughter's house.'

'We need to discover who else is part of Clay Gilbert and Jake Rhodes's inner circle,' Neil pinpointed. 'It may take time – but we can do that.'

'I hate the way people in town have ganged up against Cindy as well as against Todd,' Karen said with sudden intensity. 'She's getting hate mail left at the door. Every time Harry barks at night, Cindy says, she knows somebody's sneaking up to the house to shove some ugly message under the door.'

'We're receiving mail at the station about her,' Neil

confided after a moment. 'People want her out of town.' Karen gaped in shock. 'Some consider her as guilty as Todd. Because – they say – she knew what he'd done before, and she lied to get him into the school.'

'Todd was the best thing that every happened to our schools.' Karen blazed in indignation. 'They all know that! Wasn't he voted the town's best teacher two years in a row?'

'He was – and he deserved it.' Neil fought against an urge to reach out and draw her into his arms. *I love her passion for what's right in this world. I love her tenderness and compassion. But she has so much to offer. Could she ever be satisfied with life in a town like this? Because I'm almost certain that this is the lifestyle I need to be a whole person. I waited a long time to realize what's right for me. Don't mess up now because I'm dying to make love to her. There must be more to a lifetime relationship than what happens in bed.*

'Cindy's so grateful for your help.' The ardor in his eyes unnerved her. *Is it real – or is he using me to latch on to a terrific story for the station? The trial will command national interest. Being close to the defendant's attorney could provide a sensational scoop.* 'Todd, too,' she added.

'I told you, Karen. Once we met and talked with Tiffany Rollins, I was sure Todd was innocent. I'm convinced he's innocent this time around, too. And I think this town is stupid – irresponsible – not to realize that a rapist/murderer is on the loose. Possibly to strike again. I don't want to see what happened to Debbie Norris happen to another little girl here in Paradise.'

Twenty-Two

8.05 p.m., Thursday, September 11, 1997

He frowned as the TV newscaster wound up his brief report on the grand jury hearing of Todd Simmons. Damn the bastard! Why couldn't he give more details? But nobody was surprised that Simmons was being held for trial, he thought complacently. How could they not hold him, considering the evidence against him? He could yell that he was innocent even in his last minutes on Death Row – what would that mean when a guard and an assistant prosecutor both testified that he'd confessed? A sardonic smile brightened his face. Some of the tension eased from his shoulder blades.

Why was I sweating so? Money can buy anything on this earth. Money is power. Each time I sweated for a while – but money kept me in the clear. It was the little bitch's fault I had to kill her! Why did she have to carry on that way – so close to her house? Another thirty seconds and somebody might have heard her screeching that way. God, I was scared shitless! It was smart to have that length of cord in my pocket – just in case. I'd never come so close to being caught. I had to kill her.

Stop sweating. This town won't settle for anything less than the death penalty. Todd Simmons will go on trial. He'll be convicted. He'll be put to death. End of story. I'll be home free. Again.

Twenty-Three

Seated behind his large executive desk, Frank Bradford unconsciously moved his chair in half-circle arcs, listened with clenched teeth while Clay Gilbert delivered a stinging diatribe.

'People in this town know me,' Gilbert wound up. His face florid. 'I'm not a vindictive man – but you're asking for trouble if you run a program praising that bastard Simmons!' *How did he know about that?* And then Frank understood. The new day receptionist reported to Gilbert. 'You'll bring on violence that we can never live down! You'll destroy this town! I promise you, run it and not one of your sponsors will remain with the station.'

'I'm sorry you feel that way—' Frank began, but Clay Gilbert was stalking out of the office.

He'd have to find an excuse to fire that receptionist. Not right away, his mind cautioned – he didn't need labor troubles, too.

Moments later Neil appeared at the door.

'What's the mayor so steamed up about? He brushed right past me without even a hello.'

Frank sighed, searched for words. Neil would be upset about this.

'He got word about your program dealing with Todd. The new receptionist must be reporting to him,' he added as Neil raised an eyebrow in question. 'He warned me to drop it, or he'd see to it that we lost every one of our sponsors. And he can do that.'

161

'Are you letting Gilbert get away with that?' He stared at his father in disbelief.

'Neil, I don't have much choice.' Frank's eyes were apologetic yet resigned. 'Your mother and I invested every cent we own in the station.' How did he make Neil understand? 'We're not old enough yet for social security – all we'd have if we lost the station would be Mom's pension from the New York City school system. I got "excessed" eight months before I was eligible for a pension. That's part of our times. Sometimes you have to do what goes totally against the grain. We have to drop the program.'

Karen listened in disbelief to Neil's report on the confrontation between Clay Gilbert and his father.

'Clay Gilbert is the mayor of this town – not its dictator!' she blazed. 'How dare he tell your father what he can or can't show on his own station!'

'You're talking about a perfect world. I know how you feel – I was furious, too. But Clay Gilbert *can* pull sponsors away from the station.'

'That's monstrous!'

'The station is just beginning to show a profit. Dad and Mom never expected to make a fortune – they just want to keep the station afloat, with enough income for them to survive with a fair amount of comfort. I told you – to own a tiny station in some pleasant little town has been Dad's dream since college days. Still, he knew he'd run into obstacles along the road. He knew there would be times when he'd have to compromise.'

'So much for Mom's perfect little town.' Karen seethed with frustration.

'Sure. Paradise looks ideal on the surface – like hundreds of other small towns across the country. Then some horror erupts – and the pretty picture explodes. Locals scoff at big cities like New York and Chicago and Los Angeles. They look on them with contempt, as dens of iniquity. They don't want to see their own problems. Here in Paradise there's a new much-needed shelter for abused women. The divorce rate is shockingly high. And most of us like to forget that we have our slums here, too – like where Marie Bingham lives. Too many local kids have to leave for big cities to find decent-paying jobs.'

'When I finished law school, I never once thought about coming home to set up practice.' *Could* she set up a practice here in Paradise and build a comfortable future?

'I had no experience living in a small town – New York had been my beat all my life.' A whimsical glint in his eyes now. 'I was kind of indulgent about Dad and Mom's decision to run from the city. I knew Dad was terribly hurt that after twenty-four years on the job he could be "excessed" without a qualm.' Wrath welled in his voice. 'And Mom admitted it was time to quit teaching when she found it so hard to control a class of fifth graders. Sometimes I ask myself – what kind of parents did those kids have?'

'Parents too busy to take the time to discipline them,' Karen pinpointed. 'They spoil their kids because that's the easy way out.' Mom had never spoiled Paula and her – but she had given them love and security and a sense of responsibility.

'Dad's upset about cancelling the "one-shot" – but he's realistic. He has no choice if he wants to hang on to the station.'

'So we'll have to write off the "one-shot",' Karen accepted, fighting down disappointment. 'Let's focus on Jim Drake. *Who ordered him to lie that way?* I'll start with the newspaper files.'

'I'll ask around town,' Neil promised and hesitated. 'How's Cindy holding up? And the kids?'

'Trying to hang in there. Thank God, we hadn't told her or Todd about the "one-shot".'

'It infuriates me that people can treat Laurie and Zachie like pariahs.'

'This town is a cauldron boiling over with hate. Mom tells

me not a day passes that some customer in the shop doesn't lambaste the local police for not letting people know that Todd had a criminal record. They demand to know why the schools weren't notified that a "sex offender" lived in Paradise. Why didn't the police notify parents?'

'They forget that the laws dealing with that weren't enacted until recently.'

'In this state the "Megan's Law" didn't go through until January twenty-first of last year,' Karen recalled. 'Todd's case goes back sixteen years. Federal law bars the states from giving out information on offenders who were convicted before the law went into effect. Still, they are required to register at intervals with police as felons,' she conceded. 'Todd didn't do that. He just wanted to settle down with his family and live a normal life. He saw no chance of re-opening the case and clearing himself.'

'Which you'd like to do—' It was half-question, half-statement.

'That's what should happen. First, clear Todd in this case – then re-open the other and clear him of that. There's no question in my mind that he was railroaded by Tiffany's mother.'

'I know how rough it is on Laurie and Zachie – being ostracized the way they are.' Neil's face reflected his sympathy. 'Maybe they'd get a kick out of going on a tour of the station. I could show them how a program is put together, maybe let them watch a live telecast—'

'I'm sure they'd love it!' How sweet, how compassionate Neil was. 'Talk to Cindy about it tomorrow.'

'I will. We'll make a little party of it.'

Neil had such a warm feeling for kids. He'd be a marvelous father, she thought tenderly. Then warning signals jumped up in her brain. *How long would a man with Neil's globe-trotting background – his talent for reporting – be satisfied to stay home and play the father role? A year? Two years? I'm jumping again.*

164

Late September, 1997

In the coming days Karen settled down to the monotonous, grueling task of reading endless reels of microfilm, searching for some tiny detail. A clue to why an assistant prosecutor lied about hearing a confession. Then Neil came to her with a conviction that George Morrison masked an intense dislike for his assistant prosecutor.

'I picked up bits here and there. George slips up, gives himself away.'

'I don't understand.' Karen was bewildered. 'George was elected. Jim Drake was hired, most likely by George himself.'

'Maybe something happened along the road. I suspect that party politics are involved. He has to play the game.'

'But that doesn't tell us why Jim Drake lied.'

'We'll have to dig further.' It was Neil's turn to be dogged. 'We keep digging long enough and hard enough, we'll come up with the truth.'

Would they? How long was long enough? Todd went to trial in eleven weeks.

Karen was painfully conscious of each passing day. She dreaded each meeting with Todd because she felt his despair, his ebbing hope, his fears for Cindy and the children. His alarm at the family's financial situation – with both Cindy and himself without income. And what did *she* have to bring to the table?

Cindy tried hard to conceal her anxiety from Laurie and Zachie – but it was a losing battle. They knew something desperate was happening. *'Where's Daddy?' 'When's Daddy coming home?' 'Why can't we go to school?' 'Why won't anybody play with us?'* Even Harry seemed to sense something was terribly wrong.

Karen wished desperately that she had some substantial experience in criminal law. She must force herself to *think* like a criminal attorney. In truth, when she first considered going into law, she'd harbored grandiose thoughts – she mocked herself now – about fighting to save the innocent wrongly accused of terrible crimes. She'd allowed herself to be persuaded to believe corporate law was the path to follow.

She continued to spend hours each day at the local library – poring over endless reels of microfilm. Neil was asking guarded questions around town about the relationship between George Morrison and Jim Drake.

'I keep coming back to Jake Rhodes,' Neil confided over a Thursday evening dinner the first week in October. Neil had discovered a pleasant restaurant not far from town where they could meet away from the prying eyes of Paradise residents. *Was Neil afraid to be seen with her in Paradise? Lest it reflect badly on his parents?* 'I understand Rhodes took an active role in George's election campaign. And it's plain that George keeps Jim Drake in his office under duress. But Jake Rhodes was out of town the night Debbie was murdered. This wasn't the kind of crime where a hired hit man could be involved.'

'I'm infuriated the way the *Enquirer* and the *Evening News* are taking pot shots at Cindy. Did you read last evening's editorial?'

'I read it.' Neil grimaced. 'Next they'll be ganging up on Laurie and Zachie.'

Karen's face softened. 'They're still talking about the way you took them on tour of the TV station. They were enthralled!'

'I suspect it'll be futile, but I want to tackle that pharmacist again.' His grin was wry. 'Maybe the situation over there has changed.'

'We can't afford to overlook any possible evidence that can help Todd's case.' She was struggling to keep the discussion on an impersonal level. Why did she feel so unnerved when Neil looked at her the way he was looking at her this minute?

Why am I so distrustful of him? Is it because of what

happened with Bob? Will I never be able to trust another man again? I wish he'd forget what I said about not rushing. I wish he'd take me by the hand and run with me to some place where we could make love. I want to be in his arms. I want to be filled with him. This isn't like with Bob. It's so much more.

'Have you checked out the travel agencies?' Neil brought her back to the moment.

'No. I must. Tomorrow,' she vowed.

'Karen, you don't go to trial tomorrow,' he said gently. 'You've got weeks to work on the case. You can't follow through on everything in one day.'

When Neil drove her home, Karen sensed he was reluctant to say good-night. A feeling she shared. They lingered – talking yet again about George Morrison. Moonlight spilled into the car with an eerie brightness.

'If George had his way,' Neil surmised, 'he'd dump Drake tomorrow. But somebody wants Jim Drake to stay put. The same person who set up Drake and Amos Rogers to lie about Todd. Damn! We keep going in circles,' Neil grunted in frustration.

'I'll go on the travel circuit tomorrow. Maybe someone there will come up with a name.' Karen reached for the car door.

'We'll fight this through together,' Neil promised and leaned forward to kiss her lightly on the mouth. For an instant she froze, anticipating more. Wanting more. But reason moved in, destroyed the moment. She'd seen the question in Neil's eyes. She'd ignored it.

The house was dark except for a lamp in the foyer. Mom hadn't arrived home yet – she was staying late at the shop to redo the windows and rearrange some tables, Karen remembered. Business continued to be very slow. But it wasn't just Mom's shop that was facing a drop in sales.

This whole town was still torn up over Debbie's murder. And despite the belief of most people that the murderer was behind bars, there were some who locked their doors and were

167

watchful of their children. Some people in Paradise feared that a rapist/murderer still roamed the streets of Paradise.

As she unlocked the front door, she heard the phone begin to ring. She hurried inside, reached for the receiver.

'Hello—'

'Is this Karen Mitchell?' A young, feminine voice. Oddly strained.

'Yes.' Karen was polite, resigned to being harassed by yet another telemarketing call. No hour seemed safe from these invasions.

'You probably don't remember me,' the caller said. 'We were in the same French class our junior and senior years in high school. Carol Latham.'

'Sure, I remember you, Carol. You were vice-president of our senior class.' *Why was Carol calling her?*

'I'm a secretary in the DA's office. There's something I think you ought to know—' She paused, as though gearing herself to continue. Karen tensed in anticipation. 'It would cost me my job, of course, if anybody found out I've been talking to you—'

'Carol, nobody will ever know.' *Be cool.* 'Please, tell me,' she encouraged gently.

'There's been talk at the office about bringing Cindy Simmons up on criminal charges.'

'For what?' Karen demanded in shock.

'Nothing to do with Debbie's murder. The fact that she brought Todd into the school when she knew he'd served a prison term as a sex offender. I gather Jeannie and her father brought this up. Doug's upset that they did. Now they're all debating about whether it should be a criminal charge or a civil lawsuit.' Carol hesitated. 'I find it so hard to believe that Todd Simmons could be guilty – but he was convicted in that earlier case.'

'He was framed. We read in the newspapers about cases like that – where years later the truth comes out. And now they're trying to frame him again.' Karen paused, her mind on full alert. 'He never confessed to that guard and to Jim

Drake. *Carol, would you know why Amos Rogers and Jim Drake are lying about that?'*

'No. I'm sorry, Karen – I've told you what I know. I just felt you should be forewarned.' Now anxiety crept into her voice. 'You mustn't let on that I told you about this—'

'I won't. And I do thank you.'

'Do you remember my sister Eileen?'

'She was two years ahead of us,' Karen recalled. 'She was going to be a teacher—'

'She taught nursery school for three years. Then she got married – Bonnie was born a year later. She went back to teaching this year. She couldn't believe Todd was guilty until she heard about – about his being convicted on an earlier charge. It's hard for people to understand that – that—' Her voice faded away.

'That it could happen twice,' Karen finished for her. 'But it has, Carol. And I'm working desperately to clear Todd in both cases.'

'Ugly rumors are floating around town. About how Todd has a way of fondling kids. Kids in his class. Kids in his Little League group. People didn't think anything of it until now.'

'Todd is a warm, loving person. It's natural for him to express that warmth by hugging a child, offering a show of affection to a child starved for this. He's not a pervert.'

'I can't believe that,' Carol admitted. 'But I thought you ought to know what people are saying.'

'If you hear anything else, I hope you'll call me. Anything – no matter how seemingly trivial – that has to do with Todd and this case. He mustn't be convicted!'

Off the phone Karen's first instinct was to call Cindy – to put her on warning. No, her mind rejected – the phone might wake the kids. If she went over to the house, Harry would start barking. Hold up until the morning, then explain to Cindy how to respond to this new insanity.

I can handle the criminal charges – no way can Cindy be implicated. The civil suit will be something else. A jury might

169

strip Cindy and Todd of every cent they own. *I need more data about situations like this.*

I'll have to go to New York, research in the law library. I'll just be there for a couple of days. I'll make sure Cindy knows how to handle the situation in my absence.

Isn't it enough that they're crucifying Todd? Why must they go after Cindy, too?

Twenty-Four

6.43 a.m., Friday, October 3, 1997

K aren awoke earlier than usual this morning – after a night of restless sleep. Immediately her mind leapt into action, as though sleep had been just a refueling period. She must warn Cindy about possible new complications. She needed to go into New York for a couple of days of research at the Columbia Law Library. Some time during the course of today she must call on the three local travel agents. And Neil said something last evening about a new approach with that pharmacist – Matt Somers – in Thomasville.

Emerging from the shower, she realized that Mom, too, was up early. Though she didn't talk much about it, Mom worried about the loss of business. Expenses went on regardless of sales. She'd tried to convince Mom that she should contribute to the household expenses. Mom refused to listen to this.

'Honey, you're doing almost pro bono work for Todd, and I'm proud of that. This is a special period in our lives. I can handle it.'

Midway through breakfast the phone rang.

'Neil,' Mom predicted as Karen hurried to respond. 'He's the only one who calls at this hour.' But it wasn't a reprimand.

'Hello—' Karen was impatient to tell Neil about last night's conversation with Carol Latham. They had an ally in George Morrison's office.

'Put up more coffee,' Neil said. 'I want to come over and talk about Matt Somers—'

171

'It's up,' Karen told him. 'Mom always puts up the maximum capacity. What about breakfast?'

'You don't have to feed me this morning. Just coffee. I'll be there in five minutes.'

He would be furious when he heard what Carol Latham had told her. But they must be careful how they approached this. Carol mustn't be involved.

Neil arrived with an expression on his face that Karen had come to recognize. He was in fighting mode. He reached for the mug of coffee Helen extended with a grunt that said, 'Wow, do I need this!'

'We were too easy on Matt Somers,' he began without preliminaries. 'We must scare the hell out of him.'

'You have a plan to do this?' Karen was conscious of a flurry of excitement.

'That I have. You game for some traveling this morning?'

'Not this early,' Helen cautioned. 'The drugstore probably doesn't open before nine.'

'We'll be there when it opens.' Karen turned to Neil. 'But, meanwhile, I have some ugly news.'

'Fill me in.'

She stressed the need for secrecy, then briefed him on Carol's report.

'Can they do that?' Neil was grim. 'I mean, are there legal grounds for it?'

'I can squash the criminal situation. Still, it'll be rotten for Cindy if George tries it. It'll just add to the fire here in town. Let me run over and warn Cindy what may happen – and tell her how to deal with it. I can't stop the civil suit—'

'Except by clearing Todd,' Helen pinpointed.

'If he's cleared – *when* he's cleared,' Karen amended defiantly, 'the grounds for the suit are wiped out.' She drained her coffee mug, rose to her feet. 'I'll be right back.'

Karen heard Laurie and Zachie in noisy battle as Cindy opened the kitchen door for her.

'They're at it again,' Cindy said tiredly. 'I can't blame them, poor kids – they feel so trapped, having no one

172

except each other to play with.' Her eyes searched Karen's. Instinctively she knew this wasn't a casual visit.

'Sit down, Cindy,' Karen told her, and Cindy complied. Instantly fearful. 'I don't want you to get upset about what I have to tell you – it's a tempest in a teapot. I can handle it.'

In short, terse sentences – without revealing her source – she explained what was being hatched in the district attorney's office. 'You mustn't let on you know anything about this – and if the police show up here and try to bluff you into going downtown for questioning – insist they talk to your attorney first. Me. Of course, that's the worst case scenario. They may not show up at all.'

'Can they sue?' Cindy was ashen. 'Like with O.J. Simpson?'

'They can sue,' Karen said gently. 'But it'll take a lot of time. By then we'll have tracked down the real perpetrator.' Even to her own ears she sounded convincing. 'And pftt goes their suit.' Unlike with O.J. Simpson.

'Is there no end to this insanity?' A touch of hysteria in Cindy's voice now.

'Hang in there, Cindy. We'll fight this through.'

8.20 a.m., Friday, October 3, 1997

Karen and Neil headed for a confrontation with Matt Somers. While they drove, Neil outlined his approach.

'It's just one small item towards Todd's vindication,' he conceded, 'but if he admits on the witness stand that Todd may have tried to reach him, then Todd's explanation of what he was doing on the road at midnight will satisfy some jurors.' Karen saw his jaw tighten. 'But we still have to pin down that damned cologne and who bought it.'

They arrived at the drugstore moments after it opened. Matt Somers was in the rear. His sales clerks had not arrived. Good, Karen told herself while they walked towards the pharmacy section. As prearranged, Karen allowed Neil to make the opening pitch.

'Yeah, I remember you.' Somers was immediately on guard.

'Todd Simmons's trial is scheduled to begin on December first. We—'

'Look, I told you before!' Somers broke in, belligerent now. 'I've got nothing to do with that. He never called me.'

'But as Todd Simmons's attorney, I'm going to have to call you as a witness.' Karen saw the effect of her statement. Somers was upset – as Neil had predicted.

'You can't do that!' Somers's blustered. 'I have nothing to tell!'

'You'll be subpoenaed,' Neil assured him. 'And remember, to lie on the witness stand is to commit perjury.' This was the approach that had worked with Marie Bingham. Karen's heart pounded. *Let it work again.*

'I'm telling the truth – no matter what Simmons says. He never called me.' Somers's eyes darted from Neil to Karen. Bravado eclipsed by fear.

'But suppose you do stick to this story on the witness stand,' Neil pursued. 'And the lady you're protecting doesn't want to perjure herself—' Somers gaped in shock. 'She admits you were with her that night. Then—'

'I don't know what the hell you're talking about!' Somers face flushed. 'Get out of my store before I call the police! Get out!'

Karen and Neil left in silence. Not until they were seated in the car again did Karen voice her thoughts.

'You scared the hell out of him,' she said with satisfaction. 'He thought nobody in town knew about his affair with—' She paused. 'What's the woman's name?'

'Let's go have coffee in that restaurant again and nab that waitress. We'll get her name.' Neil exuded an air of optimism that was contagious. But this was just a minor piece of the puzzle, Karen cautioned herself. She had a long way to go to clear Todd.

But the garrulous waitress of the previous visit was not here that day.

'Oh, yeah, Gert still works here,' another waitress assured them when Neil enquired. 'But she's off today.'

Neil's working schedule required him to be at the station in an hour. They headed back for Paradise. They'd talk to Gert another day.

'I checked the telephone directory for the local travel agencies,' Karen told Neil when they drove into town. 'I'll call on all three today. Let's see what they have to offer.'

'I'll be off duty at eight tonight,' Neil said. 'What about dinner?'

'Late but fashionable. I'll snack earlier.'

'I'll pick you up about ten past.'

His eyes were full of questions again. It wasn't fair to Neil, she thought uncomfortably, to see him so much and yet hold him off the way she did. In Mom's day a woman like that was labeled a tease. But she couldn't brush aside the suspicion that her main charm for Neil was her connection to the biggest story that had hit Paradise in thirty years. *Did he have a book in mind?*

As planned, Karen spent the afternoon visiting the local travel agencies. The first two produced nothing. In both instances the only out-of-town travelers were the senior citizens who went to Alaska – as Helen had reported – and two local women teachers who'd spent eight days in Bermuda during the spring vacation. The agents were eager to help her plan a vacation out of the country 'sometimes in late January or early February'. She knew she was recognized, that rumors would zip around town that 'Todd Simmons's attorney expects the trial to last at least until late January'.

At the third agency she ferreted out the information that Jim Drake had spent a two-week honeymoon in April at a luxury hotel on St John. Fancy digs for an assistant prosecutor, Karen surmised, and headed for the library to check on local weddings this past April.

She found the account of Jim Drake's marriage to Erica Flynn, the daughter of a local judge. An old family in town. The wedding had been a splashy affair – and yes, the bridal couple spent their honeymoon on St John. Who paid for that expensive honeymoon? Was that payment linked, somehow, to Jim Drake's lying about Todd's confession?

But at dinner Karen's hope that she'd latched on to an important clue was punctured by Neil.

'Drake married Judge Flynn's only daughter. He has four sons. He bought Jim and Erica a house here in town, probably paid for the honeymoon,' Neil reported. 'But Jim Drake is still suspect. We know he lied. We don't know who arranged that.'

'I've just about decided I'll have to go into New York for a couple of days.' She saw Neil's startled reaction. 'To research at the law library up at Columbia. Once we have a strong suspicion of who is the real perpetrator in the case, I'll manage to bring him right into Todd's trial – but I need more detailed information about how to handle it. Assuming that by then we know the perpetrator.'

'We'll know,' Neil said doggedly. He hesitated. 'When do you plan on leaving?'

'Sunday. So I can be at the library first thing Monday morning. I'll be back Tuesday night – Wednesday at the latest.'

Why is he uneasy about my going to New York? Does he think I'm about to walk out on the case? I feel so drawn to him it scares me sometimes. But I mustn't jump. I must be sure.

Karen was relieved that Neil turned the conversation to amusing stories about his first two years as a foreign correspondent, his mistakes, his escapades – sometimes hilarious, sometimes dangerous. He seemed to read her mind so often, she thought with involuntary tenderness. He knew she was uptight tonight, that he mustn't push. That was one of the things that was so wonderful about him.

'I have to be at the station at 6 a.m. tomorrow,' he reminded when they lingered over coffee at close to 10 p.m. 'We'd better call it a night.' Again, that look in his eyes that unnerved her. *Was* she in love with Neil – or was it just that she hadn't made love in such a long while? *How did you know for sure?*

A Town Named Paradise

7.40 a.m., Saturday, October 4, 1997

Though Mom always urged her to sleep late on weekends, this morning Karen was at the breakfast table as on weekdays. Later she'd tell Cindy about going to New York for a couple of days. In the afternoon she'd see Todd. She remembered with pain his last words to her when she spoke with him yesterday: '*The worst of all in this mess is not to be able to see the kids. They can't understand what's happening – they must think I've just walked out of their lives. Deserted them.*'

'You're very somber this morning,' Mom intruded on her thoughts. 'Something bothering you, honey?'

'No more than usual.' She managed a wisp of a smile. 'I've been doing a lot of thinking. I've decided it's important for me to go down to the city for a couple of days. To do some research at the law library.'

'When do you plan on going?' Like Neil, Mom seemed startled.

'Sometime Sunday.'

'Oh.' Karen recognized her grandmother's disappointment. Neil's parents were coming for dinner on Sunday. Mom was eager for her to meet them. This was a legitimate excuse for her not to be here.

'I want to get settled in at the hotel on Sunday, be ready to start work at the library first thing Monday morning.'

'Take my car,' Helen said. 'I have the cell phone – in case there's any trouble on the road. Not that I anticipate that, but it's such a comfortable feeling to know you can call without leaving the car if you have a flat or any kind of mechanical trouble. I know—' She laughed indulgently. 'I bitch about the runaway technology – but some of it's great.' *Will she see Bob when she's in New York? She won't start up with him again, will she? Neil's so in love with her – they'd be so good together. Or is she going job hunting in New York? For when the trial is over. I was hoping she'd settle down here. Families shouldn't be split up the way they are these days.*

'I like the idea of a cell phone in the car.' Karen brought her back to the moment. 'And your car's less likely to have any trouble.' *Mom's worried about my going into New York. She's afraid I'm getting bored here, hankering for city life. She's praying I'll choose to set down roots here.*

'When you asked me about who from town was out of the country in the last year or so, I forgot about Jim and Erica Drake until you mentioned it last night.' Helen was apologetic. 'And like you said, the judge probably paid for their honeymoon. I hear he was thrilled that Erica was marrying a lawyer. Someone who'd follow him into the judicial field.' She paused, frowning in thought. 'There's no way the judge could be involved in Debbie's murder, is there?' Her doubt was clear.

'Mom, we're not ruling out anybody. Neil said Erica has four brothers. Jim Drake might be lying to protect a brother-in-law. We have to track any possible suspect.' Frustration crept into her voice. So many people to be investigated – and so little time in which to do that.

'I don't know the Flynns personally – only through what gossip floats around.' Mom's smile blended amusement with cynicism. 'You never know how much to believe. But the youngest brother has always been considered kind of wild.'

Karen reached for her notebook and pen. 'Which brother would that be?'

8.10 a.m., Saturday, October 4, 1997

Knowing Cindy and the children were awake, Karen went next door. Cindy responded immediately to her coded knock.

'Hi, Karen—' Laurie rushed forward to welcome her with a winsome smile. 'Zachie and I are making Christmas cards. Mom says Daddy will be home for Christmas.'

'That's right.' They prayed for that, Karen thought while her eyes met Cindy's in silent communication. Laurie and Zachie needed this reassurance. Let it come to pass!

'They're going to make ornaments for the Christmas

tree, too.' Cindy's eyes pleaded for her to play along with this game.

'And if you have time, maybe you'll make some for Mom and me?' Karen focused on Laurie.

'Yeah.' Laurie hurried off to join Zachary. 'Zachie, Karen wants some Christmas ornaments, too!'

'Todd told me yesterday that he's beginning to keep a diary,' Cindy confided while she and Karen sat at the table in the breakfast corner – beyond the ears of the children. 'He asked me to bring him a loose-leaf notebook and paper.'

'One day he might develop it into a book,' Karen said with determined cheerfulness. 'Memoirs are very commercial these days.'

Cindy appeared dubious about this. 'He says it'll help him pass the time.'

'Cindy, I'm going into New York for a couple of days—' She saw the frightened glint in Cindy's eyes. 'To do some research at the Columbia Law Library – for Todd's trial,' she added quickly.

'You're working so hard, Karen. Todd and I feel guilty that we haven't been able to pay you more.' *How long can we expect Karen to go on without more payment? She's been wonderful – but she's only human.* 'Maybe we can get a second mortgage on the house—'

'Don't even think about a second mortgage.' Karen was firm. 'This trial is great experience for me. Remember, I'm just out of law school a little over a year. I know now I want no part of corporate law. I want to work with people who need me. People like Todd – who're innocent but must prove this in the courts.'

'I'm so scared,' Cindy whispered. 'I wake up at night and remember that the death sentence can be handed out in this state. George Morrison can't seem to say that often enough to please people. If Todd is convicted, I know I'll spend the rest of my life trying to clear him. But if he gets the death penalty—' She closed her eyes in anguish.

'Cindy, don't think that,' Karen ordered. 'We can't let that happen. That's why I'm going down to New York. To be sure I can provide Todd with the strongest possible defense.'

Twenty-Five

9.50 a.m., Sunday, October 5, 1997

The town was just beginning to present its Sunday face as Karen drove through town towards the highway entrance. The morning was cool. She was glad she'd worn a light sweater with her favorite grey flannel pantsuit. Families were heading for church services. A bunch of young boys were gathering on a baseball field with their coaches for Little League practice. Who was taking over for Todd's group? Karen asked herself, and remembered that Amos Rogers's son had been in his group.

In three hours she'd be turning off the West Side Highway at the 72nd Street exit. She'd called and made reservations at the Beacon Hotel in the West Seventies. It was a long walk up to Columbia – but she was a walker. Like Neil, she thought involuntarily. *'Hey, I've been stranded in a lot of places in Third World nations where there's no other way to get from one place to another.'* It amazed her the way people out of New York would take a car to travel three blocks.

A hotel clerk had explained that there was parking nearby – on West 76th Street. She'd leave the car there until it was time to drive back to Paradise. It seemed as though she'd been away from the city such a long time, though it was not quite six weeks. But in those weeks her whole life had changed.

Traffic was light this morning, for which she was grateful. The morning chill evaporated. Now there was a feeling of Indian summer in the air. Here and there the first signs of trees saying goodbye to summer.

Why did she feel so uptight about going into New York? She wasn't returning to that other world. But walking across the Columbia campus would bring back a tidal wave of memories. The back-breaking years in law school – despite Mom's financial assistance, always concerned about escalating tuition costs, the high cost of living in the city. She'd felt sometimes as though she was afloat in the midst of the Atlantic without a life-preserver.

She'd never been confident enough to make her own decisions. When she and Paula had been with Mom, she'd depended on Mom to make decisions for her. When they were with Eve, she let Paula make the decisions – Eve always filled her with doubts. And then there was Bob.

Not until the Wednesday before the Labor Day weekend did I make my own decision. That was the day I grew up. Now it's important to trust my decisions – to know that I'm 'the master of my fate, captain of my soul'.

Mom had come down to New York for graduation exercises. Bob's parents came in from Pittsburgh. He'd made sure Mom and his parents never met. *'Let both sides enjoy the glory of a child with a law degree. That's enough for them to handle on one major occasion.'* But she'd told Mom about Bob. That she was moving into his apartment.

Mom had tried to be sophisticated about it. *'A lot of young people are sharing apartments today. You learn a lot about each other in that kind of situation.'* She'd made it clear to Mom that she and Bob planned to be married once their careers were successfully launched. And Mom was right – they did learn a lot about each other by living together. Enough to know they needed to go their separate ways. Better that than the trauma and horrible expense of divorce.

She could go into New York and not be mixed up in ugly recall. There were good memories, too. She'd loved the excitement of living in New York, yet being nurtured by the school community. She remembered summer nights of free Shakespeare in the park, of concerts in Central Park, of stolen afternoons at the city's great museums.

But once she and Bob were a duo, that life changed, she forced herself to recall. Bob liked to go to hit musicals, expensive restaurants. He enjoyed hectic weekends in the Hamptons – which they grabbed at defiant intervals – living on spaghetti or cereal for weeks afterwards. Neil relished her kind of New York.

Yet as she turned into the last stretch of highway that would take her into Manhattan, Karen felt herself floundering in an ocean of recall. She'd been so sure that the world Bob pictured for them would be marvelous, that at last she would have roots. But, in truth, she hadn't known Bob at all.

Did she know Neil – or, again, was she weaving a dream that had no substance?

It was past 1 p.m. when she at last turned off the West Side Highway and headed for the garage where she would park the car. She was conscious of a tremor of excitement, felt the pace of the city closing in around her. In truth, she'd been isolated from this segment of Manhattan once she'd received her law degree. But for the college years this had been her turf.

She'd have no trouble parking at the garage, would she? Last minute anxiety invaded her. No, on Sundays – until the weekenders returned to the city – the garage would have available space. She drove into the garage, arranged to leave the car there until Tuesday evening. With weekender in tow, she headed for the hotel, registered, settled in her room – all the while enveloped in an aura of unreality.

Now she became aware of hunger. At Mom's insistence she'd eaten a substantial breakfast, but that was hours behind her. With a pleasant sense of adventure she left the hotel, went to the American Restaurant right next door. Waiting for her turkey on rye and coffee to be served, she listened with amusement to the lively conversations around her. Actors talked about scheduled auditions. A published author comforted an aspiring author with the reminder that this was a period when 'debut novels' had their best chances in many years. A pair of senior citizens discussed a dance class at a neighborhood community center.

Her sandwich and coffee arrived. She ate with gusto. This was a small segment of time when she could push away the disturbing questions that plagued her. For now, she promised herself, she'd thrust her anxieties about Todd's defense into temporary retreat. She lingered over a second cup of coffee, then headed out into the brisk Sunday afternoon – content to walk without direction.

She'd always loved the Upper West Side, though Bob insisted the East Side was classier. More elegant. She'd loved the atmosphere here. The tables of used books that sat at the edge of sidewalks – luring prospective buyers. Citerella, Zabar's, Barnes & Noble. The writers who sat in Starbucks and made notes over coffee. She remembered with wistful recall cherished hours spent browsing in Shakespeare & Company, now gone from its home here.

After law school graduation her life had been centered – home-wise and business-wise – on the East Side. At intervals she'd met with friends who lived on the West Side. Friends who soon deserted New York for slower-paced towns. Neil had grown up on these streets. Would he be content to spend the rest of his life in Paradise? Would she?

Why am I thinking about Neil? I came to New York to work on my approach to the trial. I've wasted enough time today. Focus on what I must accomplish in the next forty-eight hours. Todd's life depends on my defense. He doesn't have a whole battery of attorneys and a staff of private investigators. He has me – and Neil.

She headed back towards the hotel. Her pace quickened as her mind probed. She knew what she must search for in the law library – but she knew, too, that what she dug from books would not be enough to clear Todd. There were elusive missing pieces that must be found. In her mind she could hear the voice of Professor Mason, who'd retired last year – '*You dig and dig – and when you think there's nothing left to be found, you dig some more.*'

Call Professor Mason, ask if she was free for dinner tomorrow night. Oh, it would be wonderful to sit down and talk with her. In sudden impatience she hurried back to the hotel, checked for Professor Mason's phone number. She felt a surge of pleasure when the phone was answered on the third ring. Somewhat abashed now – though she'd always felt a special friendship for Professor Mason – Karen explained her presence in the city.

'I know it's presumptuous to call you on short notice, but I was hoping you'd be free for dinner tomorrow night. I'm on this murder case that's driving me up the wall. I'd love to discuss it with you.'

'You've changed tracks,' the professor commented. 'But yes, I'm free tomorrow night. I'd like very much to have dinner with you.'

They arranged time and place, decided on the West End – out of sentiment. How many Columbia students – undergraduate and graduate – had spent triumphant hours, despairing hours, resigned hours – within the confines of the West End? Off the phone Karen settled down with fresh vigor to go over her notes, to plot her day's research tomorrow. First, she must acquire permission to use the law library. As an alumna that wouldn't be difficult to arrange. She'd be there when the library opened in the morning.

Somewhere in the records she'd find a case similar to Todd's – where an innocent was judged guilty and sentenced to serve time, only to face a similar situation once again. While the first case couldn't be brought into the trial, she knew any juror chosen would have heard about Todd's previous trial. The media had dragged that into the spotlight. Somehow, she must find a way to inject this into her defense, make the jury realize early on that such miscarriage of justice could happen.

She went over in her mind every minute detail of the case, dissected every possible angle. Encouraging herself with the reminder that all George Morrison had to offer was circumstantial evidence. Todd had never signed a confession. Yet she knew that in the minds of most of the town Todd had killed Debbie Norris.

Julie Ellis

At shortly past 8 p.m. she phoned to have dinner delivered to her hotel room, ate without tasting. Exhausted from the day's activities, she packed away her notes and prepared for bed while she tuned in to a 10 p.m. TV news program. Thank God, she thought with wry humor, there was nothing on the Simmons case tonight. Go to bed. Tomorrow would be a rough day.

7.20 a.m., Monday, October 6, 1997

She awoke before her alarm clock rang – sleep intruded by a raucous car alarm, a shrieking boom box, a garbage truck, plus usual city traffic noises. She lingered in bed for another five minutes, then headed for the shower. Out of the shower she checked the TV weather report. Again, this morning was unseasonably cool. Wear the grey pantsuit and a grey cotton turtleneck. If the day grew warm, she'd discard the jacket. She'd meet Professor Mason for an early dinner. *'Before the crowds descend,'* the professor had decreed.

Gearing herself for a long morning, Karen ate a hearty breakfast, headed north for the long trek to the Columbia campus. The morning air was crisp, invigorating, lifting her spirits. She approached the campus with a sense of homecoming. She'd never run away from studying – to her learning was a challenge. Bob had been addicted to last-minute cramming.

The day sped past, with one brief interruption at 2 p.m. to run out for a hasty lunch. She refused to be discouraged at not discovering cases that would be useful. It was a long and arduous search – she'd known this was a gamble. But some points that puzzled her were being cleared up. And tomorrow she'd be here again.

Reluctantly she called a halt to the day's work. It was time to go back to the hotel, change for dinner. Not that she had brought along anything special, she realized guiltily. But Professor Mason wouldn't expect her to be dressed as though they were dining at Le Cirque 2000.

186

At the hotel she changed the grey turtleneck for the black one she'd brought along – added a silver chain and matching earrings. Watchful of the time she decided to take the 104 bus uptown rather than tackle another long walk. Aboard the bus she found her mind hurtling back through the years – to evenings spent at the West End with other law students. Bob called this 'making contacts for the future'. *'You never know who's going to land in a spot that'll be a great contact for you.'* She'd relished the camaraderie, the heated discussions that to Bob were 'boring but necessary'. It was 'playing the game'.

Suddenly realizing she was nearing her destination, she sought out street signs. She left the bus at 112th Street, crossed the wide boulevard that was Broadway, hurried to the entrance to the West End. The 'outdoor terrace' section remained open – though not for much longer, she surmised. Another week or two would be its death knell until spring.

She glanced at her watch. She was twelve minutes early, but that was all right. She needed this little parcel of time alone. This was a pilgrimage to the past. She was – how long? – sixteen months out of law school, yet it seemed years behind her. With a flurry of anticipation she walked inside. She rejected the room that houses the bar and walked beyond to the second dining room.

Only a handful of diners were scattered about the faintly Tudor room. The dark wood of the tables, booths, beams, the brick walls fostered this image. Only the array of ceiling fans – available despite air-conditioning – indicated that this was a contemporary era.

She made her way to one of the booths that lined the far wall – intent on securing the privacy the booths provided. But she knew her presence would be visible to Professor Mason. She gazed indulgently at the dark wood table of the booth nicked by rough usage. No tablecloths or vases of flowers here. This was largely a student domain, though she spied a pair of fiftyish men at one of the round tables that supplied the major seating. Faculty probably, though diners often included area residents aware of the quality food served in quantities endearing to students. Many a doggie bag left the premises of the West End.

Karen's eyes focused on one of the clusters of black-framed illustrations that adorned the walls – like all the others a display speaking of earlier periods. Ragtime musicians, jazz performers who'd become icons. Bob had considered these displays campy. She'd been fascinated.

A few early diners were arriving. Now she spied the small, slim figure of Professor Mason at the entrance to the inner dining room. Instinctively she'd known that the professor would expect to find her in a booth in the second room. This evening Professor Mason had abandoned the tailored suits of her teaching days. She wore perfectly creased black slacks and a red, mandarin-collared jacket. Karen half-rose in her seat, waved. Professor Mason smiled, hurried to the booth.

'How wonderful to see you, Professor Mason!' Karen extended a hand in greeting.

'Great to see you. You know, retirement isn't all it's cracked up to be,' she said humorously. 'And let's drop the formality. Call me Pat, now that you're a member of the Bar.'

'Pat—' Karen smiled affectionately.

'I've been reading about the Simmons case,' Pat told her. 'Quite a coup for an attorney so fresh out of school.'

'Not really—' Karen sought for words. 'Todd Simmons and his wife are elementary school teachers – they can't afford "dream team" attorneys. With feelings so high against him in town no local attorney would even take the case. I was all he could get. And I worry that I don't have the kind of experience he needs. He's innocent. As he was in that earlier case. You read about that?'

'Yes.' Pat was serious. 'Of course, it can't be introduced at this trial – but I doubt that even with a change of venue you'll come up with a jury that hasn't heard about it. The media's gone all out on this one.'

'The first case should be reopened!' Karen spoke with an

intensity that startled her. She glanced about to reassure herself she hadn't been overheard. 'I know it sounds suspicious, but Todd was framed in both cases.'

'Break them down for me,' Pat ordered.

Before Karen could begin, their waitress arrived. For a few moments they focused on ordering. Karen waited until their waitress was out of hearing to resume the conversation with Pat. In meticulous detail she reported on every step she had taken thus far, explained about Neil's involvement and help.

'I understand the financial problems,' Pat began when Karen finished her summation, 'and that you can't bring in private investigators. But I'd focus on tracking down the cologne clue. That was an error on the part of the murderer – and I'd say, grab hold of that error and track it down. He's eluding you so far – some obvious little bit of the puzzle is missing. But find the man who bought that cologne. Dig and dig – and dig some more.'

'We're at a dead-end at this point—' Karen was somber. 'But yes, we'll have to dig some more.'

'Don't overlook checking on all locals who could be pressuring that guard and the prosecutor, but I'd take any bet the cologne's your major lead.' Pat paused in thought for a moment. 'What about other fingerprints in the little girl's bedroom?'

'None to my knowledge.' But she hadn't pursued this, Karen thought in sudden awareness.

'It seems unlikely that the guilty man didn't leave prints,' Pat pursued. 'Unless he wore gloves.'

'It was a humid, miserable night,' Karen told her. 'I doubt that he wore gloves – unless this was deliberate to avoid leaving fingerprints.'

'Instinct tells me he wasn't the type to be that cautious. If he were, he wouldn't have used that cologne. A cologne not familiar to American users – an exotic cologne that labeled its owner a man who'd been out of the country fairly recently. This is not a man who plotted his crime with care. He was ruled by emotions.'

'Like you said,' Karen concluded doggedly, 'we'll have to dig some more.'

And she'd call George Morrison and ask about any other fingerprints that were found in Debbie's bedroom.

Twenty-Six

11.14 p.m., Tuesday, October 7, 1997

K aren turned into the driveway with a sense of relief at being home again. Coming home to the night quiet of Paradise – after two nights of city noises – was like returning from a war zone, she thought with a touch of humor and remembered that Neil said he'd wallowed in the night quiet after the turmoil of his years in the Middle East and Balkans.

Before she reached the front steps, she saw the door swing open. Helen stood there with a glow of relief.

'I was beginning to think you'd decided to spend another day down in New York.' She reached to pull Karen close for a moment.

'I should have called you to say I'd be late—' Mom was such a worrier – she'd probably been fearful of some highway accident.

'Are you hungry?' Helen asked solicitously. 'There's chicken in the fridge—'

'I wouldn't mind a cup of decaf,' Karen said, knowing Mom would want to talk for a while before going to bed.

'Oh, Neil called this evening,' Helen told her. 'Twice.'

'Should I buzz him now?' Karen was ambivalent. Did he have something fresh to tell her – or was he just anxious to hear about her research? 'He's due in tomorrow morning at seven. He may be asleep already.'

'He said to phone no matter how late you arrived.'

'That means he has something important to tell me!'

She reached for the phone, punched in Neil's home number. As though waiting for her ring, he responded.

'How was the city?' His voice was a warm embrace.

'Noisy.' She felt a stirring deep within her. 'I had dinner last night with one of my law professors.' It was absurd to feel this way just at the sound of his voice. 'But what's been happening here?'

'Jim Drake and his bride shopped in the duty-free store on St John. For liquor and perfume.'

'Like most tourists.' *She should have guessed this.* 'How do you know what they bought?'

'My mother talked with the bride at a Women's Democratic Club dinner last night. She bought some French perfume – she didn't say what. Mom was afraid to probe. She figured we'd follow up.'

'We have to check out what she bought.' It could have been perfume or cologne on that towel. 'I'll phone Erica Drake. Pretend I'm doing a survey for some organization, checking on the popularity of American fragrances versus European. I'll mention American perfumes, then ask what European fragrances she prefers. In return for her participation we'll send her a one-ounce bottle of her favorite perfume. She'll go along with it,' Karen said confidently.

'Use some phoney accent,' Neil urged. 'We don't want this traced back to you.'

'I lived in Atlanta for almost a year – one of those times I was with my mother. I'll dig out my Southern drawl. I'll be on the phone 10 a.m. tomorrow, keep trying until I reach her.' Excitement spiraled in her. Could this be the missing bit of the puzzle?

'Karen, this may lead us nowhere,' Neil warned. 'Let's just cross our fingers and pray that it does.'

'I won't say anything to Cindy,' Karen promised. In case it wasn't a real lead.

'How did you do in New York?'

'Pat Mason – my law professor – made me realize how inexperienced I am,' she admitted. 'She wanted to know about other fingerprints found in Debbie's room. Neil, I didn't ask.'

'I imagine Todd's were the only ones identifiable. Other than family members.' Neil paused. 'But you'll ask Morrison?'

'You bet I will. Pat agrees with you about the cologne – or perfume, whichever. And she figures that somewhere in Debbie's bedroom he left his fingerprints. If he was careless enough to leave a clue like the cologne, he wouldn't have thought to wear gloves.'

'Call Erica Drake. I'll be on my early shift tomorrow. Buzz me at the station after you talk with her.'

10.05 a.m., Wednesday, October 8, 1997

Karen glanced at her watch. All right, call Erica Drake. Mom had ferreted out the information that Erica had given up her position at the day care center now that she was four months pregnant. *'She was terrified of catching German measles when one of the children came down with it.'*

She tried to get a call through every ten minutes for over an hour. Finally, Erica picked up the phone.

'Hello—'

'May I speak to Erica Drake, please?' Her voice dripped honey.

'This is Erica.'

'Hi. This is Denise Andrews,' Karen followed her prepared script, 'of American Fragrances Incorporated. We're doing a survey on colognes and perfumes. If you'll answer just a few questions, we'll send you a one-ounce bottle of your favorite perfume to show our gratitude.'

'Oh—' Erica seemed delighted. 'What kind of questions?'

Karen continued her script, mentioned popular American scents, asked if she wore any of them.

'The last cologne I bought was White Linen. That is, the last American cologne. I was on St John on my honeymoon. I bought a bottle of Chanel No. 5 in the duty-free shop there.'

They talked a few minutes more about Erica's preferences, her feelings about American fragrances in comparison to well-known foreign fragrances. Then Karen indicated the survey was completed.

'Thank you so much.' Karen oozed Southern charm, but she was drowning in disappointment. This clue was leading nowhere. 'Tell me your favorite perfume, and we'll send you a one-ounce bottle. And we do thank you for your cooperation,' she repeated.

The bottle of perfume would go out to her in a plain wrapper – mailed from a neighboring town. No return address. Erica Drake wouldn't be suspicious.

Now Karen called the station. Neil was at a taping, the receptionist reported.

'Would you like to leave a message?' she asked.

'Thank you, no,' Karen said. 'I'll try again later.'

She knew that the daytime receptionist would soon be fired for reporting station activities to Clay Gilbert. No point in advertising that she and Neil were close. Neil said the mayor hadn't trusted the station since they campaigned for funds for the shelter for battered women. He belonged to the small group that considered its existence an affront to the town.

She'd catch up with Neil later. He'd probably phone when the taping was finished. She focused on her next objective that morning. Call the district attorney's office, ask George Morrison about other fingerprints found in Debbie's bedroom.

The receptionist picked up. 'The District Attorney's office. Good-morning.'

'Good-morning. May I speak to George Morrison, please? Karen Mitchell calling.'

'He's in a meeting. May I have him call you back?'

'That'll be fine. He has my number, but let me give it to you again.'

She'd hang around the house until George called. Then she'd head for the library. The librarians were obviously curious about why she was reading so many back issues of the local newspapers – but let them gossip about it. Let this town know that she was pursuing every angle in Todd's defense.

She settled herself before her computer, brought up Todd's file, studied what little she'd been able to enter. Pat Mason was so right. She had to dig and dig – and dig some more.

Just past 11 a.m. George Morrison called.

'Simmons is reconsidering the plea bargain?' he asked good-humoredly, but she sensed his eagerness that this would go through. Because his case against Todd was flimsy. Yet she feared jurors would be quick to believe Todd was guilty. It was Todd's word against Jim Drake's and Amos Rogers' about his supposed confession. 'It would be the smart thing to do.'

'No way,' Karen said calmly. 'I have a question, George—'

'OK—' An edge of impatience colored his voice.

'What about fingerprints other than Todd's found in Debbie Norris's bedroom?'

'Nothing of any value. The parents, the babysitter, the workmen who'd been involved in bringing in the central air-conditioning.' Arrogance crept into his voice. 'Murder doesn't happen often in this town, but we know how to handle ourselves.'

'Were there unidentified prints?' she pushed.

'Karen, knock it off. We know our business.'

She hadn't expected anything else, she rebuked herself as she put down the receiver. But call Carol tonight. Ask her to keep her eyes and ears open. *Could one of the workmen be their quarry?* More people to check out.

An imperious hand on the doorbell pierced the morning quiet. She hurried to respond.

'I was tied up in a taping until a few minutes ago—' Neil hovered at the door. 'I thought you might have tried to reach me.'

'I did. I spoke with Erica Drake.' Neil came into the foyer. Avid for news of this encounter. 'Nothing there for us. She told me what she'd bought at the duty-free shop at St John.

Not what we're after. She's expecting a free one-ounce bottle of Chanel No. 5. I'll get it to her.'

From habit they strolled into the kitchen, sat at the breakfast table while Karen reported her brief conversation with George Morrison.

'About Jim Drake—' Neil frowned in thought. 'Maybe he's off the hook about the cologne, but he lied about the confession.'

'I can't believe they're taking orders from Clay Gilbert—' Yet he was so damned anxious to have Todd convicted. So sure Todd was guilty.

'My gut tells me Gilbert isn't the guy. He blusters a lot, but from analyzing his past history I'd say he's a man who takes orders.'

'Jake Rhodes?' Karen shook her head. 'No.'

'Rhodes has a solid alibi for that night. But tell me about New York.'

'I told you about my meeting with Pat Mason – and my research at the library.'

'That's not what I meant.' His eyes searched hers. 'How did it feel to be back in the city?'

'It was as though I'd been away for many months—' She managed a shaky smile. 'Instead of just a few weeks—' But that wasn't answering Neil's question. He was asking, *Could you be happy putting down roots in Paradise?*

'I missed you,' he said softly. 'I'd got used to seeing you every day.'

She was unnerved by what she read in his eyes. 'Would you like some coffee?'

'Not now.' A hint of laughter in his voice. 'Believe me, 1402 Maple Drive isn't just my favorite coffee hangout. It happens to be the place where you live. It amazes me,' he mused, his eyes making love to her, 'that I had to roam all over the globe and end up finding you here.'

'Neil, I have a case to solve before I can have a life of my own,' she said unsteadily. *Let him ignore what I say, pull me out of this chair and into his arms. Isn't there a life for me beyond this case?* 'But the trial comes up in a few weeks—' *If he will just reach out, I'll forget the trial. I'll forget everything except how sweet it is to be in his arms.*

'We'll have much to talk about when it's over. I want to spend the rest of my life with you, Karen. But for now,' he exuded confidence, 'we'll fight to clear Todd. I'm with you on this – all the way.' *I'll play it as she calls it. I can't take a chance on losing something that could be so beautiful. If this trial doesn't move her out of my reach—*

8.10 p.m., Wednesday, October 8, 1997

Doug Norris sat in grim silence at the dining table – eating without tasting – while his wife and father-in-law talked with savage intensity about their shared insistence that District Attorney Morrison demand the death sentence for Todd Simmons.

'Don't you worry, baby,' Clay Gilbert soothed. 'Todd Simmons will die for what he did to our little angel.'

'I want to be there,' Jeannie said in slow, determined tones. 'I want to see his life ebb away. His daughter is alive while mine is gone forever.'

No way would he ever believe in the death penalty, Doug told himself. Too many times prisoners were scheduled to die – and then proved innocent. The courts couldn't bring back life they'd destroyed. Just last week he'd watched a TV program that gave shocking statistics about men who were proved innocent long after their execution.

To Jeannie and Clay it was treason to say he believed Todd hadn't killed Debbie. But he couldn't see Todd Simmons as a killer. And Todd was right in claiming he'd been in Debbie's room that afternoon – to pick up Laurie. Jeannie had been furious at Marie for not insisting Todd didn't have time to go into Debbie's room. But she didn't let on to Marie – she wanted Marie to stay on the job.

But *he* knew Todd had been in the room. He'd found that volunteer fireman's pin that had, somehow, been kicked under the chest of drawers. Marie never cleaned any more than she absolutely had to. It stayed there until he found it. Todd must have stood by the chest of drawers while Debbie and Laurie showed him Debbie's new Barbie doll – the way he'd claimed. He didn't notice that the pin fell off. Whoever took Debbie wouldn't have been near that chest of drawers – he scooped her up and hurried through the window again.

How could he go on pretending he hadn't found the pin when Jeannie and Clay talked about Todd's being given the death penalty!

Doug waited until his father-in-law had gone and he and Jeannie had cleared the table, were stacking the dishes in the dishwasher, to bring up his discovery of the pin.

'Jeannie, it was like he said – he was in that room in the afternoon. That's why his fingerprints were there.'

Jeannie stared at him in shock. 'You found Todd's pin in Debbie's room? There's more proof he's guilty! He lost it when he came back into the house at midnight and took her away!' She was white with rage. 'How could you think anything else?'

'I have to give it to the police,' Doug said unhappily.

'You will not!' Jeannie shrieked. 'That'll be giving Karen Mitchell something else to twist around to her way of thinking! Don't you dare, Doug!'

'Jean, I have to. It's been bugging me ever since I found it.'

'I don't want you in this house anymore!' she blazed. 'You're not the man I married. You're some weird stranger. I don't want you here another night, Doug. Pack up and get out!'

10.33 p.m., Wednesday, October 8, 1997

Doug paced about his small hotel room – his mind in turmoil. What was happening to his life? Tomorrow he'd have to look around for a furnished apartment – he couldn't afford to stay here on his salary. How could Jeannie break up their marriage this way? Wasn't it terrible enough that they'd lost Debbie?

He didn't talk much about it, but he missed Debbie so much. His sleep was disturbed by such awful nightmares – knowing what that monster had done to Debbie before he killed her. His son needed him – couldn't Jeannie understand that? He understood how Jeannie was hurting – but don't take it out on him this way!

He stopped pacing, stared at the phone on the night table beside the bed. Tomorrow morning he would go to George Morrison's office and give him the pin. But first, call Karen Mitchell and tell her. He owed that to Todd.

His heart pounding, he waited for the phone to be answered at the other end.

'Karen's Coffee House,' she greeted him blithely.

'Karen Mitchell?' For a moment he was disconcerted.

'Oh, I'm sorry,' she said with an apologetic laugh. 'I was expecting someone else.'

'Karen, this is Doug Norris—' All at once he was uneasy.

'Hi, Doug.' She sounded friendly yet curious.

'I know it's late to be calling, but—'

'Not late for this house. I just this minute stopped working.'

'There's something I have to tell you.' He paused, fighting for strength to say what Jeannie and her father considered treason. 'I just can't believe that Todd is guilty—'

'He *isn't*, Doug. Anything you can do to help me prove this will be a godsend.'

Karen tensed in anticipation, listened to Doug's report of finding Todd's pin in Debbie's bedroom.

'I know George Morrison will grab it as proof that Todd sneaked into Debbie's bedroom that midnight – but whoever took our little angel wouldn't have gone that far into the room. The chest of drawers is at the entrance – no point in his going there. Todd must have dropped it when he was there in the afternoon – as he claims.'

'Doug, thank you for telling me. Todd thanks you. George

Julie Ellis

will have to report this to me as new evidence – but what
you've pointed out about the placement of the pin will be
helpful.'

'The word will be all around town tomorrow,' Doug said
tiredly. 'Jeannie and I are separating.' He took a long,
anguished breath. 'She threw me out tonight. Supposedly
because I insist on handing over the pin. But that's just the
surface reason. She blames what happened to Debbie on me.
Because we didn't have a dog on account of my allergies.
Because I hadn't been able to get repairman in to take care
of the air-conditioning system. In a corner of my mind I was
afraid of this.'

'Doug, she's terribly hurt. Give her some time – the
situation can change.' How rough this must be for him,
Karen thought.

'I'll be here if she changes her mind. But the chances are
slim. I hope you can clear Todd,' he added. 'And when you
do, I pray you nab the monster who killed Debbie.'

Karen sat immobile, digesting her conversation with Doug.
Tomorrow morning Doug would go to George Morrison's
office. George would call her later – as required by law – to
report on this latest bit of evidence in the case. What a fine
person Doug was to come forward this way.

'Was that Neil?' Helen stood in the doorway with a
warm smile.

'No. It was Doug Norris—'

'Oh?' Helen lifted her eyebrows in astonishment.

Karen explained why Doug had called – and how it had
been the catalyst that drove him from his house.

'You'll set up the facts to show that Todd lost the pin that
afternoon,' Helen deducted. 'That – and Marie's admission
that he could have gone into Debbie's bedroom – should plant
plenty of doubt at his fingerprints having been left later.'

'That's a help. But I still have to prove that Jim Drake and
Amos Rogers were lying when they said Todd confessed to
raping and murdering Debbie Norris. That's the crucial point.
Because proving they lied will lead us to the real perpetrator.'

200

'You'll do it, Karen.' Helen exuded confidence.

'Mom, I don't know. Time's so short. Todd's life is in my hands – and I don't know if I'm capable of saving him.'

Twenty-Seven

11.12 p.m., Wednesday, October 8, 1997

K aren prepared for bed – knowing she'd have difficulty falling asleep tonight. It was too late to call Neil, her mind told her. He had to be at the station at 7 a.m. tomorrow. Yet she needed to talk with him, to tell him about the call from Doug. Heart winning over mind, she reached for the phone, tapped out Neil's number, waited for a response. *Can I use the development about the pin to strengthen the case for Todd – or will George twist it around to his advantage?*

'May I speak to Neil?' *Why am I stammering this way?*
'Oh, I'm sorry, I just realized how late it is— I—'
'That's all right,' Arline Bradford soothed. 'I'll put him on.'

Moments later Neil's voice came to her. He'd been asleep, she thought guiltily.

'Neil, I'm sorry – I didn't realize how late it was.' A little 'white lie'. 'I know you're on duty early tomorrow—'

'It's OK, Karen.' *If I'd done this to Bob, he would have screamed at me.* 'What's on your mind?'

With fresh excitement she reported her conversation with Doug.

'That's good!'
'It's not much—' *I have to be honest.*
'It's a small piece in the puzzle – but every little bit helps. You'll know how to use it well.'

Would she? 'Everybody in town thought Doug and Jeannie

had a solid marriage.' *Is there such a thing as a solid marriage?*

'They've been through a terrible crisis. There's a good chance they'll reconcile in time.' He paused a moment. 'I would have thought they'd seek comfort in each other.'

'Jean's looking for someone to blame. She's made Doug her whipping post.'

'I'm glad he insisted on taking the pin to the district attorney's office. You'll use it well,' he reiterated.

'I'll be standing by for a call from George. He'll have to report it to me. Sorry I woke you up.'

'You didn't,' he insisted. 'I was just lying in bed and staring up at the ceiling.'

'I'll talk to you tomorrow,' she wound up in sudden haste. 'Good-night, Neil—'

A few minutes later she settled herself in bed. Knowing sleep would be elusive.

Could the perpetrator be one of the workmen at the house? Fingerprints supposedly left there during the air-conditioning installation – but, in truth, left when he stole into the house and took Debbie? Check out every workman on the job. Get names from George. He can't refused to give them to me.

In mid-morning George Morrison phoned to report on the missing pin – though it was clear he considered this another plus for the prosecution. Karen pursued the question of other fingerprints, demanded – and was promised – the names of the air-conditioning crew.

'Look, we know our job.' He was testy now. 'We checked out other fingerprints. The family, Marie Bingham – even her boyfriend,' he recalled and chuckled. 'He had a one-time record for drunken driving. Marie babysat one night – he came over. Not that night,' he emphasized. 'Your boy did it, Karen. We've got him nailed.'

Karen buckled down to what Bob had always labelled 'donkey work'. She and Neil agreed that every man of any local importance must be profiled in depth. Now to that list she

Julie Ellis

must add the workmen on the air-conditioning job. She continued to be haunted by the elusive fragrance that she was convinced was a major clue. And not for a moment should she ignore the fact that Jim Drake and Amos Rogers were lying about Todd's confession.

In the days ahead she spent hours at the library – ignoring the librarian's avid curiosity, knowing they whispered about her work here. She traveled to Albany to check on what might have appeared in the Albany papers about the men on her 'search' list. She studied the pages of the East Sedgewick newspapers, to which she had subscribed – along with those of Thomasville, where Matt Somers lived. Nothing must be overlooked.

She was grateful that Helen and Neil's parents were adding little fragments of information to her expanding profiles. She didn't have a paid investigative staff, she thought – but she had dedicated helpers. Still, she was ever conscious of each passing day – one day less until Todd went to trial.

She visited Todd at regular intervals – not just to try again and again to ferret out some bit of evidence that might have slipped his mind, but to bolster his spirits. She stayed with Laurie and Zachie while Cindy went to see Todd. He spent his days making longhand notes about the current case and the previous one. Cindy put each day's output through the computer, provided Karen with copies.

'The writing is what sees me through each day,' Todd confided to Karen at an early November meeting. Both conscious of a lack of progress in clearing him. Of the passage of time. 'Searching my mind for something that might just be helpful to you. I miss the kids so much. Cindy brings me these little pictures they've drawn.' His eyes lingered lovingly on the crayon drawings taped to the walls of his cell. 'They make me feel less alone.'

He seemed so tired, she thought compassionately – so frustrated. But Todd knew that others believed in his innocence. Few compared to those who screamed for revenge, she forced herself to admit – yet he clung to this knowledge.

204

Once the trial began, the town would be invaded again by the media. Reporters and photographers would clog the town's streets. There wouldn't be an empty room in either of the hotels. The local radio station would screech its stream of invectives. And the TV station – Neil's station – would be an impartial reporter of each day's news. Neil's parents didn't dare take the unpopular side.

And George Morrison kept hawking for the death penalty. He knew the publicity value of achieving the first death penalty sentence in New York State. That would give him the statewide recognition he wanted. Already there was talk in town about his running for Congress in the year 2000.

I won't be able to live with myself if Todd is convicted and executed. I'd never be able to take on another case.

Tonight, Karen remembered, as she headed for an afternoon session at the library, she was having dinner with Neil. What he called a 'working dinner'. They'd consolidate any fresh information either had picked up about the men on their lists. Each time they felt themselves at the edge of a breakthrough, they were derailed.

Face it – we're no further along than we were four weeks ago, and in less than four weeks we go to trial. I need to know who killed Debbie before I can clear Todd.

Leaving the library at close to 6 p.m. she realized the weather had taken a deep drop. Shivering in the unexpected chill, she hurried to the car. Dusk had already arrived. The days were growing shorter.

Mom was having dinner tonight with the fund-raising committee of the women's shelter. They were having a rough time. The mayor was looking into zoning laws to close up their temporary quarters. The TV station was opposing him.

Neil would pick her up in about forty minutes. They'd be early enough to have their choice of table. Neil liked a quiet corner table that provided privacy. Bob had been annoyed if they didn't have a table in the center of the room – which she had loathed.

Change into something warmer than this pantsuit, she

reminded herself. Winter was close at their heels. The Colonial, which they now considered 'our place', featured a huge brickfaced fireplace. Perhaps tonight there'd be logs burning there. Instinctively she knew that – like herself – Neil would enjoy a blazing fire.

Conscious of the time Karen changed quickly from pantsuit to a smokey-blue wool dress in the long length that had been favored by the big wheels at Clifton, Ambrose, Taylor & McNeil. She had bought it – shuddering now as she recalled the astronomical price tag – because she'd loved its graceful lines. Not because she'd been trying to make an impression on her then new boss, she thought with pleased defiance.

She heard a car pull into the driveway. That would be Mom. With a flick of a brush across her hair, she left her bedroom, went out to greet Helen.

'God, it's cold!' Helen strode into view. 'I'm not ready for this.' She paused, inspecting Karen's dress. 'That's lovely, Karen.'

'One of my "bought for the career" dresses,' she said with a faint laugh. 'But I love it.'

'Oh, about Thanksgiving – I know, it's almost three weeks away, but we have to plan. For the past two years I've gone to the Bradfords for Thanksgiving dinner. Arline called this morning to remind me we're expected. I bake a couple of pies and Arline and Frank do the rest.'

'But I thought we'd have Cindy and the children over,' Karen said uncertainly. She hadn't realized it was so close! 'And Harry, of course. Cindy says he goes out of his mind for turkey.' *Thanksgiving with Neil's parents? That's intimidating.*

'Arline told me to bring Cindy and the kids. I called Cindy and talked to her. She said she doesn't feel up to going out for Thanksgiving. You can understand that—'

'Sure.' *But I'm not ready yet to meet Neil's parents. I know what they're thinking. I know what Mom's thinking.*

'I'd better change for dinner,' Helen said briskly. 'This suit won't be warm enough. By the time I get home again it'll probably be another ten degrees colder.'

Helen changed in record time, swept off to her meeting. Restless – trying to erase from her mind the vision of a meeting with Neil's parents – Karen switched on the television. Watch a bit of early evening news. Neil would arrive any minute – he had a passion for promptness. Too soon, her mind traitorously reminded, reports on Todd's trial would be headlining the evening news.

She heard a car pull up before the house. She switched off the TV, hurried to the hall closet for the smokey-blue winter coat she'd hung there earlier. Neil was charging up the path to the house. He pulled open the door.

He stood immobile for a moment. 'Wow, you look beautiful.' He took her coat, held it for her.

'Winter's arrived.' She struggled for lightness while his arms closed in about her for an electric moment.

'Does your living-room fireplace work?' His eyes were asking disconcerting questions.

'Mom would never have a house without a working fireplace.' Her heart was pounding.

'I build a great fire—' His smile was eager. 'Maybe we could just order in pizza or Chinese?' But before she could reject this, he dismissed the thought. 'No, not till after the trial.'

He knew she considered him special – but that the trial came before anything else in her life now. She'd made it clear too, that she needed time. That she'd just broken up a bad relationship.

It would be so easy to say, 'Yes, let's have pizza here before the fireplace.' We'd have the whole evening to make love. Doesn't he realize how easy it would be to convince me?

While they drove to The Colonial, Neil confirmed what he'd told her earlier about the foreman on the air-conditioning job. He'd had a scrape with the law – a fling with an over-heated fifteen-year-old – about six years ago. He'd married her two years later.

'He was out of town on a job that whole week,' Neil said ruefully. 'Another lead shot down.'

'Mom is on dozens of mailing lists – she receives a batch of catalogues every week. Some sell discount cosmetics and perfumes. She wrote away. Nothing on their list that we didn't know.'

'The cologne had to have been bought in either the Balkans, in France, or in Switzerland. Your professor thought it was a strong lead,' he reminded, sounding exasperated. 'I can't figure out where to go with it.'

'Somebody here in Paradise had to have been in one of those countries.'

'We're overlooking one possibility. There's the chance that the cologne was shipped here by somebody in one of those countries.'

Karen was startled. 'We hadn't considered that.'

Neil's hands tightened on the wheel. 'How do we find out who has family – or friends – over there?'

'It wouldn't look good for either you or me to try to track that down – but suppose Mom has developed a fascination for foreign stamps? The philatelist scene. She has friends at the post office. Let's ask her to do some spadework.'

Neil chuckled. 'Somebody is sure to tell her my folks used to receive letters from Europe and Asia and Africa. But I have an alibi for the night Debbie was murdered,' he joshed. 'I was two hundred miles away – on an assignment.'

'You're off the hook.'

Neil swung off the road into The Colonial's parking area. Only a few cars sat there.

'We'll have the place practically to ourselves,' Neil surmised, leaning across to open the door on Karen's side. They stepped out into the crisp cold night and gazed up at the star-splashed sky.

'They have a fire going!' Karen clutched at Neil's arm while she sniffed the aromatic scent of burning birch logs. 'Lovely.'

'The power of positive thinking. I put in a special order.'

They walked into the restaurant – conscious of its caressing warmth. The music a gentle whisper. The hostess greeted them with the special cordiality accorded regular patrons, led them not to the candle-lit table they considered 'theirs' but to one that flanked the fireplace.

'This table all right?' The hostess was solicitous. A romantic glint in her eyes.

'This is great,' Neil approved.

They ordered. Neil began to probe about the day's activities, added minute details of his own.

'Helen will come up with leads for us.' He nodded with conviction. Right off, Karen noted, Mom had put him on first-name terms with her. 'This philatelist kick could be the edge we need.'

'Todd is piling up pages about both cases. A lot of it is repetition – as he said – but he's hoping he can come up with something useful.' Her face softened. 'I think it's part of his survival kit—'

'What a book this whole situation will make! An innocent man framed twice. This town – where he's given so much of himself – so quick to turn on him.' Neil exuded excitement. 'A small town stripped of its pretty veneer. That'll reach out to millions of readers.'

Karen felt enveloped in a sudden cold. *That's what this is all about. Neil means to write a book about the case. That's why he's so involved. That's why he's attached himself to me.*

'I'll talk to Mom tonight about the post office deal,' Karen said. 'It was stupid of me not to have thought of that right away.' That had been Neil's contribution, she thought conscientiously. *I can't afford to break off with Neil – even though I'm sure he plans to write a book about Todd. He's helpful. For Todd's sake, I can't afford to break off.*

She made a pretense of listening to his report of a comic incident in Bosnia. *I was close to believing this would be the love of my life. We think alike about so many things – we're on the same wavelength. He touches my hand –*

209

and fireworks shoot off in my heart. Or am I back to my old weakness – needing somebody to lean on? In this age of independent women, am I a replica of Eve?

'You're not hearing me—' He intruded gently on her thoughts.

'I'm sorry.' She managed an apologetic smile. 'I keep thinking about how little time there is before we go to trial. It's terrifying to realize that Todd's life is in my hands.'

'It's like your law professor said—' Neil comforted. 'The murderer left two clues. The cologne and, probably, finger-prints. Track down the first, and we'll have a road map to the second.'

Twenty-Eight

Normally Neil gave her a casual good-night kiss when he left her at her door. Tonight – for a moment – there was a new urgency. Then he released her mouth with an air of apology. He was fearful of pushing too hard, she told herself – lest she put an end to their meetings. Irrationally, she'd wished – for a moment – that he'd been more persuasive.

'Talk to you tomorrow,' he said gently and strode back to the car.

Mom was home. Her car in the driveway. A light in the kitchen.

'Karen?' Helen's voice drifted down the hall as she unlocked the door.

'It had better be,' Karen called back, grateful for the cozy warmth of the house. 'Unless you're expecting a secret lover.' She slid out of her coat, hung it in the foyer closet.

Helen came into view. 'How was dinner?'

'Pleasant. They had a fire going. We sat around forever. The food is always good.'

'Any meal I don't cook is good,' Mom said, her eyes appraising Karen. 'And a firelit room is so romantic in weather like this.'

'There's nothing romantic in searching for evidence to clear an innocent man.' Let Mom understand this wasn't a romantic rendezvous.

'I have coffee up.' Helen ignored the rejection. 'It should be ready now.'

Meaning, Karen interpreted, that Mom wanted to talk.

'Great.' She followed Helen into the kitchen.

'How was your meeting?' Karen sat at the breakfast table while Helen poured coffee, then brought two mugs to the table.

'We decided to postpone our "cabaret night" from early December to late January.' Helen was serious now. 'Everybody feels it would strike a wrong note to have a splashy affair while the trial is on.' She hesitated. 'It should be over by then, shouldn't it?'

'I hope so – for everybody's sake.' But she lived in a haze of apprehension.

'Oh, I came up with a bit of information for you. You know, about who in town has connections out of the country? There's a family named Rousseau, who come from a French-speaking island in the Caribbean – they have close relatives in Paris.'

Karen was instantly alert. 'Where do they live? What do they do?'

'They live on the other side—' Paradise's 'low-income' area. 'The father works with a construction crew. The daughter is a shampoo girl at Elaine's beauty salon. The son's a waiter at The Colonial.' Karen lifted an eyebrow. Somebody she'd encountered there? 'Mama is a housewife.'

Karen searched her mind for a waiter with a French accent. 'Do you know the son's name?'

'Leon, I think. He's supposed to be very good-looking—'

A face leapt into her mind. 'I know the waiter.' *This could be the elusive missing piece.*

'I hear he has a rotten temper. He was fired twice – but they took him back each time.'

'He can be very ingratiating,' Karen recalled. But with that temper dangerous. 'We'll check him out.' A handful of people in town knew Neil was her unofficial assistant. She needed him – don't forget that. Todd needed him.

'I was thinking, it might be nice if you and I prepared Thanksgiving dinner for Cindy and the kids – and Harry,' she added humorously. 'We aren't due at the Bradfords until two o'clock. I'll bake the pies – including one for Cindy and the kids – the night before, then Thanksgiving morning we can do a small turkey and the trimmings and take them over before we leave.' She sighed. 'What a sad time it'll be for them without Todd.'

Both started at the sudden sound of Harry's angry barking. That meant somebody was at Cindy's mailbox again, stuffing it with a vicious note. Harry would shut up in a moment when he realized the trespasser had gone.

'It doesn't stop, does it?' Karen, too, had received a share of ugly notes.

'If the radio station would stop its nasty campaign, people might not react that way. Nobody will ever push Arline and Frank on that bandwagon.' Helen rose from the table, took her mug to the sink and rinsed it. 'I'm going to get into bed with my mystery and forget how rotten this town is behaving.'

Karen went into her office, sat before the computer. Her mind dwelling on the French-speaking waiter with a bad temper. Was it he who crept into Debbie's room that night and took her away? Now – knowing it was futile – she called up the voluminous files on other men who'd been suspect. Either she or Neil had tracked down their whereabouts that awful night. Everyone was in the clear.

All right, run with this newest lead. He had family in Paris. The perfume – or cologne – could have been sent to him. He was the type, she judged, who'd flaunt an exotic cologne. *Where was he that night?*

Earlier than usual Karen began to prepare for bed. She felt drained by the tension of these past weeks. Restless – knowing sleep would be elusive – she headed out into the living room to choose a book to read. The phone rang – shrill in the stillness of the night.

'I'll get it, Mom—'

She went back into her bedroom, picked up the receiver there.

'Hello—'

'For a lawyer who was looking for the quiet life, you've roamed far afield.' Bob's voice – blending gentle rebuke with amorous undertone. 'I never expected to see your name in the tabloids.'

'It wasn't planned.' Of course, Bob would call late at night.

'I've missed you—' That charismatic approach she remembered. 'I keep expecting when I turn on the TV news to see your face staring at me. Hoping,' he added.

'When do you have time to watch the TV news?' *Why is he calling? Doesn't he know it's over between us?*

'Do I hear a touch of reproach? But this is the time in our lives when we're building for our whole future. I've been waiting for the right moment – I didn't want to call you until I was sure, but I'm convinced that if you apologize prettily to the old man now, he'll take you back into the firm. Sure, the big wheels look down on the tabloids, but they recognize you've acquired name recognition. That's money in the bank.'

'Bob, I don't want to go back to the firm. I'm—'

'Baby, you've rebelled – now get back into the swing,' he ordered indulgently. 'Why don't we head out to Montauk for the long Thanksgiving weekend? Call that great real estate broker you know – what's her name?'

'Kathy Beckmann.' Karen strained to be casual.

'She was great about finding us a house for the Labor Day weekend. Tell her to do her thing again. A house right on the water. We'll cut ourselves off from the world for four gorgeous days and—'

'Bob, I'm not going back to the firm. I go to trial here early in December.'

'Honey, they understand that. After the trial. We'll—'

'You don't understand. I've begun a new life for myself here in Paradise. I don't want to go back to the firm. I loathe corporate law. Manhattan is a great place to visit.' *Why doesn't he stop this nonsense?*

'You've really reverted, haven't you?' Contempt undercoated his voice. 'You're satisfied with being small time. A nobody.'

'I wish you luck, Bob.'

'I thought you were bright. You're just another stupid bitch.'

She flinched as he slammed down the phone. There went the end of an era. She *didn't* want to go back to New York. But would she ever be able to practice law here, after the hostility towards her for taking on Todd's case? If she won, yes, she considered – *but would she want to stay?*

8.40 a.m., Thursday, November 6, 1997

'I'm dropping the heat,' Helen told Karen – pausing at the thermostat en route to the front door. 'The outdoor temperature is up to sixty-one degrees already. A break after last evening.'

'That was just a hint of what's to come.' Karen reached for the phone. Neil would be in the clear at the station now – the morning news finished.

'A cold snap might be good for business. This is the worst fall season in the past dozen years.' *Slow all over town because of the murder – especially slow for Mom because she was representing Todd.* 'But with luck we'll have a smashing Christmas. See you tonight, honey—'

It would be a smashing Christmas if she won a 'not guilty' decision for Todd, Karen told herself. *But she mustn't think otherwise.* She tapped Neil's number, waited for a reply. Moments later the receptionist connected her.

'Hello—' Neil's voice disconcertingly welcome this morning after that brief ugly conversation with Bob.

'Hi. Have you got a minute?'

'Sure. What's up?'

'Mom has a lead for us. There's a family in town from one of the Caribbean islands – they have relatives in Paris. Do you remember the tall, dark waiter – thirtyish – at The Colonial? The one with an accent?'

'Yeah.' A touch of excitement in his voice now. 'I think his name is Leon.'

'That's the one. I hear he's hot-tempered, was fired and re-hired twice. We need to know where he was the night Debbie was murdered. The restaurant closes at 10 p.m. – so we know he wasn't there.'

'The kind of guy who would favor an exotic French cologne,' Neil mused. 'That could have been sent to him from Paris by family. Let's do a profile on him. I'll ask questions around town—'

'I'll check the newspapers for the past six months – see what I can come up with.' She sighed. 'I know – it's a long shot, but I'll dig.'

Like Pat Mason said, 'You dig and dig – and then you dig some more.'

10 a.m., Thursday, November 6, 1997

Karen waited impatiently at the library entrance. It should be open now. There – someone was coming to the door.

'Good-morning.' One of the librarians greeted her – polite but reserved. She had spent two-thirds of her life here, but she was the enemy because she was defending Todd. Damn people for turning on him this way! What had happened to the old cliché about being innocent until proven guilty?

Knowing the curiosity her presence here always created, Karen made out her call slips, waited for the microfilm to be brought from the files for her. She knew the odds of finding some incriminating evidence against Leon Rousseau were dismal, yet this must be done.

She pored over microfilm until past 1 p.m., then left for a quick lunch at a neighborhood coffee shop. Forty minutes later she was back at the library, filling out more call slips. Muscles aching from hours of sitting hunched before a microfilm machine – eyes strained from studying what seemed to be miles of film – Karen decided to call it a day at 5 p.m.

At 4.50 p.m. a name in a very small segment of news leapt out to command her attention. Not what she'd hoped to find. A vindication of Leon Rousseau as a suspect in Debbie Norris's murder. He had been in a fight at a local bar. At midnight – on the night Debbie was taken from her bedroom – he was in the emergency room of Paradise General Hospital.

9.20 p.m., Monday, November 10, 1997

Dreading yet another day of 'donkey work' at the library, Karen welcomed the arrival of the morning's mail. An acceptable brief diversion. She walked out to the mailbox, brought out the contents. Bills, catalogues, a letter from Paula, and yesterday's copy of the East Sedgewick *Sentinel*, she catalogued as she hurried back into the house in the grey chill of the morning.

Depositing the other mail on the living-room coffee table, she dropped into a chair to read Paula's letter. They were all fine, but Paula missed Mom and her. *'It's been so long since I've seen either of you. Why don't you two fly out for Christmas? It'd be such fun.'* She'd dismissed their flying to Paradise. Probably because of Ron's work.

Couldn't Paula understand that she couldn't make any plans until after the trial? And it was so weird the way Paula was fascinated every time her name was mentioned in a newspaper article or a TV or radio newscast. *'I tell my neighbors – that's my little sister!'*

Paula missed giving up on chasing after a career, she suspected. She was often bored and lonely, with Ron away from the house so much. *'He just lives for his job, I think sometimes – but he's a wonderful father when he's with us.'*

Sure, she'd love to go out there with Mom for Christmas – but she couldn't allow herself to think that far ahead. At this point clearing Todd took precedence over everything.

Traitorously her mind turned to Neil. Talking to Bob made her realize how much Neil meant to her. But that wasn't meant to be. Once the trial was over – and, please God, Todd was cleared – Neil would take off for New York and publishing circles to work up a great book deal for himself. He'd never settle here in Paradise. But she knew now that this was where she meant to spend the rest of her life.

She folded Paula's letter and shoved it back in its envelope, reached for the East Sedgewick *Sentinel*, perfunctorily began to turn the pages. All at once her eyes clung to a name on the obituary page. Lottie Rollins – Tiffany's mother – had died. With attention to every word she read the obit. Lottie Rollins had died on Friday. She was being buried this morning. Karen's mind charged into action. Would this make any change in Tiffany's attitude towards Todd? At least, she thought, she ought to send flowers.

Working on instinct she phoned Neil at the station. He was in a meeting but should be free shortly, the station secretary reported. Karen waited impatiently for him to return her call. Probably she was making too much of this, her mind cautioned – yet she wanted Tiffany to know that she was aware of Mrs Rollins's death.

Five minutes later Neil called. She told him about the obit in the East Sedgewick *Sentinel*.

'The funeral is this morning. Shouldn't I wire flowers?'

'It'll be too late for the funeral,' Neil pointed out. 'Let me wire flowers from the two of us. To Tiffany. Not that it's likely to change anything,' he cautioned, 'but we'll do it.'

In a black dress more suited for a cocktail party than a funeral – but the only black dress in her limited ward-robe – Tiffany dropped into a corner of the sofa in her chintz-splashed living room. In deference to the occasion her face was devoid of make-up except for pressed powder and lipstick.

'It was a nice funeral, Tif,' her friend Mollie comforted. 'Your mom would be pleased.'

'She'd be pissed at how much it cost,' Tiffany flared. 'It's weird. All that loot just to put her in the ground.'

'It was a beautiful coffin.' Mollie was almost wistful. 'You could have bought yourself another car for what it cost. Your old heap – if you don't mind my sayin' – is ready for the dump.'

'How could I afford to buy another car with Mom's doctor bills and hospital bills comin' in the way they did? She was sick for eleven years. We didn't have no health insurance – and she was too young for Medicare.'

'I don't have no health insurance, either. Of course, the boss did say he'd pay half – but I couldn't spend all that money every month.' Mollie winced at the thought.

'I was gonna try for it – remember? When I figured I'd get Mom on the policy with me – but no deal.'

'Did you mean it, Tif? About sellin' the house and leavin' town?' Mollie's eyes were reproachful.

'What else can I do? I had to take out a second mortgage – to meet the payments of the first mortgage and keep up with Mom's bills. Mom's little insurance policy pays for the funeral.'

'It was sweet, the way she always pretended you owned the house outright.'

'Mom bought it outright with the money from that newspaper – but then she had to stop work and the medical stuff kept pilin' up. We couldn't get her on Medicaid because we owned the house and I was workin'.'

'When will you put it up for sale?'

'Tomorrow.' Tiffany's face was set. 'I hope it don't take too long to move. If I'm lucky, I might have a thousand or two after payin' off the mortgages. Then I'll blow this town.'

'Where will you go?' Mollie seemed shaken.

'I don't know.' Tiffany shrugged. 'Anywhere but here. In this town I'll never be anything but trash.' Her eyes settled on the red roses that had arrived just as they returned from the cemetery. 'You don't see anybody rushin' over here to console me.' Her voice softened. 'You're my only real friend, Mollie.'

'I don't wantcha to leave town, Tif. You're my only real friend.' She hesitated. 'Maybe we can go together—'

'Would you go with me?'

'In a minute!'

'Let me sell the house, then we'll make plans.' Suddenly she felt less alone. 'I got cousins in Boston – but they didn't even bother comin' for the funeral. Yeah, we're a team, Mollie.' She hesitated a moment. 'Why don'tcha move in here with me for now instead of payin' rent to your creepy old aunt?'

Mollie's face lighted. 'Hey, that'll be cool.'

'Go home and pack up your gear,' Tiffany said resolutely. 'Then you come here when you get off at the bar.' It was understood that she would not return to work for another two days. *'Out of respect for my mom,'* she'd told her boss.

'Great.' Mollie nodded in approval. 'I hate that closet of a bedroom she does the favor of rentin' me. Things are gonna work out good for us. You'll see.'

Alone in the house Tiffany was restless. Mom couldn't say she didn't see her through, she thought defensively. She was right there to the very end. Again, her eyes strayed to the red roses. He didn't look at her like she was trash. He and that woman lawyer sent flowers. That was nice.

She'd never felt right about what they did to Todd. He hadn't been like the other boys – who looked at her and made filthy cracks. But when she wanted to tell the police it wasn't like she'd said, Mom had smacked her rear until she couldn't sit down. *'You change your mind – I'll get in real trouble. Don't even think about it.'*

Mom was real proud of the house. It made her feel she was somebody. Not just a waitress in a two-bit gin mill. If Mom hadn't got sick when she was half-way through beautician school, she might have had her own shop by now. She left school and took over Mom's job because it was a fast paycheck. She didn't expect to stay in that creepy joint all these years. She'd thought Mom would get better – and she'd go back to school.

She was glad Mollie would be staying with her. This creepy house stank of ugly memories. Maybe – just maybe – before she left town she ought to clear the slate. They couldn't blame her for what happened when she was twelve years old, could they? Mom had made her lie like that – when she'd wanted to tell the truth at the trial. Mom said the lawyers would make her look like a whore. She said it would make *her* look bad.

Her heart all at once pounding. Tiffany crossed to the table where she'd tossed the wrappings and card that came with the flowers. *Where's the card? Oh, here it is. Neil Bradford – that's his name. He works for the TV station. I can talk to him, make sure I won't get into trouble if he tries to reopen the case.*

In defiant determination she crossed to the telephone directory, flipped open the book. What was the number at the TV station?

I'm not makin' no commitment. We'll just talk about what happened that night sixteen years ago. Mom's dead – and the cops can't do nothin' to me. Neil Bradford will be so pleased. He'll think I was doin' the right thing.

Twenty-Nine

4.40 p.m., Monday, November 10, 1997

With towering excitement Karen listened while Neil reported on his phone conversation with Tiffany Rollins.

'She may have called on impulse, then deny everything she said when I talk with her tomorrow,' he warned. But Karen sensed he, too, was excited by this development. 'Still, it looks as though a door might be opening for Todd—'

'She admitted he thought she was seventeen and that she came on to him!'

'That won't hold up if she denies it when you try to reopen the case. She must follow through or it's useless.' He paused for a moment. 'She was quiet all these years because of her mother.'

'Let me go with you—' *Tiffany mustn't change her mind.* Neil was ambivalent. 'She might balk.'

'Explain that I'm an attorney there to protect her interests,' Karen plotted. What could they say to assure Tiffany's cooperation? 'Remind her that while the reopening of her case can't be presented at this trial, it'll be a newsworthy story. There's a good chance that there'll be tabloid interest. She could make a lucrative deal. "The loyal little girl who couldn't hurt Mom, waited until her death to come forward with the truth."'

'Complete with sexy photographs of Tiffany.' Neil grunted in approval. 'She just might buy that. Still, we can't be sure—' Reservations crept into his voice. 'Don't get too

222

high on this. Tiffany could turn around and deny she ever talked to me.'

'Perhaps you should tell her you're bringing me—' Karen tried again.

'No,' Neil rejected. 'Let's don't give her a reason to abort the meeting before it happens.' *Then he means to take me with him.* 'We're due at her house around 4 p.m. tomorrow – when her girlfriend is awake and off to work.'

'It'll take time to reopen the case even if Tiffany plays along with us.' Karen was thoughtful. 'But if it's in the works, we can make sure the media picks it up. Even if it's inadmissible at the trial, it'll be important.'

'The station can do a story on it,' Neil said with confidence. 'That'll be reporting the news – not taking sides. But cross your fingers that she doesn't get cold feet.'

3.55 p.m., Tuesday, November 11, 1997

For the past fifteen minutes Neil and Karen had been cruising about East Sedgewick. Karen had cautioned against their arriving early for the appointment with Tiffany. *'Don't let her feel we're pushing her.'*

Now Neil approached the Rollins house. 'All right,' he said briskly. 'Let's call on Tiffany Rollins.'

Karen's mind was assaulted by conflicting visions. Tiffany fallen prey to a guilty conscience, eager to recant. Tiffany determined to hoist herself onto the tabloid pages again. Tiffany backtracking at the crucial moment, denying all she's said to Neil. Tiffany screeching she'd been pressured to refute her earlier testimony. Was Tiffany ready to provide the first positive note in the battle to clear Todd – or was she about to add fresh insanity?

Neil pulled up before the Rollins house. He reached out to squeeze Karen's hand for a comforting moment. 'Don't be upset if she balks at your appearance. We'll handle her.'

'Sure.' The skepticism in her eyes belied her smile.

Tiffany reacted as Neil had feared.

'What's *she* doin' here?' Tiffany stood squarely in the doorway, blocking their entrance.

'She's Todd's lawyer,' he reminded with studied casualness. 'She'll be the one to request a reopening of the case. When you testify, then—'

'I didn't say I was goin' to testify about anything.' All at once she was defensive.

'Tiffany, that's why you brought me here.' It was a gentle rebuke. 'We all want to see the case reopened. People will applaud you for coming forward. And when the tabloids come after you for a story, Karen will represent you. She'll negotiate the contracts, see that you don't get cheated.'

He's getting through. She's visualizing herself on the front pages of the tabloids again. She's hungry for the money – and for the attention.

'I won't get in trouble with the cops?' Her eyes pleaded for reassurance. 'I mean, I was twelve years old – my mom made me say those things.' She was retreating into the living room, allowing them to enter.

'I'll make sure that doesn't happen, Tiffany.' Play it low-key. Nothing intense, Karen ordered herself. 'You make no official statement until the district attorney guarantees you immunity.'

'What about him? Todd? Will he try to sue me?' Tiffany's eyes darted from Karen to Neil. 'He'll blame me for havin' to go to prison. This is a rotten idea. I musta been out of my mind to call you!'

'Todd won't sue,' Karen insisted. 'I'll have him give me a written statement to that effect. It'll be notarized, legal. You're just righting a terrible wrong.' She had geared herself for a hard sell. 'It'll be a terrific human interest story. People will understand that you were acting out of love for your mother. I'll represent you when you're approached by the tabloids.'

'You show me that paper from Todd. And somethin' from the cops sayin' I won't be punished because I was a little kid when it happened. Then I'll go with you to the district attorney. I'll tell him what really happened.'

The next twenty-four hours were chaotic. Karen acquired the notarized statement from Todd that he wouldn't sue. She approached the district attorney in East Sedgewick and outlined the need to reopen the old case. He was skeptical. Cagey. She prepared for a battle. *She had her witness. She would have the case re-opened.*

Ever conscious that in less than three weeks jury selection for Todd's trial would begin, Karen plotted her course. On Friday morning she went to the local newspaper with the story about her campaign to reopen the Rollins case. Neither the *Enquirer* nor the *Evening News* would run the story.

'*Come back when it's official.*'

That same evening – on the 6 p.m. TV news – the town was told about Karen's efforts to reopen the Tiffany Rollins case.

The station was besieged by phone calls. This was labeled a sleazy effort to whitewash Todd, to save him from the death penalty. Tiffany was savaged as an opportunist, being paid off to revise her testimony. After the first three obscene phone calls to Karen, Helen unplugged the line.

'We don't need to listen to that garbage.' She was upset that her town could behave this way.

Late that evening, George Morrison appeared at the front door.

'You've unplugged your phone,' he told Karen without preliminaries when she responded to the doorbell. 'I know what you're doing, and it won't work. You're trying to affect the jury pool!'

'I'm trying to right an old wrong,' she said calmly.

'Who's behind this? Who's paying off that little slut to lie for you?'

'She lied before. She'll tell the truth now.'

'None of that will be admissible at the trial!'

'I'm aware of that. Todd was framed back then – as he's

being framed now. But Tiffany Rollins will go into court and tell the truth this time. Before she was a scared little girl, acting under her mother's orders. Now she's a grown woman. She realizes how wrong that was.'

'We'll fight this! This town wants to see justice down!'

'The Rollins case is out of your jurisdiction, George.' She fought for calm. He saw her making inroads on his case – and he wasn't happy.

'You're trying to affect the jury pool,' he repeated through clenched teeth. 'It won't work, Karen. Todd's guilty as hell. We'll prove that in court.'

Karen stood immobile at the door, watched him stalk towards his car. All he had against Todd was a circumstantial case. She had to keep chipping away at what little he had. Yet she was fearful of the kind of justice that would be meted out by a local jury. She knew, too, that it would be futile to seek a change of venue.

Suspecting it would lead to another dead end, she tracked down the whereabouts of Leon Rousseau's father on the night of the murder. He was in the clear. Desperate, she dug up the whereabouts of the boyfriend of Leon's sister – with similar results. She was haunted by the knowledge that an exotic fragrance stood between her and the discovery of who killed Debbie Norris.

Jury selection began. Karen challenged every prospect fearful of pre-set decisions. George displayed a new confidence that was unnerving. What did he have up his sleeve? She was ever conscious of a conspiracy that she and Neil were convinced existed yet couldn't penetrate.

On the Tuesday evening before Thanksgiving Karen received a phone call from Carol Latham. As on the last such occasion, Carol seemed nervous.

'Karen, this must never get back to me,' she prefaced the information she was about to share. 'I'd lose my job.'

'I promise you, Carol, nobody will ever know.'

'It may mean nothing at all, but Morrison is all upset because some of the fingerprints lifted from Debbie Norris's room have never been identified – and he'd thought they'd been checked against the workmen in the Norris house just before the murder. That was Jim Drake's job, but he screwed up. Anyhow, George has given orders to have them checked out as soon as possible.'

'Because one of those fingerprints might belong to the real murderer,' Karen pounced. 'He wants everything tied up neatly so he can focus on Todd.' It was like Pat Mason had said. *The murderer surely left fingerprints.*

8.28 a.m., Wednesday, November 26, 1997

Karen tried for the third time to get through to George Morrison. She knew that these mornings he was in his office no later than 8 a.m. Why didn't he pick up his private line? She drummed with one finger on the edge of her desk while she listened to the ringing at the other end.

'Hello—' His voice telegraphed his annoyance at this intrusion.

'George, this is Karen Mitchell. I have one quick question. I was going over all the facts in the case again last night – but I don't find any definite statement about fingerprints other than Todd's that were lifted from the bedroom. I have notes about various workmen and so on – but were there any prints that were not identified?' He'd suspect a leak, but he couldn't attribute it to any one person.

'A couple.' He was brusque. 'They probably belong to the kid who mowed the lawns or to a delivery boy—'

'In Debbie's bedroom?' Her tone was skeptical.

'It could happen. Who's been feeding you crap about unidentified fingerprints?'

'I had a long talk last night with a favorite law professor,' Karen fabricated. 'She says the murderer left two clues to his identity: the cologne or perfume dumped on the towel that was wrapped about Debbie's body, and his fingerprints. I want to know about those unidentified fingerprints.'

'You'll know – provided they can be identified. I'll see

227

you in court later.' The jury was set – just some procedures to settle. 'Oh, it'll be a half-day because of the holiday tomorrow.'

The customary Thanksgiving excitement was missing in Paradise this year. Instead, the town was conscious of the imminence of its first major murder trial in thirty years. Hotels were receiving reservations from members of the media. Restaurants took on extra help – knew that on the Monday after Thanksgiving they must prepare for the presence of hordes of newcomers.

Karen tried to gear herself for Thanksgiving dinner with Neil and his parents. In the morning she would stay with Laurie and Zachary while Cindy went for a brief visit with Todd. She and Mom would carry Thanksgiving dinner over to the Simmons house before going on to their own mid-afternoon dinner.

By Wednesday noon local college students were arriving in town for the long weekend. Family members coming together for what in Paradise had always been a cherished holiday. Karen tried not to remember that Todd's trial would begin on Monday. She still felt painfully inadequate.

Normally this was the day when Paradise began to set up Christmas decorations. Strings of red and green lights to be strewn across street corners. Christmas trees positioned at strategic spots on Main Street. Stores vied with one another for the most eye-catching displays. But that would be muted this year.

In one of the guest bedrooms of the Rhodes house Olivia Madden, Jake's older daughter, was hanging up the contents of the valise she'd brought along for the long weekend. Bill was tied up at the office – he'd arrive late tonight. The lively chatter of her seven-year-old daughter Betsy was fading in the distance as she accompanied Althea downstairs to the kitchen for cookies and milk.

She never felt truly comfortable in this house. Not since

her father re-married all those years ago. Not even when the second marriage broke up. She'd never felt comfortable with Adam – just sorry for him because Dad treated him so coldly. Before Adam's mother was thrown out of the house, Dad had spoiled him rotten.

She heard the phone ring on the lower floor. Moments later Althea called up from the foot of the stairs.

'It's for you, Olivia. Your father.'

She hurried to the doorway. 'Thanks, Althea. I'll take it up here.' She picked up the extension on the bedside night table. 'Hello, Dad.'

'Olivia, I can't get away from the office to pick up Adam. Will you run over to the airport? He's arriving at one forty.'

'I'll pick him up.' She checked her watch. 1.10 p.m. 'There's plenty of time.' He hadn't asked how she was, how Betsy was, when was Bill arriving. He liked the image of family; all he cared about was the business.

'We're running the usual schedule,' Jake continued. 'Althea will be at the house till noon, when she goes to her family. Everything for dinner will be ready – Clarice will handle it. She'll serve, clear away and stack the dishwasher before she leaves. Oh, we're having guests. Clay Gilbert, and his daughter and grandson. Don't discuss the case – Jean's still traumatized.'

'I won't.' In a way it would be a relief to have others at the table. Thanksgiving was usually such a grim occasion, though she always tried to create an air of festivity.

'You'd better leave for the airport,' he said brusquely. 'Be there when Adam's plane arrives.'

Betsy would stay with Althea. On the few times each year when they were here at the house, Althea made a delightful fuss over her. It was Althea who always hung Christmas decorations about the lower floor, arranged for the Christmas tree.

She stopped by the kitchen – where Betsy was listening with avid attention to Althea's description of the cake she was about to make for tomorrow's dinner.

'Because I know, Betsy, that you don't like pumpkin pie.'

'Chocolate inside and out?' Betsy asked eagerly.

'Inside and out – and you can lick the frosting bowl,' Althea promised.

'I'm going to pick up Adam,' Olivia told the other two. 'I'll be back soon.'

'OK, Mom.'

Betsy would cling to Althea every moment she was in the house. And Althea would be warm and loving – as though to make up for the grandfather's lack of affectionate display. But Dad had established trust funds for both of his grandchildren, Olivia forced herself to acknowledge. That was being a good grandfather. A delicate peace existed between Dad and Bill. Neither liked the other.

She arrived at the tiny local airport ten minutes ahead of Adam's scheduled arrival. Usually their father delegated these tasks to her. Sometimes she wondered if Adam's allergies were actually that serious – that he couldn't remain here in town for more than ten days without suffering a bad allergy attack. Dad didn't want him home. Adam was a constant reminder of the marriage their father wished to forget.

The plane arrived right on the button. Adam didn't seem surprised to see her waiting to meet him. He was used to this.

'Don't tell me,' he jeered good-humoredly. 'Dad had an important business meeting.'

'You got it.' She smiled in affectionate conspiracy.

How charming and handsome he was, she thought as they headed for the car. Her baby half-brother who always seemed to yearn for attention.

'That's a real cool pair of earrings,' he teased.

'I think so, too.' Adam had sent them to her for her last birthday.

At one time – when he was small – he'd resented their sharing a birthday. Mrs Raymond – the housekeeper before

Althea – had solved that just three years before she walked out on the job so unexpectedly. For three years there had been two – small – birthday cakes, each with the appropriate number of candles. Resentment put to rest, Adam began to feel their sharing a birthday was a special bond between them. Each year since he was ten they'd exchanged small birthday gifts.

En route into town Adam talked about school activities.

'You like the new school, I gather.' Dad had been annoyed that he'd complained mightily about the last one.

'It's OK.' Adam shrugged.

They were approaching town now. Adam was going to be so bored, she thought – he'd spend most of the time holed up in his room reading. He'd lost touch with the kids here in Paradise.

'Adam, would you like to stop off at the bookstore?' she asked on impulse. 'Maybe you could pick up a good mystery.' He was an avid mystery buff. 'An advance Christmas gift from Bill and me.'

Adam's face brightened. 'Thanks. Maybe there's a new Dean Koontz out.'

'While you're in the bookstore, I'll run down the block to the Oasis.' She always shopped at the Oasis when she was in town. Helen had such superb taste. 'I'll meet you at the car.'

She parked before the bookstore, pulled bills from her wallet and handed them to Adam. 'Don't leave town with the change,' she joshed.

Adam strode towards the bookshop. Olivia headed for the Oasis. She paused at the window, admired a beige cashmere sweater on display. If Helen didn't have it in her size, she'd order it and ship it on, Olivia thought in pleased anticipation.

In the shop Helen came forward with the warmth that endeared her to local shoppers.

'I have it in your size,' she said when Olivia explained her presence, and reached on a shelf for the sweater. 'I was thinking of you when I selected it.' She gazed admiringly at Olivia's tall, svelte figure. 'You have an eye for its kind of unusual details.'

For a few moments they talked about clothes, then Olivia brought up the subject that dominated local thoughts.

'I suppose everybody in town is waiting for the trial to start.' Dinner conversation tomorrow would be difficult, Olivia thought unhappily. Dad said Jeannie was still traumatized. That was understandable.

'It's a difficult time.' Helen was somber. 'But nobody will ever convince me Todd Simmons is guilty.'

'I couldn't believe at first that something so awful could occur in this town. I was two years ahead of Jeannie in school – I didn't really know her. But what happened to Debbie has made me so watchful of Betsy.'

'Those are gorgeous earrings.' Helen inspected the intricate silver designs. 'So unusual.'

'They were a birthday present from Adam. He sent them to me from Switzerland. He was at camp there this summer,' she explained because Helen was staring at her so oddly. 'The mountains are great for his allergies.'

Helen was trembling with excitement as she waited for Karen to respond to her phone call. *Let her be home.*

'Hello—' At last, Karen's voice came to her. Faintly breathless, as though she'd rushed to pick up the phone.

'Oh, I was afraid you hadn't got back from East Sedgewick,' Helen said in relief.

'I just walked in the house. What's up?'

'Karen, *Adam Rhodes* was in Switzerland this summer. Olivia just told me so. And he was here in Paradise over Labor Day weekend – when Debbie was murdered—'

Thirty

Her heart pounding – her mind digesting every word Helen had said – Karen put down the phone. Logically, she shouldn't jump to the conclusion that she had just identified Debbie Norris's murderer. So Adam had gone to camp in Switzerland. That was nothing to take to the district attorney. Hundreds of American students went to camp in Switzerland each year. But it was a lead she must follow up.

Someone high up in this town forced Jim Drake and Amos Rogers to lie about Todd's confession. Someone like Adam Rhodes's father. Adam was here in town after returning from camp in Switzerland and before returning to boarding school. He had the opportunity. Only a small wooded tract separated his house from the Norrises'. He could have bought the cologne in Switzerland. Would a seventeen-year-old boy buy cologne? *That's what I must discover.*

But Jake Rhodes offered a $50,000 reward for the arrest and conviction of Debbie's murderer. Could he have not realized that Adam was guilty – or was that a grandstand play? *How do I find out if Adam bought the same cologne that was poured onto the towel wrapped about Debbie's body?*

In a surge of impatience – blended with frustration and anxiety – she phoned Neil. He was away from the station.

'When do you expect him back?' she asked the receptionist. Knowing she sounded overwrought. But Adam was home for the Thanksgiving weekend. He'd be returning to boarding school sometime Sunday.

'He's out on an interview in Albany,' the receptionist explained. 'Would you like to leave a message?'

'Yes. Please tell him to call Karen Mitchell as soon as he can. He knows the number.'

She sat immobile. Mentally reaching for her next move. Then in a burst of energy she phoned the shop. Helen answered.

'Mom, we need to find out if Adam bought cologne in Switzerland.' Mom knew what cologne she meant. 'If he brought the bottle home. I can't make a move without that. Will Althea help us?'

'I don't know.' Helen was troubled. 'You're asking her to spy on Adam. How can she do that to Jake Rhodes?'

'Look what he's trying to do to Todd!'

'Karen, we don't know that—'

'Mom, explain to Althea how important this is! It can lead to clearing Todd!'

'I'll talk to her,' Helen said after a moment. 'That's putting her in an awful spot.'

'Does she want Adam to be loose in this world – if he is guilty?'

'I'll talk to her,' Helen reiterated. But she seemed distraught at the prospect.

'When, Mom?' *Time was so short.*

'I'll leave the shop early, drop by the Rhodes house on pretext of taking her a book. One I promised to loan her. But Karen, this sounds so – so far out.'

3.05 p.m., Wednesday, November 26, 1997

In her small office at the rear of the shop Helen reached into a desk drawer for the suspense novel she'd finished reading last night. She'd found it fascinating. Now Althea was eager to read it.

'Frances, I have to run out on an errand,' she called to the idle saleswoman. Della was going into a dressing room with a customer. 'I'll be back in an hour.' She hurried from the shop to her car.

Could Adam Rhodes be the one who raped and killed Debbie Norris? Was Karen so anxious she would leap at any possibility? But Todd's life hung in the balance. Any lead must be followed.

At the Rhodes house she parked in the circular driveway, noted that Olivia's car was not there. Could Althea be alone in the house? Clarice usually left between 2 p.m. and 3 p.m. It was past that now. She rang the bell – struggling to appear casual. Althea responded.

'Oh, you brought me the book—' She smiled and reached out for it.

'I finished it last night. Althea, are you alone in the house? I need to talk to you. Privately.'

'Olivia and Betsy went into town to buy some puzzles for Betsy. There's nobody here except Adam and me—' She frowned as Helen winced. 'Adam's in the den, watching some football match on TV. Come out to the kitchen with me. We can talk there.'

The kitchen was at the other end of the house from the den, Helen recalled. Together they walked down the long hall that led to the kitchen. From behind the closed door to the den came the voice of a TV commentator reporting on a football game. Adam would hear nothing else, Helen told herself.

In the privacy of the kitchen Helen explained the situation. Althea was horrified.

'Helen, you're asking me to go up to Adam's room and look for a cologne bottle?'

'You don't have to take the bottle,' Helen soothed. 'Just let us know the name of the cologne. Althea, it's urgent to Todd's case.'

'I'll try,' Althea said reluctantly. 'But I can't promise.'

'If he killed Debbie, how can we know that he won't strike again? Sex offenders are often repeat offenders, Althea. Do you want to see other little girls meet the same fate as Debbie?'

'I'll try to find a time when I can get into his room,' Althea said after a pregnant pause. 'But I can't be sure I can.'

Helen contrived to talk about the book as Althea walked her out to the car – in the rare event their conversation might be overheard. Althea was more concerned about being caught, she thought uneasily, than in proving that Adam had raped and murdered Debbie Norris. *Did Althea know more than she was telling?* But immediately she felt a rush of guilt that she could harbor such suspicions.

Althea stood at the door and watched Helen drive away. She was remembering stories Clarice had told her about Adam. How he'd often been in trouble at school. How her predecessor had walked out of the job and out of town with her little girl with no more than a day's notice. Clarice hinted she'd left with bad feelings – and right after that Adam was shipped off to boarding school.

She remembered with anguish those first traumatic days after Debbie was kidnapped – and then her body found. *No, she wouldn't want to see that happen to another little girl.*

She hurried back to the kitchen with a sharp awareness of the time. Olivia and Betsy wouldn't be back for probably another hour. She just might be able to handle this.

In the kitchen she reached into the refrigerator to bring out the chocolate chip cookie dough she'd prepared this morning – to be baked tomorrow or Friday. Bake a batch of cookies to take in to Adam while he watched the football game. He'd watch the football game and eat the cookies. He wouldn't stir from the den. That would provide her with time to go up to his room and look around for a bottle of cologne.

Fighting guilt she put a tray of cookies into the oven, set the timer for twelve minutes. If she was caught going into Adam's room, she'd say she'd brought up another blanket because the weatherman predicted a steep drop in temperature overnight. A hundred to one, she comforted herself, Karen was way off base on this. She'd find no bottle of cologne. But if he was guilty, then she should do this.

She busied herself with washing cranberries, removing the less than perfect. The timer rang. She brought the tray of cookies from the oven, transferred them to a plate, poured a glass of milk. She hesitated before taking them in to Adam. Oh, leave a few cookies for Betsy.

The cookies should cool first. No, no time for that. Adam wouldn't notice that they were still warm – he might even prefer that.

With cookies and the glass of milk in tow, she walked to the den, knocked.

'Yeah?' Adam was annoyed at this intrusion.

Althea opened the door, walked inside, smiled ingratiatingly. 'I thought you might like some cookies and milk.'

'Hey, that's cool.' He hurried to take the tray from her.

Her heart pounding, Althea strode down the hall to the stairs, headed for the upper floor. She stopped at the linen closet for a blanket to validate her possible alibi at being in Adam's room. Her hand was unsteady as she turned the knob and let herself inside. In the den the TV commentator was reporting in high excitement. No chance that Adam would suddenly come upstairs.

Careful to leave no traces, she searched his dresser drawers, the night table beside his bed, the bookcase loaded with the suspense and horror novels he devoured when he was home. Nothing. Her eyes focused on the closet. She opened the door, felt in the pockets of the few garments hanging in the closet. Nothing there. Now she bent to look on the floor.

Excitement spiraled in her. In a dark corner wrapped in paper toweling, was a bottle. She bent to pick it up, thrust aside the toweling. A bottle that once held cologne but was now empty. The name on the label, she suspected, was French.

She couldn't take the bottle with her – that would be a giveaway if Adam happened to look in the closet. She reached into a pocket, pulled out a tissue, opened the bottle and tried to elicit a few drops that might linger. She lifted the tissue to her nose. A pungent scent was there.

Take this to Karen. She'll know what to do.

Downstairs again, she heard a car pull up in front of the

house. Olivia and Betsy were returning. Her mind in high gear, she went to the door to admit the other two.

'I have a few chocolate chip cookies out in the kitchen,' she greeted them. 'I thought you might like them, Betsy.'

Betsy's face lighted. 'Sure.'

'I'm going over to the grocery store to pick up some sage,' she fabricated. 'I don't think I have enough for the dressing.'

'I'll get it for you, Althea,' Olivia offered.

'Oh, I don't mind, Olivia – but thanks. I could use a little fresh air. I haven't been out of the house today.'

'Dress warmly,' Olivia said. 'It's getting so cold.'

'I will. The cookies are on a plate on the kitchen table,' she told Betsy and moved towards the foyer closet for the coat she kept there. 'I won't be long.'

She drove first to Helen's shop – reminding herself to pick up sage before she returned, to justify this small excursion. Helen was in her office working on inventory figures. She glanced up at Althea with an air of hopeful anticipation. Sensing this wasn't a casual visit. She rose quickly and closed the office door.

'I found an empty bottle of some French cologne hidden away in a corner of Adam's closet.' She reached into her purse, withdrew a piece of tissue. 'I managed to get some of the fragrance on this. It's faint but definite.'

'Althea, you're wonderful!'

'Does this mean Adam killed Debbie?' Her face was anguished.

'If this is the same scent that was found on that towel, yes. Of course, it could be something else,' she conceded. 'There could be a legitimate explanation.' But her face refuted this. 'I'll give it to Karen—'

Karen paced about the house, impatient to hear from Neil. All the while chafing at Mom's strange phone call twenty minutes ago: *'Something's happened, but I don't think we should discuss it over the phone. I'll be home early.'* What had happened?

The phone rang. She darted to pick up the receiver.
'Hello—'

'Vicky said you called.' Neil sounded expectant.

'Can you come over to the house?' Mom's caution was contagious.

'I'll be there in ten minutes.' His voice crackled with excitement.

Each minute seemed ten until she heard his car pull up before the house. She hurried to the door to greet him.

'We know who from Paradise was in Switzerland last summer,' she told Neil as he walked into the foyer. 'Adam Rhodes.'

Neil whistled softly. His mind following hers. 'He was here in town when Debbie was murdered. He could have gone to the house through that patch of woods between his house and the Norrises'. Nobody would have seen him.'

'His father knew. That's why he's been trying to frame Todd.'

'Let's sit down and figure out where we go from here—' Neil dropped into a corner of the sofa. 'Next question: did he buy the cologne?'

'Mom's talking with the Rhodeses' housekeeper. Hoping she'll track that down for us.'

'Great!'

'If Adam bought the cologne, then our next step is to get his fingerprints, compare them with the unidentified prints that were found in Debbie's room. Then we—' She paused, alert to sounds outside. 'There's Mom—'

'Karen, this sounds hot – but we could be way off-base,' he warned. 'Without setting Adam in Debbie's room, we're nowhere.'

'I know.' Neil worried that she'd build her hopes up to the sky, only to be disappointed.

Moments later Helen charged into the house. 'Oh, what a day,' she gasped tiredly. 'But Althea came through.' She reached into her purse and brought out a folded-over tissue. 'Adam had hidden an empty cologne bottle in a corner of

239

his closet. The label had some foreign name on it – French, Althea thought. She managed to get some scent on this tissue—'

Karen reached for the tissue, held it to her nose. 'I think this is it!' She handed the tissue to Neil, waited for his reaction.

Neil sniffed. His body telegraphed his excitement. 'This is what was on that towel! Adam Rhodes killed Debbie. But we need more than this to convict him.'

It was just as Pat Mason had said. Two clues would lead to the real murderer – the cologne and the fingerprints he must have left in Debbie's room. 'How do we get Adam's fingerprints? To compare with those unidentified prints lifted from Debbie's room?' The ones George Morrison insisted belonged to the kid who mowed the lawn or to a delivery boy.

'It has to be fast,' Helen reminded. 'Adam goes back to school on Sunday.'

'I have an idea that may work,' Neil said softly.

'Then tell us!' Karen ordered.

'First, give me a rundown on what you surmise happens at the Rhodes house on Thanksgiving morning.' He gazed from Karen to Helen.

'It's pretty routine,' Helen began, squinting in thought. 'As I recall, like a lot of families they go to special Thanksgiving services at their church. Except for Adam,' she pinpointed. Neil's face brightened. 'Adam never goes. It's Jake, Olivia and her husband and Betsy. Once three years ago the younger sister came with her husband. They went to church, too. Jake loves to present the solid family picture. But Adam always refuses to go, Althea told me once.'

'Then Adam will be home alone,' Neil pounced.

'Except for Althea,' Helen told him. 'The family will be at church. Clarice – the maid – won't arrive until eleven o'clock. To be there to serve dinner and clear away.'

'Adam doesn't know me,' Neil plotted. 'I'll play a delivery man, bringing a bottle of champagne from the liquor store. You'll have to make sure Althea doesn't answer the door. I want Adam to come to the door, accept the package – and sign for it.'

'How do we know Adam will go to the door?' Helen was ambivalent. 'Althea will ask him to go!' she said in momentary triumph.

'Adam has to be downstairs. I'm not sure Althea can manage that.' Yet hope surged in Karen. 'We'll have to take our chances. Remember to dress the part, Neil. You're a delivery man for the liquor store – working for little more than minimum.'

Could this be the end of the road? For a moment she churned with optimism. Let this be a true Thanksgiving day for Todd and Cindy! Or would it be another dead end?

Thirty-One

8.42 a.m., Thanksgiving Day, 1997

The morning air was crisp and cold, the sky a cloudless blue canopy. A picture book Thanksgiving, Karen thought as she gazed out the kitchen window. The pungent aroma of pumpkin pies – blending with that of freshly brewed hazelnut coffee – emerged from the oven. In another twenty minutes the pies would come out, to be replaced by the small turkey being roasted for Cindy and the children. Karen crossed to the range to check on the cranberry sauce. It would be done in moments.

'Be sure you dress warmly when you go out,' Helen said. 'It's cold—'

'I will.' Karen wore a turquoise cotton turtleneck and black jeans.

Mom was trying so hard to create an air of festivity this morning. Yet she knew that – like herself – Mom was tense, apprehensive of what the morning would bring. Were they being naive to put such emphasis on the cologne Althea discovered in Adam's closet? Was that just a coincidence? But his fingerprints might prove it wasn't.

Althea promised to call to Adam to answer the door when Neil arrived with the package requiring a signature. But suppose Adam was asleep? Althea said he liked to sleep till noon when he was home. By noon Jake Rhodes and the others would be back from church services.

On Monday Todd's trial would begin. She had so little to offer in his defense. Please God, let this business of securing

242

Adam's fingerprints go through without a hitch. *But would Adam prove to be their quarry?*

'I'm going to sauté the turkey heart and giblets for Harry,' Mom interrupted Karen's introspection. 'After I have my coffee.' She glanced at the kitchen clock. 'No, I'll leave that for later. I have to go over to Cindy's in a few minutes.' Cindy had been granted a fifteen-minute visiting privilege this morning at 9 a.m. Karen had been scheduled to sit with the children while Cindy was away – but Helen was replacing her so she could accompany Neil on his urgent errand.

'This is a grim Thanksgiving for them.' Karen flinched, reflecting on this.

'But with a little luck – and God's help,' Helen said with determined optimism, 'that may change very soon.'

Anger flared in Karen. 'I'll never forgive this town for turning on Todd the way it has.'

'Once the Rollins case is reopened – and Tiffany clears Todd, it'll be a whole different ball game. That made him look so bad.'

'That's going to take time.' Karen was somber. 'Though I'm making progress. I talked—' She paused,, listened to street sounds. 'Is that Neil – this early?' But she was already on her feet.

'Could be—'

Karen opened the door. Neil grinned down at her. 'I've had breakfast – just coffee. I know I'm early—' His eyes made silent love to her.

'We're both punctuality nuts—' Bob had never been on time anywhere in his life, she thought involuntarily. *I can think of him so impersonally. Because of Neil.*

'How do you like my wardrobe? Suitable for the occasion?'

Karen inspected his beat-up L.L. Bean boots, his ripped-at-the-knee jeans, the time-worn, faded grey down jacket, and nodded with approval.

'Oh, I have a cap to complete the outfit.' He reached into a pocket, pulled out a red knit cap. Playing the scene lightly, but both knew the impact of what lay ahead.

'You can deliver to me anytime,' Helen greeted him. 'Where's the champagne?'

'It's in the car. I drove over to the next town to buy it last night – just to cover our tracks.' Liquor stores were closed today.

'That jacket looks as though it's lived through a lot.' Helen brought him a mug of coffee.

'Three bitter winters in the Balkans.' His eyes glinted in recall. 'There were nights I slept in it.'

'I talked to Althea,' Helen told him. 'She's going to do her best to have Adam answer the door. But there's no guarantee she can bring it off.'

Neil refused to relinquish his air of optimism. 'So Jake Rhodes will receive a free bottle of champagne. Domestic.'

'This whole thing could backfire.' Karen ordered herself to be realistic. 'Even if you do get Adam to sign for the champagne—' She stopped short. 'You have a delivery pad for him to sign?'

'Yes, ma'am.' Neil produced this from another pocket. 'With phoney earlier deliveries on the sheet. Plus a plastic bag to store it once he signs.' *If he signs, she tormented herself.*

'There'll be a big blow-up with George Morrison,' Karen predicted, 'when I walk in and demand that Adam's finger-prints be checked against those unidentified ones. Without telling him whose fingerprints they are.' She frowned. '*If* they're still unidentified.'

'You spoke with him just yesterday morning. It isn't likely anything happened since then.' He chuckled. 'Things don't happen that fast in this town.'

'It's time for me to head next door,' Helen said briskly. 'Karen, take the pies out when the timer goes off. Oh, test them first with a knife,' she reminded. Two pies, the small one for Cindy and the kids, the over-sized for dinner at the Bradfords. 'If they're OK, take them out to cool and put in the turkey. I won't be more than half an hour. I'll be back before you two leave.'

'We should be stalking the Rhodes family by nine thirty-five,' Neil computed with an effort at humor. 'Services at their church start at 10 a.m.'

'Calm down,' Helen clucked. 'They're giving Cindy only fifteen minutes with Todd. She'll be back by nine twenty-five. And if they're generous and let her stay a few minutes longer, the turkey will manage without my presence.' She rose to her feet, lifted a fist in a playful poke at Neil's chin. 'You do good, you hear?'

9.28 a.m., Thanksgiving Day, 1997

Neil slid behind the wheel of his car. Helen had returned to the house moments ago. He was anxious that the Rhodes family might decide to leave early, that he wouldn't know when they'd departed.

'The car will be warm in a few minutes,' he promised Karen while he adjusted the heat. The sun had disappeared behind threatening clouds. The temperature had dropped several degrees.

'I'm fine.' Her smile belied her anxiety.

The first churchgoers were heading for Thanksgiving services. Here and there teenagers were rollerblading in high spirits. The pleasing scent of logs burning in fireplaces drifted into the morning cold. Neil slowed down to a crawl as they approached the Rhodes house.

'It's early,' Karen reminded. *Please God, let Althea manage to send Adam to answer the door.*

'There's Rhodes.' Neil drove past the house, focused on the rear-view mirror.

'He's headed for the garage—' Karen twisted about in her seat to follow Rhodes's progress. 'The others are coming out now.'

Neil turned at the next corner, then backed out onto the road again. They saw Jake Rhodes bring his white Mercedes – the only Mercedes in Paradise – out of the three-car garage, pull up before the entrance. Olivia and Betsy climbed into the rear. Jake's son-in-law joined him on the front seat.

'So far so good,' Neil said with an air of relief and continued on the road.

Minutes later the white Mercedes – its driver impatient with Neil's slow pace – sailed past in a burst of speed.

'I hope Adam's up this early—' Karen was anxious.

'Let's stall for ten minutes before I go up to the house. Just in case the family returns for something or other.' His eyes left the wheel for an instant to rest on Karen. 'Will it bother you if I park here by the woods?' Where they had discovered Debbie's body that awful night.

'No,' she lied. She never passed the woods without remembering how Harry had led them to that so shallow grave. 'It's the best observation point.'

They sat in the car beside the woods, stripped of its autumnal hues, winter gauntness taking over. Neil reached for her hand in comfort, launched into a story of a bitter winter in Sarajevo – in which he managed to inject a thread of humor.

Karen checked her watch. 'It's ten minutes – they're not coming back.'

'No. I'll walk there from here. Drive around and pick me up at the house – that way you can turn on the heat.' He leaned forward to kiss her lightly, reached in the back of the car for the package and notepad. 'Think positive, sugar.'

Neil walked with compulsive swiftness past the woods and onto the Rhodes property. He strode to the front door. The house was dead-of-night quiet. *Was Adam awake? Could Althea get him to answer the door?* He shifted the parcel to his left arm, positioned the pad and pencil in preparation for the plotted scene. He rang the bell. Waited. There was no response. He pushed the bell with new insistence. Then a shrill feminine voice filtered from inside.

'Adam! Will you please answer the door? It might be somebody for your father. I can't leave the kitchen.' A moment of silence, then Althea tried again. 'Adam!' A peremptory yet anxious tone in her voice. 'The others have gone to church. There's somebody at the door—'

Neil felt his throat tighten. *The little bastard wasn't coming down.*

'Adam, you have to go to the door!' Something akin to panic in her voice now. 'If it's something important for your father, he'll be furious if we don't answer.'

'All right, all right.' Adam was angry but complying. 'I don't know why you had to wake me so early when you know I never go to church with them.'

Neil heard Adam charging down the stairs now. He was crossing the foyer. He swung the door open. A hostile seventeen-year-old in jockey shorts and tee shirt. 'Shit, it's cold,' he bellowed. 'Come inside—'

'I have a delivery from the liquor store,' Neil said casually. 'I need somebody to sign for it.'

'I thought the whole town was closed up for the day.' He glared at Neil.

'Sure, but Mr Rhodes is a special customer,' Neil said with a show of respect as he extended pad and pencil. Play this cool. Todd's life was on the line. 'I guess he wanted champagne for Thanksgiving dinner.'

'My old man?' Adam jeered. But he took the pad, was signing the delivery page. 'Sorry, no tip,' he said and shrugged.

'That's OK. Have a nice Thanksgiving.' But Cindy and Todd and the kids weren't having a happy Thanksgiving. Jeannie and Doug weren't having a happy Thanksgiving.

'Yeah. Happy Thanksgiving.' Adam closed the door with a thud.

Neil pulled a plastic bag from a pocket of his jacket, carefully slid the pad inside and pressed the bag into locked position. Now he strode down the long driveway. His eyes searched for Karen. *Here she came.* He lifted a hand in greeting as she pulled up at the curb. His face telegraphed his triumph.

'You got it!' she interpreted, her smile radiant.

*   *   *

Neil lingered at the house briefly with Karen and Helen.

'I know it's a holiday,' he said ruefully, 'but I'm one of the working stiffs.'

'We'll see you at two,' Helen said in high spirits. 'Go work.'

Karen tried to steel herself for Thanksgiving dinner with Neil and his parents. Like Neil, his parents were eager for a story that would thrust the station into the limelight, she reminded herself. They were Mom's friends, yes – but the station was in a shaky financial position. Neil admitted that. If they broke the true story of the Debbie Norris murder, they'd be in a strong position.

Even if Neil meant what he said about the two of them, how could she expect him to remain here in Paradise? This would be a personal coup for him. After the hooplah died down, he'd be bored. He'd take off for some troubled spot in Asia or Europe or Africa. *He'll dash off and I'll never see him again.*

At shortly past noon Karen and Helen transported the 'small Thanksgiving dinner' from their kitchen to Cindy's. Harry sniffed hopefully at the roasting pan that contained the turkey. Laurie and Zachie were intrigued with the prospect of pumpkin pie.

'With ice-cream?' Laurie asked.

'With ice-cream,' Helen assured her, pulling the two children to her for an affectionate hug.

'Daddy likes pies with ice-cream—' All at once Laurie seemed incredibly sad. *A little girl should never feel that way.* 'When's he coming home?' Her eyes darted from Helen to Karen – as though knowing her mother could not provide a definitive answer.

'Soon,' Karen promised – knowing this was rash.

'From your lips to God's ear.' Cindy mouthed the words.

'And we've got something special for Harry,' Helen told the children with an air of conspiracy. 'But he can't have it till you all sit down at the dinner table.'

'Harry, too?' Laurie giggled at the vision of Harry at the table.

'It's not that he hasn't tried.' For a moment Cindy seemed to shed her ever-present anxiety. 'One day last week he climbed up on a chair and ate my scrambled eggs when I went out to the kitchen for a few minutes. He looked reproachful that there was no bacon.'

'Harry loves bacon,' Laurie reported. 'But Mommie says it's not good for us or him.' She sighed. 'We don't have it much anymore.'

'Tomorrow,' Cindy promised. 'The four of us will have bacon and eggs for breakfast. Once in a while it's all right.'

'We should go back and clean up the kitchen, then take off for the Bradfords,' Helen decided.

Karen debated in silence for a moment. 'Cindy, it's too early to know for sure – but we have a strong lead.'

'Something to clear Todd?' Cindy's face was luminous.

'I don't know for sure—' Karen forced herself to be honest. 'But I'm very hopeful.' Immediately Karen chastised herself for lifting Cindy's hopes. *Why did I tell her that? This whole deal can blow up in my face.*

Within ten minutes of sitting down with Neil's parents in their elegant yet cozy living room – an eclectic blend of eighteenth- and nineteenth-century reproductions – Karen understood why her grandmother was so fond of them. They were warm, bright, compassionate people. They hated what was happening to this town. They were so concerned for Todd. Yet she felt self-conscious, too, because she knew they and Mom were so hopeful that she and Neil would build a life together. Didn't they realize Neil wasn't going to stay here?

Could she ever build a practice in this town after all the ugliness she'd encountered? Maybe another small town somewhere – where the pace was slow and people worked to make their town special. But here was where – deep in her heart – she knew she wanted to put down roots. Here was Mom.

When his mother began to fuss over a delay in bringing the turkey from the oven, Neil at last arrived.

'Mom, I'm sorry to be late.' He turned to Karen – a glint in his eyes. 'You know my call-in show? There was one caller I spoke with after we went off the air.'

'About what?' His father leaned forward expectantly.

'He used to live in East Sedgewick. He's a pediatrician now in Linwood.' A small town eighteen miles away. 'He saw our 6 p.m. newscast on November fourteenth – when we reported on the request that the Tiffany Rollins case be reopened. He says he kept thinking about it.' He turned to Karen. 'He says he was at that party. Like Todd, he figured Tiffany was sixteen or seventeen. And she came on to Todd. He wanted to testify at the trial, but his family ordered him to stay out of it. I have his phone number and his address. Karen, he wants to talk to you.'

'Great!' The East Sedgewick district attorney was dubious about Tiffany's turn-around. *This was what she needed.* 'Of course, it won't clear Todd of the Debbie Norris murder. We still have hurdles to jump.' She exchanged a loaded glance with Neil. He hadn't told his parents about this morning's venture. The plastic bag with the pad that must be covered with Adam's fingerprints was safely tucked away in her desk. She ached to talk to George Morrison about the unidentified prints found in Debbie's room. It was going to be agonizing to wait until tomorrow morning to talk with him.

Now – with the two older women bringing Thanksgiving dinner to the table – there was a silent pact to put aside worrisome discussion. Neil's father launched into reminiscences about the sixties.

'Neil, you were with us at the Democratic convention in Chicago in 1968 – though I don't expect you to remember.' He turned to Karen. 'He was about fourteen months old and sporting a baseball cap that said "Humphrey for Prez". When his cap got knocked off, his mother decided it was time for us to cut out.' He winced in recall. 'Just before the rough stuff began.'

'Today people have a tendency to badmouth the young of the sixties,' Neil said somberly. 'But there was a lot of good going on back then. And some of it lingers,' he said defiantly. 'I remember a group of doctors from Columbia-Presbyterian down in New York – all with fancy practices – who took time out to come to Bosnia to help treat the wounded and sick in the worst of conditions. God, were they welcomed.' He chuckled. 'A throwback to the young of the sixties who also cared.'

But despite the concerted effort by those gathered about the festive table to generate a holiday spirit, Karen was restless, impatient to talk with George Morrison. She needed to give him Adam's prints – without naming Adam – to discover if they matched any of the prints found in Debbie's bedroom and that were as yet unidentified.

'I may never eat again,' Neil declared, demolishing the last of a wedge of pumpkin pie. 'Everything was so good.'

They lingered at the table over coffee, as though reluctant to relinquish the holiday mood. Yet Karen knew that – like herself – Neil was impatient for tomorrow morning to arrive, when she could confront George. With candid reluctance Helen and Arline Bradford announced they would clear the table, stack the dishwasher.

'Two sessions,' Frank Bradford commented. 'I'll help,' he offered and rejected their insistence that this wasn't required. Yet Karen suspected there was an unspoken conspiracy to leave her and Neil alone.

Karen and Neil settled themselves on the living-room sofa that faced the fireplace, where birch logs emitted a rosy glow.

'I'll put on more logs.' Neil rose to perform this small task – erecting a pyramid of astonishing height, poking and rearranging until flames spiraled to new heights.

'It's beautiful—' Karen felt herself almost relaxed as she watched the mesmerizing performance in the grate.

Neil returned to the sofa.

'You hate waiting until morning to talk to George—' He shared this feeling.

'Neil, would it be awful – unprofessional – if I tried to reach him at home right now?' By this time of day most residents of Paradise had consumed their Thanksgiving dinner, she suspected – were feeling mellow.

'You don't know where he's having his Thanksgiving dinner—'

'It's worth a try, isn't it? To see if he's home.'

'I'll look up the number.' Neil was on his feet. He crossed to the telephone table, reached for the book, located the number. 'Shall I dial for you?'

'Please.' In her mind Karen sought for words to explain the situation in a way that would not create hostility in the district attorney, while Neil dialed on the Victorian phone that blended with the traditional furniture of the room. Hearing a ring, he handed the phone to Karen.

'Hello—' A soft feminine voice replied at the other end.

'I'm sorry to intrude this way,' Karen apologized, 'but may I speak with George Morrison? This is Karen Mitchell.'

'Oh—' She sounded astonished rather than annoyed by the intrusion. 'Hold on, please.'

Moments later George was on the phone.

'What is it, Karen, that can't wait until tomorrow morning?' Irritation underlying an effort at jocularity.

'You said yesterday, George, that there were unidentified fingerprints in your files on the Norris case.'

'Yes.' Wariness blended with irritation now. 'So what has come up that can't wait until morning?'

'I have fingerprints that I'd like you to check against those. It's—'

'Karen, the prints go to a lab in Albany. They're very busy over there – I can't ask them to waste time on a wild-goose chase.'

'It's important to know if these match the prints found in Debbie's room. Then we'll—'

'Whose prints?' George demanded.

'I can't tell you that until I know he was in Debbie's room,' she began. 'I—'

'Are you working on a hunch?' he derided. 'Come on, Karen. This is a murder case.'

'It's more than a hunch. I assume you're aware of the cologne on the towel about Debbie's body?'

'Yeah, we know about that. We couldn't track it down.'

'Because it was made and distributed only in Europe. I traced it to the man with these fingerprints. If the prints match those unidentified ones in Debbie's room, I'll give you his name. George, you want to catch this killer as much as I do.'

Karen waited – her throat tight – while George Morrison considered this in silence.

'OK.' He was brusque. 'Bring me the prints first thing tomorrow morning. I'll see what I can do.'

George Morrison sat motionless while he recycled the information Karen had given him. She was on to something. Sure, he wanted a conviction. It would be a tremendous boost to his political career. But was Karen Mitchell just trying to undermine his case? Could he trust her?

What the hell was going on? He reached for the phone, tapped out a familiar number. Moments later a masculine voice greeted him.

'Hello—' Annoyed at this intrusion.

'We need to talk,' George said grimly. 'Shall I come over there or would you prefer to come here?'

'I'll be there in fifteen minutes.' A terse communication before George heard the receiver come down with a thud.

Thirty-Two

Triumph blended with unease in Karen as she considered the deal with George Morrison. She sat tense, shoulders hunched, and gazed without seeing at the smoldering logs in the fireplace.

'You don't trust George Morrison.' Neil read her thoughts.

'I don't know that we can,' she confessed. 'He's so determined to get a conviction. Will he lie to us about the fingerprints?'

Neil mentally debated this for a moment. 'We have to play it by ear. If he thinks you're about to upset his applecart, that he'll lose the case, he may go along with you.'

'He accepts Amos Rogers and Jim Drake's testimony about Todd's confessing to them – and we know that's a lie.' Exasperation lent sharpness to her voice.

'See what he comes up with on the unidentified fingerprints,' Neil urged. 'Take it from there.'

'You're counting on his being honest with me.' *Will he be?*

'We don't have much choice – we have to believe he will be.'

'You have a copier at the station?' Karen's mind was in high gear.

'Sure.' Neil raised his eyebrows in question.

'Make a copy of the page where Adam signed. Then cut out the signature on the original. If George is playing on Jake Rhodes's side, we don't want him to know whose fingerprints you're giving him.'

The other three strolled into the living room. Frank inspected Karen and Neil. His gaze was quizzical.

254

'You two look somber. Do you know something we don't know?'

While Neil's parents and Helen sat in flanking chairs, Neil explained about their tracing the cologne to Adam Rhodes – and about this morning's venture.

'Karen just spoke with George Morrison. She told him that if the fingerprints matched the unidentified ones found in Debbie's room, she'd give him the man's name.' Unexpectedly Neil chuckled. 'Today any boy over fifteen is a "man".'

'We realize we may be way off-base,' Karen conceded. 'It could be nothing more than coincidence that Adam bought that cologne in Switzerland. His fingerprints may not match those in Debbie's room. But it's a *possibility*.'

'You've done all you can today,' Helen said gently. 'Let's try to put it out of our minds for now.'

'I have to run over to the station for an hour.' Frank grunted in self-reproach. 'Why did I think running a TV station would be an easy life?' But his eyes said it was the life he loved.

'I picked up two videos yesterday.' Arline rose to her feet. 'Let's relax with an old Cary Grant film.'

'I'll buy that.' Helen nodded in approval. 'I complain about the rush of technology – but I love my VCR and my computer.'

'When they're working,' Karen joshed. 'I never knew Mom had such a colorful vocabulary until her computer malfunctioned one day last month.'

'Hurry back, Frank,' Arline ordered tenderly. 'This is Thanksgiving Day.'

The others settled down to enjoy *Bringing Up Baby*. Karen found her mind trailing off at intervals, though this was an old film she loved. She was haunted by the realization that Todd's trial was to begin on Monday morning. *She felt so unprepared.*

It was past five when Frank returned to the house.

'All quiet at the station,' he reported. 'I'm clear until 9 p.m.'

'Why don't we polish off the rest of that pumpkin pie?' Arline suggested. 'Helen, you do magical things with pies.'

'It's the bourbon mixed with the pumpkin.' Helen chuckled. 'Karen accuses me of trying to make us lushes. I love cooking with liquor.'

'Pumpkin pie on one condition,' Frank stipulated and grinned. 'I have a hankering for a big chunk of vanilla ice-cream to go with it.'

'Who's open on Thanksgiving Day?' Arline chided. 'You'll take it straight and be grateful.'

'That ice-cream place at the edge of town has a big sign out saying they'll be open Thanksgiving Day until 7 p.m.,' Neil recalled. 'I'll go pick up a carton. Come with me, Karen, since I've ingested bourbon with dinner?' Via the pumpkin pie.

'Yes,' Karen accepted. 'Though I'm not sure either of us could pass a breathalizer test. Mom put a wicked amount of bourbon into that pie.'

Karen and Neil left the house, climbed into his car. They didn't notice a dark green sedan parked across the road. A man slumped in the driver's seat – his face hidden by the newspaper he was reading. They were unaware that he abandoned the newspaper when Neil pulled away from the curb, reached for his ignition key. Followed them at a cautious distance.

Karen stared up at the darkening sky. 'It's getting dark so early now.'

'This is the end of November,' Neil reminded. 'It's just over three weeks until we arrive at the shortest day in the year.'

'I miss the long stretches of daylight,' she said wistfully.

'You'd hate living in the Arctic Circle.'

'I like living here—' Involuntarily she turned to Neil. How much longer would he stay here in Paradise?

'I came home expecting to stay three months,' Neil mused. 'Now it's over eight months.' But that didn't answer the question that haunted her.

'We're not the only ones with an urge for ice-cream.' Karen

gazed in amusement at the line-up of cars at the parking area of their destination. Neither she nor Neil were aware that the dark green sedan followed them onto the area.

Here the holiday atmosphere was on display. Motorists lined up to buy ice-cream, frozen yogurt or more elaborate concoctions. Karen and Neil left the car, joined the line. The sky darkening into night as they waited their turn to be served. Watching a pair of ebullient little ones, Karen thought with a surge of compassion about Laurie and Zachary at home with Cindy on this familial occasion and so conscious of the absence of their father.

'Cold?' Neil was solicitous when Karen – feeling Cindy and the children's sense of desolation – involuntarily shuddered.

'No, I'm fine.' But she welcomed his arm about her as they waited. Not because of the cold.

With the quart of French Vanilla in tow, Karen and Neil returned to the car. Total night had descended. Not a star in the sky, not even a sliver of moon relieved the darkness. Headlights seemed garishly bright as they drove out of the parking area. Both oblivious to the dark green sedan that followed them once more.

'We should have bought ice-cream to take to Cindy and the children,' Neil said in self-reproach. 'Shall we go back?'

'Cindy bought ice-cream when Mom drove her to the supermarket before going into the shop yesterday morning.' How considerate of Neil. 'They're all set.'

Karen was astonished by the amount of traffic on the road this evening. Still, the dark green sedan allowed no more than one car to separate them. At the next turn Neil headed for the short cut to his parents' house. Now the traffic dwindled. Only their car and the dark green sedan behind them appeared interested in this route.

'Cindy gave me another dozen pages that Todd wrote. He's so depressed about the way this town has turned on him.'

Neil stole what was meant to be a fleeting glance at Karen, then suddenly shouted, 'Karen, get down!'

Not waiting for her response, he shoved her down on the seat, shielding her with his body – no more than a second before a shot rang out, whizzed over his head and out the driver's side window. Simultaneously he swung off the road onto a vacant lot, slammed on the brakes. The car came to a rough, clamorous stop.

'Oh, my God!' Karen straightened up in shock. 'Somebody meant to kill me!'

'It was dark – and too quick – for me to get a look at the driver. It was a dark green sedan with 'MP' somewhere on the license plate.' He switched on the interior light. 'You OK?'

Karen nodded. 'You could have been killed! You saved my life—' *How could she have ever doubted Neil?*

'We're all right – both of us.' He pulled her – cold and trembling – into his arms.

She lifted her face to Neil's, welcomed the warmth of his mouth on hers. They clung together, for a few moments oblivious to the near-tragedy that had shadowed them.

'I've waited so long for this.' Neil pressed his face against hers. 'I was afraid to rush you—'

'I was afraid you were playing games with me,' she confessed, hearing his heart pound against her. 'That after the trial you'd take off for some far-off place, and I'd never see you again.'

'I knew that first day – when you charged out of the Norrises' house and lit into me that way – that you were the one woman who could fit into my life. And I was afraid, too – that once this trial was over and you were a big-name attorney – you'd take off for New York again.'

'Wherever you want to be, I'll go with you,' she said recklessly. 'I know that'll be right for me.'

'Oh God,' he shuddered. 'How close I came to losing you!' Now his face grew taut with rage. 'You must report this to George Morrison immediately. As district attorney he has to investigate this attempt on your life.'

'We're getting too close to the truth about Debbie's murder. Somebody's scared. Neil—' She stiffened in his arms.

'George could be part of this! Just two hours ago I told him about the fingerprints – and the cologne.'

Neil pondered for a few moments. 'George is as ambitious as hell – but I don't see him as a party to murder. But we'll know fast enough if he is. Call him when we get back to the house. Tell him somebody tried to kill you. Somebody in a dark green sedan with a license number that incorporates the letters "MP". Let's see how he follows this up.'

The driver in the green sedan was sweating despite the coldness of the night. The driver's side window still open. *Hell, did I get her? I won't know until we hear the late news.*

The boss said, 'Go to the house after dark. You'll be close enough for a good shot. If you think the old lady is about to cause trouble, get her, too.'

Now he closed the window, slowed down. This wasn't the night to get picked up for speeding. There was no way he could get at the house with all those folks around. He had to go back a block, pick up the car and trail her and the boyfriend. No way he could have been seen – the night pitch black, no street lights. *But did I get her?*

Pumpkin pie and ice-cream were forgotten while Karen and Neil reported on what had occurred en route to the house. Helen and Neil's parents listened – faces drained of color.

'This is a nightmare.' Helen's voice was shrill with shock. 'Who would do such a thing?'

'Somebody who's terrified that Karen knows who raped and murdered Debbie Norris,' Frank pinpointed.

'If the fingerprints Neil collected this morning match the unidentified ones in Debbie's bedroom, we'll know that Adam Rhodes killed Debbie – and that his father is behind the attempt on my life.' Still unnerved by her close brush with death, Karen left her chair and crossed to the phone. 'Let's see if George Morrison is playing games with me about those fingerprints.'

Karen punched in George Morrison's home phone number. This time he answered.

'Hello—' A guarded greeting, Karen thought in a corner of her mind.

'George, something quite unpleasant just occurred.' She struggled to keep her voice even. 'About ten minutes ago somebody took a shot at me from a passing car. Only because Neil Bradford has quick reflexes am I alive to report this.'

'Good Lord!' George sounded shaken. 'Did either of you get a look at the car? The license plate?'

'We were on Sycamore Road – there are no street lights back there – and it's a dreary night. We know it was a dark green sedan with the letters MP somewhere on the plate.'

'We'll work from there.' George was terse. 'And first thing tomorrow morning I want you to bring me those fingerprints,' he reminded, 'I'll take them right over to Albany, explain this is a rush.' He hesitated a moment. 'I'll have a police car cruise around your block for the rest of the night.'

6.30 p.m., Thanksgiving Day, 1997

Olivia welcomed an excuse to take Betsy up to her room and go through the bedtime ritual. These holidays at home with her father were always fraught with tension. Thank God, Dad and Bill maintained a truce – none of the verbal battles that erupted in earlier years because Dad resented Bill's refusal to come into the business. Bill disapproved of Dad's business tactics.

But this was Betsy's only living grandparent, she reminded herself. This was the reason for the holiday visits – so Betsy could have a sense of family. So missing from her own growing-up years.

'Mommie, when are we going home?' Betsy was restless here.

'Sunday night, darling. Oh, tomorrow Althea said she's going to let you help her make a fancy layer cake.'

'All right.' Betsy seemed resigned. 'But we missed the Thanksgiving Day parade on television again.'

'You'll see it when we get home,' Olivia soothed. 'Don't you remember? Cathy's mommie taped it for you.'

Olivia endured the usual bedtime delays, then returned downstairs. She heard her father on the phone in the den as she reached the bottom of the stairs.

'Damn it, George, we don't want any sideshows to halt the trial. You tell Judge Reagan no shenanigans. I wouldn't be surprised if that bitch Mitchell cooked up this whole story about a murder attempt on her life. She's looking for headlines. Mayor Gilbert's a good friend – he wants to see his granddaughter's murderer receive the death penalty. Don't screw up, George.'

Olivia returned to the living room, where her husband and Adam were watching the news from a neighboring TV station. Dad rejected the local station as 'a bad influence in this town'. She sat down – recoiling from the commentator's graphic description of the sensational rape and murder of Deborah Norris. That's all this town seemed to think about these days.

Dad talked scathingly about Doug Norris, Jean's husband. Was he serious about firing Doug for saying he wasn't sure that the police had the right man? Sometimes it scared her – the power Dad wielded in this town.

'Hey, I know we had a huge dinner – but what about an early supper?' Bill grinned. 'You got two growing boys here.' Like herself, he sometimes felt much sympathy for Adam.

'We'll have dinner leftovers in a little while,' Olivia promised. They both knew they'd wait for her father's announcement that he felt the proper time had arrived. Bill, too, detested the way Dad set himself up as the rulemaker in the family as well as in the town. Dad was the major reason they'd moved away from Paradise. 'Do we have to watch this?' she demanded impatiently as the commentator began to recall Todd Simmons's earlier conviction for rape.

'I want to see it,' Adam said doggedly. 'Dad says the guy's sure to be convicted. Everybody knows he's guilty.'

8.20 a.m., Friday, November 28, 1997

George Morrison drove into the parking area shared by the town's offices and the local police precinct. He stifled a yawn as he left his car. Damn, he'd had a rotten night's sleep.

He should have insisted that Karen Mitchell tell him who owned those fingerprints she was pushing him to check out. And who the hell took a shot at her? Did it have something to do with Debbie Norris's murder?

He left the car and headed for the side entrance to the building. Stopped short. His mind replayed Karen Mitchell's description of the car she claimed was driven by a man who tried to shoot her last night. *'We know it was a dark green sedan with the letters MP somewhere on the license plate.'*

His eyes focused on the dark green sedan to his right, zeroed in on the license plate. The letters 'MP' jumped out at him. The driver of this car tried to kill Karen Mitchell last night. *Why?*

Thirty-Three

T he morning was dank and grey. Fog hung low over the town. Stepping from the cozy warmth of the car into the parking area adjoining the district attorney's offices, Karen shivered for a moment in silent reproach, then reached for the zipper of her red down jacket. Neil had emerged from the driver's side. They hurried towards the side entrance to the building.

Ushered into his office, they found George Morrison at his desk – on the phone in brusque conversation. He waved them to chairs. Moments later he slammed down the phone, turned to them.

'You have the fingerprints?' he asked without preliminaries.

'Right here.' Neil handed over the plastic bag sheltering the notepad.

George took it, frowned at the cut-out segment of the page, where Adam had signed for the package. 'What's this crap?'

Karen refused to relinquish her aura of confidence. 'Never mind that I cut out the signature. The lab will find fingerprints.' But she tensed as he glared at her. 'I told you, George. Unless the prints were found in Debbie's bedroom, I see no reason to implicate him.' She'd have no case against him.

'I can't ask the lab to waste time because you have a hunch.' He'd said that last night. 'I need to know his name.' Last night's air of cooperation replaced by hostility.

'Tell me these prints match ones found in Debbie's room, and you'll have it,' Karen reiterated.

The atmosphere was suddenly super-charged. Karen's heart began to pound. Last night he'd said, *'Bring me the prints first thing in the morning. I'll see what I can do.' What's happened since last night?*

George ruminated for several moments that seemed minutes. He cleared his throat, hesitated. 'I have something interesting to report. I have a lead on the driver of that green sedan with MP on its license plate.'

Neil leaned forward intently. 'Who is he?'

George gazed from Neil to Karen. 'Tell me who belongs to these prints, and I'll tell you who drives that green sedan.'

'Adam Rhodes,' she said quietly. 'Jake Rhodes's son.'

George gaped in disbelief. 'You're off your rocker!'

'Adam was here in town at the time Debbie was murdered. He was in Switzerland last summer – where he bought a bottle of cologne. The same fragrance found on the towel wrapped around Debbie's body. A fragrance not distributed in this country.'

George squinted in thought – absorbing these facts. Still, he exuded doubts. 'You can prove this business about the cologne?' Suspicion lent harshness to his voice. *He was reluctant to accept what was staring him in the face.*

'Get a warrant to search Adam's bedroom.' George snorted contemptuously. Karen read his mind: *'A warrant to search Jake Rhodes's house?'* 'Hidden in a corner of Adam's closet you'll find an almost empty bottle. The scent still lingers. The same as on that towel,' she reiterated.

George reeled. His face was drained of color. Karen understood; facts unknown to her were leaping into an ugly pattern in his brain.

'The cologne plus the fingerprints – if they're the same as the unidentified ones in his room,' she conceded, 'will prove that Adam Rhodes raped and murdered Debbie Norris.'

George deliberated a few seconds. 'I'm driving to the Albany lab right now. I'll get a fast check on the prints.

If Adam Rhodes's fingerprints—' He paused, attacked by fresh distrust. 'How do I know these *are* Adam's prints?' he challenged. 'In this town you don't question Jake Rhodes's son without knowing you have good cause.'

'OK, we used a ruse to get Adam's fingerprints.' Neil turned to Karen. 'Show him the copy of the original with Adam's signature.'

Karen reached into a pocket, pulled out a copy of the original sheet, handed it to George. He studied it, suspicion waning. His mouth settled into a thin tight line.

'If this backfires,' George warned Karen, 'I'll have your head. If I make a move against Adam, and it won't hold up, I'm dead in this town.'

'If his fingerprints match those in Debbie's room – and you find the bottle of cologne, how can you be wrong?' But Karen was trembling. 'That's a tight case.'

'You haven't told us yet who owns a green sedan with MP on its license plate,' Neil reminded. 'We had an agreement.'

'The car belongs to Amos Rogers.'

'Who lied about Todd's confessing to him,' Karen pounced. 'Under Jake Rhodes's orders.' She saw George flinch. He'd believed – like so many others – that Todd was guilty.

'I'm issuing orders to have Rogers taken into custody on suspicion of attempted murder.' George's face was taut with rage. 'Then I'm heading to Albany.'

'May we go with you?' Karen asked.

'Why not?' George shrugged. 'But first, give us a statement about what happened to you last night. A statement from both of you,' he emphasized. 'Amos Rogers has a lot of explaining to do.'

9.40 a.m., Friday, November 28, 1997

Karen was impatient that the fog had not yet lifted. The car moved ahead with frustrating slowness. At intervals George swore under his breath as another vehicle swerved perilously close.

Neil grunted in disgust. 'It's taking us twice the normal time because of the fog.'

'I have a crew standing by at the lab to check out the fingerprints,' George said. 'They'll give us an answer pretty damn quick.'

Now – at last – Karen and Neil sat waiting in an office at the fingerprint lab. After what seemed an interminable time, George emerged from an inner office. Karen searched his face – inscrutable at first. Then he nodded. Karen rose to her feet. *What had he learned?*

'The fingerprints match. I'm bringing in Adam Rhodes for questioning. On charges of raping and murdering Deborah Norris.' George shuddered. 'God, that'll turn this town upside down!'

'There'll be a lot of changes made,' Karen predicted softly. Jake Rhodes no longer the town's dictator. 'Let's hope it'll be better for all that's happened.'

George's eyes appraised Neil. 'I'll want prime time on the station to report my findings once I've questioned Adam. Karen will appear with me. We worked together to bring the real murderer to justice.' He was throwing her a bone, Karen understood. *But Todd would be cleared.* 'And I'll want a tape on the segment.'

'You'll have the time,' Neil promised. 'And the tapes.'

For future political campaigns, Karen pinpointed.

'Wait for me in the car,' George ordered. 'I have a phone call to make.'

Karen and Neil left the lab to return to the car. George retreated to an office where he could make his phone call. His mind was in turmoil. Sure, he danced to Jake's music. The old man helped put him in office. He couldn't have made it without that extra push. He'd paid his dues – got jobs for people at the old man's orders. Even Jim Drake – whom he didn't particularly like. But this was more than rough politics. How could he help cover up a murder? Not even when it meant bringing in Jake's son. But he felt a tightness in his throat. His stomach churned.

266

Can I handle this? Suppose Jake manages to extricate Adam from this lousy situation? Where will I be? He's played footsie with Clay Gilbert for at least twenty years – Clay owes him big. What happens if Clay lies for Adam, says, 'Naturally Adam's fingerprints were in Debbie's room – he was there that afternoon. Bringing a gift for Debbie.' What happens to me then? Shouldn't I go to Jake before I bring in Adam?

12.28 p.m., Friday, November 28, 1997

Karen was conscious of an odd withdrawal by George Morrison as he drove them back to town. He wasn't playing a game with them, was he? No, he'd identified the fingerprints as belonging to Adam. He didn't try to cover for Adam. But apprehension infiltrated her earlier jubilation.

Not until she and Neil had left George at the parking lot did she confess to him her mounting fears.

'He has to bring in Adam. He may go through another fingerprint check – but the results will be the same.' Neil refused to relinquish his air of satisfaction. 'Todd won't be released instantly – there're formalities to go through. But George knows Adam is his murderer.'

'Which tells him that Jake Rhodes engineered that fake confession. That Rhodes hired Amos Rogers to kill me.' How would George react to prosecuting Jake Rhodes? 'Neil, we're on dangerous ground—'

Neil's hands tightened on the steering wheel. 'George issued orders for Rogers to be taken into custody. Rhodes will try to push George to release Rogers for "insufficient evidence". We can't let that happen.'

'By now Amos must have been picked up and taken to the police precinct.' Karen's mind charged ahead. 'Let's go talk to Amos's wife. She must have a strong suspicion – if she doesn't actually know – that Amos was following Jake Rhodes's orders. Let's make her understand she must convince Amos to cooperate with the police—'

Neil nodded. 'Spill his guts. Name Jake Rhodes. Before Jake can make a move to get him out of jail.'

'That's the scenario.' *Could they handle it?*

'Let me talk to Amos's wife,' Neil urged. 'It could be judged a conflict of interest if Todd's attorney approaches her. I'm from the TV station, following up the story,' he improvised. 'I'll make her understand the court will be much lighter on Amos if he cooperates. If he behaves himself in prison, his sentence will be cut even shorter. It's for his own good to tell everything that happened.'

'Call Information on the cell phone – get Amos's home address. Every minute is important!' The local phone company would give out the address.

Amos Rogers lived in a modest section of town. Arriving at his street, Neil drove slowly while Karen searched for the house number.

'That's it!' Karen pointed just ahead. 'Where the squad car is pulling away.' A small, white frame house that hungered for a coat of paint. 'Detectives must have been here questioning his wife.' *Even if George allows himself to be manipulated by Rhodes, he'll have to put up a pretense of investigating the case. How many dark green cars in Paradise, New York have 'MP' on their license plate?*

'We'll drive around the area for about five minutes,' Neil said. 'Allow what's happening to her husband to sink into her mind. There's no car in the driveway – she isn't going anywhere.'

Karen sat in the car, parked a hundred feet beyond the house, and waited while Neil strode to his destination. In the rear-view mirror she saw him ring the doorbell. The door was opened. He was talking to the woman who responded.

'Mrs Rogers, I'm Neil Bradford – from the local television station. We're following up a police report that your husband has been arrested in charges of attempted murder. His car was identified as—'

'I don't want to talk to you!' Visibly distraught, she made a frantic attempt to close the door, but Neil forestalled this.

'You can be helpful to his case,' Neil pursued. 'There are ways to lighten his sentence.' Her eyes told him she expected Amos to go to prison. 'The police know he owns the car from which shots were fired at Karen Mitchell last night. Please, let's talk about this. It's for your husband's good.'

She debated a moment, then pulled the door wide, admitted him into the small, neat but shabby living room. Pale and trembling, she sat at one end of the sofa, gestured to Neil to join her there.

'The police know that Amos was not working on his own,' Neil said with an air of sympathy. 'He'll have to go to prison – but his sentence will be cut much shorter if he cooperates with the police. If he tells them everything he knows. And if he behaves himself in prison, his sentence will be cut even shorter. He could be out in eighteen months,' Neil guessed. 'If he cooperates with the police.'

'I don't know—' She wavered. 'He don't even have a lawyer.'

'The TV station will provide him with a lawyer,' Neil promised. 'We'll—'

'We don't have no money,' she warned. 'We're payin' off a mortgage on the house, the car loan, dentist bills for my root canal—'

'The station will pay the lawyer – if Amos cooperates with the police.'

'Why?' Suddenly she was suspicious. 'Why would you do that?'

'We want an exclusive interview with Amos,' Neil fabricated. 'He has to agree to that.'

'Suppose he won't talk to the cops? He's awful stubborn sometimes.'

'Make him understand he's going to prison – but he can cut his time way back by cooperating.'

'He's such a dumb jerk.' All at once she was furious. 'I told him over and over again – you're headed for trouble, doin' Jake Rhodes's dirty work—' She stopped dead, shaken by this inadvertent revelation. 'How do I know you ain't just

269

handin' me a line? How do I know the TV station will pay for a lawyer for Amos?'

'Give me a sheet of paper and a pen. I'll write it out for you. I'm an officer of the company – I can make that commitment.'

A few minutes later – her eyes trained to the entrance to the Rogers house – Karen saw Neil emerge with Amos's wife. Hastily she reached into the glove compartment for the sunglasses Neil kept there. She heard his casual remark as they approached the car. 'My girlfriend's in the car. You don't mind, do you?'

Contriving not to introduce her to Mrs Rogers, Neil seated the other woman in the rear of the car. She was agitated but seemed determined to go through with the deal she'd made with Neil.

He reached into the car for his cell phone and – standing outside – he made a call. To the station, she surmised. To make arrangements for the station attorney to represent Amos Rogers – as they'd plotted before Neil talked to Mrs Rogers. No doubt in his mind that his father would go along with this.

En route to the police precinct, Neil told Mrs Rogers that he would go in with her and explain that she had to talk with her husband about legal representation. That would be allowed.

But would Amos Rogers agree to talk?

Neil argued good-humoredly with the desk sergeant about who would be playing in the Rose Bowl this year. Only a tic in his left eye – unnoticed by the sergeant – revealed his anxiety. If Amos Rogers wasn't scared into talking fast, there was a strong chance that Jake Rhodes would send in a team to handle him.

Neil tensed when Mrs Rogers walked into view.

'My husband Amos has got somethin' to say,' she told the sergeant. 'He wants to make a deal with the prosecution.'

'Yes, ma'am!' The desk sergeant reached for the phone. 'We'll take care of that.'

'His lawyer will be comin' over soon—' She turned to Neil. 'Ain't that right?'

'That's right. I'll drive you home now.'

Karen was impatient for Neil to come into view. Mrs Rogers was talking avidly, hands gesturing. What happened inside? *Neil was smiling. Amos had bought their offer.*

In the car Amos's wife appeared relieved at the results.

'Amos ain't dumb,' she rejected her earlier accusation. 'He knows he could go up for a long stretch. And it don't make no sense for him to go on protectin' that fat cow Jake Rhodes. It was Rhodes who hired him for the hit. He didn't say why he wanted that lawyer woman out of the picture, but Amos has a pretty good idea.' Karen slid down in her seat. Mrs Rogers didn't know she was 'that lawyer woman'. 'I told him not to do it – but he wouldn't listen. Adam's been in trouble almost since the day he was born. The old man's been payin' off the housekeeper before this one for over five years because Adam was messin' around with her seven-year-old. When he was only twelve. Jake Rhodes thinks nobody knows, but things like that get around. The man that does his yard work told us. The housekeeper caught them doin' it.'

Amos's wife talked compulsively about her efforts through the years to straighten him out. Then they arrived at her house.

'You did the right thing,' Neil told her as he pulled up at the curb.'

'I don't know how I'm gonna manage while Amos is away,' she fretted. 'He's one of them guys who don't want his wife to work. We been married since I wuz sixteen – I never held no regular job.'

'We'll help you find a job,' Neil promised, including Karen in this.

'We'll get together with you early next week,' Karen said gently. 'I'm sure we'll come up with something.'

'Todd won't be released right away,' Neil reminded Karen while they drove away. 'You know, there're formalities.'

'I know.' But her heart was singing. *Todd would be cleared.*

'You'll tell Cindy – she'll take the word to Todd before he can be officially notified.'

'I can't believe it's really happening. I was so scared – I felt so inadequate to defend Todd.'

'You pulled it off.' Neil took a hand from the wheel to reach for hers. 'He'll be cleared in the Rollins case, too.'

'I couldn't have done it without you.' In such a short span of time Neil had become such an important part of her life.

'We're a team. I think that together we can make a difference in this town. I think this is where we should set down roots.'

Karen's face was luminous. Neil wanted to stay here in Paradise. He meant it.

'Yes,' she whispered. 'I'd like that.'

'How would you feel about a December wedding?'

'Late December,' she pinpointed. 'Paula and Ron and Jill will be able to come out here for Christmas. It wouldn't be legal for me to be married without Paula present.'

'Now that the wedding date is set,' he murmured, 'do you suppose we can indulge in a pre-wedding night rehearsal?' His eyes were eloquent.

'First we have to tell Cindy what's happened,' she stipulated, her heart pounding. 'She and the kids will be so happy. Let's stop at the florist shop and pick up flowers—'

'I'll agree to that,' he said huskily. 'But let's keep it brief. I need to make love to my future wife.'

Thirty-Four

6.03 p.m., Friday, November 28, 1997

N eil took his place before the cameras, waited for his signal. He'd been churning for hours for this moment to arrive, when he could release the latest news about the murder – and attempted murder. Just four minutes ago George Morrison had given him the go-ahead.

'And now for "breaking news."' His voice anticipated the drama sure to be evoked by his message. 'New developments in the tragic murder of Debbie Norris vindicate Todd Simmons. Now in police custody are Adam Rhodes, seventeen, on charges of rape and murder; his father, Jake Rhodes, on charges of complicity in the murder plus additional charges of ordering a "hit" on Simmons's attorney, Karen Mitchell; and Amos Rogers and Jim Drake on perjury charges connected with the murder cover-up. Also, attorney Karen Mitchell has just received confirmation that the East Sedgewick district attorney is reviewing new evidence in the Rollins rape case of some years ago that will clear Simmons of that charge, also. Now let me return you to your early evening newscaster.'

Neil left the studio, headed for his father's office. His 'breaking news' reached out to invade the personal lives of many local residents. But after the initial shock, he reasoned, they would understand that their fate as employees of Rhodes Shirt Factory would not be in jeopardy. In truth, their situations should improve. Olivia's husband – well-liked, Dad said, during his brief tenure – would move in to take over the company. And local politics, Neil told himself with statisfaction, were due for a vigorous housecleaning.

In his father's office, he found both parents on phone calls.

'Sorry, we have no further information at this time,' Frank said with strained patience and put down the phone. 'God, all at once this is a madhouse!'

'Marcie, I know – the phones will be ringing off the hook until we go off the air at midnight,' his mother soothed on another phone. 'Don't put through anybody else. Tell them all the same thing. When new information comes through, we'll provide "breaking news".' Returning the phone to its cradle, Arline uttered a long, anguished sigh.

'Mom, you ought to be happy,' Neil chided good-humoredly. 'This is great news.'

'I know – but I worry. How can we keep Cindy and Todd and the kids here in town?' She smiled at Neil's startled reaction. 'If it were you, would you want to stay? And if they leave, this town will never recover from its shame.'

9.18 a.m., Saturday, November 29, 1997

The atmosphere in the Simmons' cozy living room was joyous. Reflecting this mood, morning sunlight laid ribbons of gold across the floor, the furniture. For the dozenth time since Karen had arrived twenty minutes ago, Cindy fussed with sofa pillows. Laurie and Zachary sat with rare immobility in their diminutive rockers with a poignant air of expectancy.

'Cindy, relax,' Karen coaxed. 'The room looks lovely.' Cindy had cleaned and polished since dawn. The red roses that she and Neil had brought yesterday sat in colorful display on the large, square coffee table.

All at once Harry leapt up from his prone position, paused an instant, then charged towards the door – barking exuberantly.

'They're here!' Cindy rushed to the foyer, opened the door, pulled it wide. Karen following her. Todd and Neil were striding up the path to the entrance. 'Todd! Oh, Todd, we've missed you so!' Cindy rushed into his arms.

Laurie and Zachary darted forward to greet their father. Harry jumped in welcome. Tears filled Karen's eyes while she watched the emotional reunion.

'Hey, Cindy, you're not supposed to cry,' Todd joshed tenderly. 'You're supposed to be happy.'

'Darling, I've never been so happy.'

'You know what I want?' Todd said in high spirits – Zachary in one arm, Laurie clinging to the other. 'A decent cup of coffee. I haven't had one in almost three months. Cindy, I'll bet you have coffee up.'

'Oh, honey, yes!' Cindy was radiant. 'We've waited breakfast for you. Your favorite banana fritters.'

For a little while they were all content to sit around the table in the dining area and focus on breakfast. Everyone seemed ravenous this morning. As though, at last, it was acceptable to relish small pleasures. Not until Laurie and Zachary were persuaded to settle themselves on the living-room floor to demonstrate their growing skills with puzzles did the conversation acquire a serious note.

'The most horrendous part of all,' Todd said with remembered pain, 'was not knowing what would happen to Cindy and the kids without me. I was so—'

'That's over,' Cindy broke in. 'You're home.'

He reached for Cindy's hand, turned to Karen. 'I owe my life to you – and to you, Neil, and to those who came forward to help you.'

'We owe you so much in legal fees, Karen,' Cindy added. 'But we'll—'

'No more fees,' Karen dismissed this. 'You've paid enough. This was a learning experience for me. And Todd, the East Sedgewick district attorney wants to speak with you. It's a mere formality now – Tiffany's testimony will clear you.'

Todd managed a faint smile, but his eyes were serious. 'We'll have to pull our lives together again. It's too late to find regular teaching jobs this school year – but—'

'We'll put the house up for sale, clear out of this town,' Cindy interrupted. 'I can't wait to put all this ugliness, this horror behind us.'

'Cindy, don't rush into such a huge decision,' Karen urged. *This was what Mom feared.*

'Why don't you and Todd try to unwind for a little while?' Neil suggested. 'Enjoy being together again.'

Karen saw their eyes meet, felt their hunger for each other, their need to be alone. 'Why don't I take the kids over to the petting zoo? They open at ten on Saturdays.' Without waiting for a reply she called to them in the living room. 'Laurie, Zachie, would you like to go over to the petting zoo with me? Remember what fun it was last time?'

'Yeah! Yeah!' Laurie and Zachary abandoned the puzzle, darted into the dining area.

'Mommie, can we?' Laurie clamored, while Zachary hovered hopefully before her.

'I'll go with you,' Neil offered and grinned. 'It's my day off – and I haven't been to a petting zoo in twenty years.' A sympathetic glint in his eyes, he turned to Cindy and Todd. 'We'll be back in about two hours—'

'Let me get your coats, kids.' Cindy was on her feet. She pantomimed a grateful 'thank you' to Karen. 'And wear your gloves,' she ordered Laurie and Zachary. 'It's cold outside.'

'Remember,' Karen said. 'Mom's expecting the four of you over for a small welcome home dinner party tonight. Just us and Neil's parents and Mom's friend Althea Jackson – who was a big help in nailing Adam. When Laurie and Zachie get tired, we'll put them to bed in my room.'

'When shall we be there?' Cindy reached for Todd's hand.

'Around seven o'clock,' Karen told her. 'Todd, it's so good to have you home.'

Helen checked the roast in the oven while Karen finished setting the dining table – expanded to accommodate ten.

'I can't bear the thought of Cindy and Todd moving away,'

Helen repeated for the twentieth time. 'Though I understand how they feel.'

'Mom, you're friendly with the Millers, aren't you?' A campaign was taking root in Karen's mind.

'Beth Miller and I serve together on the committee for the women's shelter.' Helen's face brightened. She read Karen's mind. 'Do you suppose, if the Millers asked them to come back to the school, Cindy and Todd might change their minds about leaving?'

'It's worth a try. Cindy knows the Millers never believed Todd was guilty. They were pressured by parents to fire them.'

Helen glowed. 'I'll call Beth now.'

Karen listened while Helen talked with Beth. First they discussed the awful past weeks, then the shattering discovery that strong evidence indicated that Adam Rhodes had raped and murdered Debbie Norris and that his father, Amos Rogers, and Jim Drake had collaborated in a cover-up.

'Oh, there's no doubt that they'll all be found guilty,' Helen told Beth. She listened for a few moments while Beth talked, then picked up on her end. 'Karen and I are so upset. Cindy and Todd plan to move away. It would be such a loss to this community. I'm wondering, Beth – if you and Fred offered to take them back on the faculty, would they—'

Helen paused, her face luminous. 'Yes, I think it would be great if you made that offer to them! They're coming over for dinner – they'll be here in ten or fifteen minutes. Why don't you come over and talk with them?'

Again, Helen was listening. 'Yes, do come right over. Both you and Fred!'

She put down the phone, waited for the disconnect, dialed again. 'Cindy, could you all could come over a little early – say, in the next ten or fifteen minutes? I have something to show you before the others arrive.' She put down the phone. 'They're coming.'

'Oh, Mom, let's hope this works!' Still, Karen was anxious.

'That's step number one,' Helen said. 'We need to do more.'

'Some kind of public apology?' Karen searched her mind. 'A committee from the town approaching them?'

'Stronger.' Helen exuded determination. 'A town dinner,' she plotted. 'A benefit for the women's shelter – with Cindy and Todd as honored guests and Clay Gilbert offering the town's apology. We—'

'Will the mayor do that?' Karen was dubious.

'You bet he will. He's been too close to Jake Rhodes. He could lose the next election if he doesn't redeem himself. We've been talking about a benefit dinner – but holding off because the town's been in mourning over Debbie's death. But the time is right now.'

Karen was ambivalent. 'Cindy's so bitter—'

'Pray that we can bring it off,' Helen said softly.

Moments later Neil arrived.

'Mom and Dad will be along later,' he said. 'I drove Althea Jackson home from the station and—' He paused, chuckled at their startled air. 'We just filmed an interview with Althea to appear on the eleven o'clock news.' He saw their air of astonishment. 'It was a quick decision on her part – she called me to say she was distrustful of the police – knowing Jake Rhodes's influence. She wanted to go on record telling what she knew of Adam's background.'

'Althea felt she owed Jake her loyalty.' Helen was sympathetic. 'But now she sees him for what he is.'

'Rhodes's daughter Olivia is distraught over what's happened. She told Althea that Rhodes pays off his previous housekeeper – in monthly checks rather than a lump sum, to avoid continuous blackmail – because Adam molested her little girl when he was twelve. Adam was thrown out of his boarding school two years later for molesting the small daughter of a faculty member. Jake hushed that up by giving the school a new gym. Adam was at a sanitarium in Switzerland last summer – not in a summer camp. Olivia kept telling herself Adam had just touched these little girls in an unacceptable manner. That it was a sickness. She'd always made sure that Betsy was never alone with him. When she realized he'd raped and murdered Debbie Norris, she fell apart.'

'I think Althea will acquire a new job,' Helen said. 'We'll need a competent woman to handle the battered women's shelter. I don't know a soul who'll vote against hiring her.'

Karen glowed. 'Cindy and Todd and the kids are coming—'

She hurried to the side door to admit them. Laurie and Zachary chattered in high spirits about their visit earlier in the day to the petting zoo. Helen rushed to embrace Todd, expressed her relief and joy that justice was at last arriving in Paradise, New York. Karen focused on the children.

'I have a new puzzle for you two,' Karen cajoled, extending a hand to Laurie and Zachary. 'It's in the den. Would you like to do it?'

'Yeah—' Both were enthusiastic, followed her into the den.

'I know now what I want to do with my life.' Todd's face was etched with commitment. 'I never believed in the death penalty. It's not just from a moral standpoint – that I don't believe we have a right to take another life. But I know how close I came to dying for a crime I didn't commit.'

'Helen, you said you had something to show us,' Cindy began, stopped at the sound of the doorbell.

'In a minute,' Helen said while Karen rushed to respond to the doorbell.

Beth and Fred Miller walked from the foyer into the living room. Cindy and Todd froze.

'Cindy – Todd – I know what we did to you was wrong—' Beth's voice was husky with remorse. 'But the parents were at our throats. We were in danger of losing the school.'

'What Beth is trying to say,' Fred pursued, 'we hope – and pray – that you'll come back to the school. You brought something special to our kids.'

Karen saw the exchange between Cindy and Todd. But their rage and hurt were not put to rest.

'Mom tells me that her committee is scheduling a benefit dinner for the battered women's shelter – and they'll ask you two to be guests of honor,' Karen told them. 'You'll be offered a public apology for what happened.'

Todd hesitated. 'We – we'll think about it.' But Karen feared this was no more than polite temporizing.

'We'll be richer for your presence here,' Beth Miller pleaded. 'Whatever we can do to make amends, we'll do.'

'We'll think about it—' Cindy reiterated Todd's offer.

'The replacement teachers understand they have only substitute status.' Fred tried to appear optimistic. 'I guess in a corner of our hearts we knew we'd beg you to come back to us.'

'We should get home—' Beth exchanged an anxious glance with Fred. 'My parents are coming for dinner—'

Helen walked Beth and Fred to the door. Uncomfortable in this encounter, Cindy escaped to the den to check on the children. Todd seemed to be fighting inner demons. It was too much, Karen tormented herself, to expect Cindy and Todd to put aside their rage and hurt. Not even the proposed dinner could wash away the horror of these past three months.

'My parents should be here any minute.' Neil tried to lessen the tension. 'You know how it is with the station. There's always some last minute hassle to deal with.' He paused, listening to sounds in the foyer. 'Ah, they're here now—'

'Oh, this is a wonderful day!' Arline charged into the living room, crossed to embrace Todd. 'Welcome home!'

'Where's Cindy?' Frank asked.

'In the den with the children,' Karen said. 'I'll tell her you're—'

But Arline wasn't waiting for her to finish. 'Cindy! We have something to show you—'

Cindy emerged from the den. Somewhat defensive, Karen observed. She was fearful of more entreaties to remain in Paradise. 'I was helping Laurie and Zachary with their puzzle—'

'We have something important to show you and Todd.' Arline turned to her husband. 'Frank—'

But he was already pulling a sheaf of papers from his briefcase. 'This is a plea from the citizens of Paradise that you stay here and continue to enrich our town, as you have so nobly in the past. We have over two thousand signatures – and there'll be more—'

In startled silence Cindy accepted the papers Frank extended. In silence she and Todd read the brief but eloquent plea, began to scan the parade of signatures. Cindy lifted a hand to brush away the tears that spilled onto her cheeks.

'We're touched—' Cindy's voice was unsteady.

'But I've made a vow,' Todd said uncertainly. 'I promised myself that – if by some miracle I wasn't convicted and executed – I'd spend the rest of my life fighting against the death penalty—'

'Todd, you can do that and still live and teach here!' Neil insisted. 'Write about your experiences – make people understand how an innocent man was so close to receiving the death penalty!'

'I wrote all that material in prison for myself. I couldn't bring it together as a book.' Todd seemed alarmed by the challenge. 'I couldn't—'

'Neil will help you,' Karen rushed in. 'Together you can bring this off. Show the world how close you came to being convicted of a murder you didn't commit. Make them understand that even in this country innocent men have died in the name of justice. They can take a life – but they can't give it back.'

Todd turned to Cindy. She nodded in agreement. His eyes sought Neil's. 'We can do this book together? A publisher will buy it?'

'I don't doubt that for a minute,' Neil assured him. 'It's your duty to do this. You have a message to send to the world.'

Todd was caught in inner debate. The atmosphere electric. Cindy reached for his hand, pressed it. Their eyes met in silent communication. He turned to Neil. 'We'll write it together.'

'And in time,' Karen said softly, 'this town will heal. We'll bring that about together. All of us.'